TO GET
TO THE
OTHER
SIDE

TO GET TO THE OTHER SIDE

A Novel

KELLY
OHLERT

alcove
press

Published in the United States by Alcove Press, an imprint of The Quick Brown Fox & Company LLC.

Alcove Press and its logo are trademarks of The Quick Brown Fox & Company LLC.

Library of Congress Catalog-in-Publication data available upon request.

ISBN (trade paperback): 978-1-63910-138-2
ISBN (ebook): 978-1-63910-139-9

Cover design by Carolina Melis

Printed in the United States.

www.alcovepress.com

Alcove Press
34 West 27th St., 10th Floor
New York, NY 10001

First Edition: December 2022

10 9 8 7 6 5 4 3 2 1

For my mom, who is my first reader and is endlessly supportive.

CHAPTER ONE
TRIXIE

Leave it to a chicken to throw my life into a tailspin. My heart raced as I gripped the steering wheel with white knuckles.

Only moments before, my ride home from work had been tranquil. Music flowed from the car radio and worked its way into my soul. I hummed, and my arms swayed with the practiced grace of years of competitive dance ingrained in my muscle memory. Stopped at a light, I smiled and waved at a man crossing the busy road.

He squinted in confusion with a hand raised to return my wave.

No, you don't know me. I smiled harder, trying to laser beam positivity at him. It was a shame you couldn't even smile at a stranger anymore without it seeming odd. He shook his head and continued his trek.

The light changed to green. All around, skyscrapers towered above me. At street level, their greatness cast a shadow. Above, light gleamed off their shiny exteriors. As I pressed the gas, a white blur flashed in the corner of my eye.

What in the name of hiccupping hippos . . . ? The blur moved in front of my car. I slammed on the brakes and swerved to the curb. Behind me, horns blared. Someone shouted colorful curses out a window, shoving a middle finger in my direction. I lifted my hand and smiled back with a guilty shrug. *Oops.* I flipped my gaze back in front of me, in search of the blur.

Then I saw it. It was the scraggliest-looking chicken I'd ever seen, hobbling toward the sidewalk. I didn't have much experience with chickens, other than at the occasional petting zoo as a child. I had zero reason to encounter a chicken in my adult life, given I lived in downtown Chicago.

What the heck was a chicken doing here?

I flung my door open and ran to scope things out. A fresh symphony of car horns and angry shouts rose in response to my exit from the vehicle. Heat radiated from the asphalt. The road was too narrow for the cars behind me to get around, and there was a constant stream of vehicles going the other direction.

"What the hell are you doing, lady?" the man behind me yelled.

"There's a chicken!" I shouted, kneeling to get a look at her. Blood. Flies. Not good.

"A what?"

"A chicken!" I called, glancing up and down the street, searching for the chicken's owner. Streams of pedestrians moved down the sidewalk. I wasn't sure what I was looking for. Someone waving their arms, yelling, *Hey, that's my chicken*? Maybe a random coop wedged between buildings? I saw nothing. The chicken was as out of place as a chicken roaming the streets of downtown Chicago sounds.

"Well, why was it crossing the road?" he yelled. I couldn't help but giggle at the perfect setup he'd given me. Ah, the age-old question.

"Presumably to get to the other side!" The quip bought me a moment, but a quick glance down the street told me the line of cars behind us was getting longer. The horns were getting louder too. I needed to hurry.

The poor chicken looked at me with her sad little chicken eyes and tilted her sad little chicken head. A soul that sad deserved to be loved. I could empathize. That decided it. The chicken was coming with me . . . just as soon as I figured out how exactly one picked up a chicken.

If I couldn't pick her up, I had no business taking her with me, but the horns were getting to me and people were yelling, and I couldn't leave her there. It was not an environment for sound decision-making.

"I don't give a shit about the chicken, lady. Get out of the way!" the man yelled.

Steeling myself, I went for it. I lunged toward my new feathered friend. She squawked and gave a weak flap and hobble but didn't make it far. I freaked out at the last minute, afraid too strong a grip would crush her already fragile body, and she slipped away.

"You all right?" a deep voice asked. At least one lone soul in the swarm of pedestrians had bothered to check on us.

"Just rescuing a chicken," I said cheerfully, if a little stressed. Eyes on the prize, I kept my gaze on her, not sparing him a glance.

The shouty guy in the car behind me blared his horn again, as if I were not aware of his presence. *Kill 'em with kindness, Trixie.* I smiled and waved, then went back to sizing up my opponent for my next attempt.

"Come on, lady!" the guy behind me yelled. People have no patience these days. So rude.

"I'll deal with him. You focus on her," the deep-voice guy said. I glanced up to see him step between shouty and me. I couldn't see his face, but he was standing in a cowboy-before-a-shootout stance, minus the weaponry, thank goodness. Then again, he was intimidating all on his own. He towered over me, which doesn't say much, given my fun-sized stature, but he could have towered over most, and was built like a tree. Even in my frazzled state, the mouthwatering way his jeans framed his butt did not escape my notice.

The glare I presumed he was giving shouty must have worked, because the yelling trailed off and he ducked into his car, sulking. Taking advantage of the momentary reprieve from harassment, I ran after the chicken again. If she had been in better health, I probably would have wound up chasing her for an hour. In her current state, she was easy to keep up with. I scooped her up and petted her in a feeble attempt to soothe her.

"Got her!" I stepped around my protector and got a look at his face. Oh. Oh wow.

I think he checked me out, but the roving eyes were quick enough that I couldn't say for certain. He nodded. I hesitated, considering introducing myself. He had the kind of rugged good looks that ought to be illegal. He was silent, but he had loud thoughts. I could practically see the gears turning in his mind. I wanted to know what he was thinking.

"Thanks for your help," I said.

He opened his mouth to speak, and a strangled sound escaped. He coughed a bit and settled for a shrug. Hmm, a bit of an awkward conversationalist. A hint of color tinged the top of his cheeks above the edges of his beard. I needed to give him an out. Maybe I'd suggest he was quiet rather than uncomfortable as an excuse.

"Don't talk much, do you?" I asked.

"I guess not. Sometimes it's better to watch."

I side-eyed him. Was he mocking the ridiculous show I'd put on with my chicken chase, or was that an implication he liked what he saw? I didn't think I'd object either way, not when each additional feature I noticed pulled me in further. He had this thin strip without hair on his upper lip, where a scar must be. How inept had I become at dating that I couldn't tell if I was being flirted with?

A fresh wave of horns from the line of cars behind Mr. Shouty broke the moment, and I knew I needed to leave before people went wild.

"I'd better go," I said.

He nodded and stepped back onto the curb. I caught one side of his mouth quirking up in amusement at my struggle to wrestle the chicken into the car. She feebly flapped about, straining to escape. "I'm trying to save you," I muttered through clenched teeth.

Finally settled, I shouted, "Have a nice day!" with a wave and a grin and took off.

In the rearview mirror, I watched the man who'd helped me. He held up a hand in farewell, then scratched at his beard, fading from view as I got farther away. I frowned at his diminishing figure, unable to fight the flutter in my belly that said I was going to regret driving away from him.

Once my unlikely pet could see the car wasn't any imminent threat, she settled down onto the passenger seat, looking exhausted. I watched her in my peripheral as I drove. "Please don't poop in my car."

She squawked.

"Does that mean you're going to poop in my car?"

The chicken bobbed her head. Was she bobbing in acknowledgment? No, the chicken didn't understand me. I was losing my mind.

Then reality screeched in, crackling and popping like a firecracker. Oh my god, I owned a chicken. I couldn't own a chicken! I lived in a no-pets-allowed apartment. One not willing to make exceptions for any pets if history repeated itself. *Oops, did it again.*

I pulled into a convenience store parking lot and stopped the car to assess the situation.

My heart thumped in my chest, and my breathing was heavy. What had happened back there? Had I entered some sort of fugue state that left me incapable of logical thought? What now?

A fly buzzed by my face, and I swatted it away. No, I hadn't lost my mind. I'd let my heart gag my brain, tie it up, and stuff it in a closet—otherwise it would have intervened and stopped this. The poor animal needed my help. So, time to put on my big-girl panties and help. No problem was too big when tackled one piece at a time. I pasted on a smile and leaned in to look at my new pet.

"Who's a good chicken?"

First things first: prevent chicken poop from covering my seats. I looked at the fly-bitten bird next to me and grimaced. Okay, the seats were going to need a good cleaning anyway. Still, a chicken-poop-free seat was decidedly better than a chicken-poop-covered seat.

Having dropped off my recycling earlier, I had an empty bin in the trunk. I lined it with a T-shirt from my gym bag and placed the chicken inside, standing back to admire my handiwork.

The chicken looked at me. I looked at her.

"Well, what do you think?" I asked.

She flopped on the shirt and pecked at it.

"I don't speak chicken, but I'm going to take that as you like it."

Another squawk.

"If you're going to hang with me, you're going to need a name. I can't keep referring to you in my mind as *the chicken*."

Squawk!

"Chickira? Henrietta? Princess Lay-A. Hennifer Lopez! Clucky Charm? I'm going to call you Chick-Chick."

* * *

As the vet looked her over, I paced in the quiet room. I'd have preferred to let Anastasia, the resident vet at the animal shelter where I work, check on her. When I called, she'd been adamant that she specialized in cats and dogs and knew nothing about chickens. No knowledge of chickens. An inner-city vet— imagine! Still, a referral was the next best thing.

There was a soft tap on the door, and the gray-haired receptionist popped her head in. "Some tea, sweetheart?"

"Thank you." I accepted the cup, amazed as always by what a smile could accomplish, even if I wasn't a fan of how that knowledge had been forced on me. *Smiles win judges' hearts, Trixie.* The best way to ensure my smile stayed in place was to practice at all times. No exceptions.

Even after a truce with my parents that was shaky at best, the practice had stuck. As a reward, I got tea.

I sipped while I waited and tried (and failed) not to stress. The chicken was a mess. Her poor little body was caked in dry blood, and that was far from the worst of it. I shook my head to clear the unpleasant image. She'd been injured, but her condition was the result of far more than a roadside injury. That kind of health deterioration took time. The idea filled me with rage, not an emotion I felt often. When I did, it was generally directed at the previous "caretakers," if you could call them that, of some of the animals that come to our shelter.

The chicken, however, would not be one of our shelter animals. We didn't accept chickens. I knew I could beg until blue in the face, but nothing would change that policy. I'd seen others try it with a variety of animals; I'd tried myself. To provide the best care, we had strict rules, and we took in only the animals we were equipped to handle.

That meant Chick-Chick was now mine.

What was I going to do with a chicken? Free from prying eyes in the exam room, I buried my face in my hands and groaned. Now that I had a chicken, I wouldn't get rid of her. I already knew abandoning her wasn't in me.

The door to the exam room creaked open again, and Dr. McAlister slipped in. Her face was somber. The news would not be good.

"So, Miriam tells me this isn't actually your chicken?"

I exhaled, glad she'd delayed the bad news and I'd have more time to muster some composure.

"No, I found her," I said.

"So, you found a chicken, roaming down busy city streets, and you . . ." The vet met my eyes, waiting for me to finish the sentence.

"Scooped her up," I finished.

"Scooped her up," she repeated, her head shaking in a subtle way.

"Well, when you see a chicken crossing the road, you don't not help it," I clarified. "Or, rather, you have to help it. Right?"

"I suppose so." She watched me with a curiosity that gave me the impression she didn't suppose. Maybe your average person would not scoop up a random chicken. Was what I'd done so ludicrous?

Dr. McAlister wrung her hands, then, seeming to realize she'd done so, shoved them in her pockets. "She's dehydrated and in desperate need of fluids, and has one of the worst cases of mites I've ever seen. Her coloring is off, which tells me she hasn't gotten the nutrition she needs and may have some other underlying issues that we'd need to investigate further. That all stems from neglect, but unfortunately those aren't the only problems. She sustained some injuries, probably from cars before you found her."

My heart shattered all over again for this sweet, unappreciated creature who had charmed me the moment we'd stumbled into each other's lives. I understood on the surface all the things the vet was telling me, but when they were all tied together, the picture got fuzzy.

"What does all that mean?"

"The prognosis isn't good. If she can make it through the night, she might survive. We'd need to put her on fluids, and gradually add food, and pump her with a slew of medications to deal with infections and the bugs." She paused, then sighed. "I never want to advocate against a patient, but even if we do those things, it's going to take a lot for her to recover. She's going to need a lot of extra care, and a lot of medication. For tonight alone, you're probably looking at nine hundred dollars."

Nine hundred dollars! While I didn't struggle to pay my bills, I didn't have discretionary income either. I had what I needed and not much else, and I was okay with that. Nine hundred dollars was more than I could afford, and that was for one night. It wasn't like I had pet insurance. Until today, I hadn't had a pet to insure.

"What would you like to do?" Dr. McAlister asked.

A stabbing pain wrenched my chest. A powerful wave of guilt crashed into me at the idea of doing anything but agreeing to help her.

She was just a chicken. Not one I had any connection to. I'd known her for an hour.

"Can I see her?" I asked.

"Of course," Dr. McAlister said, and turned toward the door, waving me to follow. "Right this way."

Chick-Chick sat glassy-eyed in a cage, fresh from X-rays. I knelt and met those beady little eyes again, as if I hadn't already made up my mind. She was down but not out. I'd always been held to such high standards myself that I'd never had it in me to hold others to them, especially innocent animals. I always rooted for the underdog.

"Do what you can for her," I said, and minutes later I signed the paperwork agreeing to the charges.

CHAPTER TWO
BEAR

"Please come out Friday night? It'll be fun! I promise." My little sister Zoey looked up at me with pleading vibrant green eyes similar to my own. The five Ross siblings all had green eyes and round noses.

These traits came from our biological father, Lyle. If I couldn't have my mother's features, I'd much rather have shared genetics with Russell—the man she remarried when I was nine and whom I'd always consider my dad.

"No, Zo," I said. "You know clubs aren't my thing. And isn't the cover at that club like thirty dollars?"

"Aha!" Zoey jabbed her finger in my face. "Money troubles?"

From anyone else, the blatant exposure of my financial situation would have stung, but with one of my sisters, it was a fact of life.

"The cost of living in the city is bull," I said noncommittally. She didn't need to know I was getting fewer hours with work, at a job I didn't like, and doing commissioned projects around the neighborhood for extra income in order to pay the mortgage.

"True," she agreed. "But you should have told me. I can pay your cover. Please come with?"

I scowled at her suggestion. "I can pay for myself. But standing in the corner uncomfortably at a club isn't worth the money."

She studied me, suspicion all over her face. I needed to tread carefully, or the whole family would be planning some kind of financial intervention. My family took care of each other and was always glad for an excuse for a family meeting. We'd had many a meeting when I was growing up, either around the dining table at home or around the table in the back room of the shop when Mom couldn't get away or we were all helping with arrangements on a busy day.

"If I'm paying for it, you don't have to balance the scales to figure that out," she said.

"How can *you* afford it? What is it you do again?" I asked.

She rolled her eyes. "I'm an entrepreneur with my hand in a lot of pies. I know none of you want to believe it, but I'm doing well. The point is, I can. You aren't turning this back around on me. Let me pay."

"Not happening." I clicked off the TV and walked to the kitchen. "Do you want some pancakes?"

Zoey followed me into the kitchen. I flipped on the stove and retrieved the pancake mix and a pan. She blinked at me. "It's three in the afternoon."

"Your point?" I asked.

"It's not any mealtime, let alone breakfast." She hopped on the counter and swung her legs back and forth, and they thumped against the cabinets. I scratched at the edges of my beard in annoyance. I'd worked damn hard to remodel this kitchen and racked up a mountain of debt in the process. I'd be pissed if she scuffed them up.

"There is never a bad time for pancakes." I nodded toward her thumping feet. "Please stop doing that."

"Sorry." She stuck her tongue out at me, with the kind of attitude only a little sister can manage. "Quit changing the subject. Are you coming or not?"

"Not." I focused my eyes on the pancake mix as I stirred, avoiding her gaze.

The back door banged open, letting in a waft of sweet floral smell from the garden, along with my stumbling elder sister Fawn. She nudged her five-year-old, Bella, ahead of her, and balanced at least five grocery bags in her arms.

"Hello, baby brother," Fawn said.

"Do you ever knock?" I asked.

"No," Fawn said, dumping the contents of her bags onto my counter before leaning in to kiss my cheek. I shrugged her off, not that I minded the affection. I loved my sisters as much as they loved me, but the intrusion, although a regular occurrence, annoyed me, since it came on the tail of Zoey's nagging.

"What're you doing here?" I straightened the fallen baking tins, bags of powdered sugar and flour, sticks of butter, and more.

"My oven crapped out, and I need to make cupcakes for Bella to bring to school for her birthday tomorrow. So I'm commandeering yours," Fawn answered.

"You could just *buy* cupcakes," Zoey said, resuming her leg swinging. I winced, but decided the thumping wasn't worth badgering her. If I continued to chide her, she'd only kick the cabinets harder, knowing my little sister. Whenever she was with family, her immaturity seemed to amplify, like she needed to make sure everyone remembered she was the youngest sibling. Not that we could ever forget.

"Honey, can you get the rest out of the car?" Fawn asked Bella. As soon as the little girl had skipped out the door, Fawn spun on Zoey.

"No. I absolutely cannot buy them. You don't understand. This stuff is a vicious competition. If they aren't Pinterest worthy, we'll get uninvited to play groups! She's only five, and I can already see the PTA cliques developing. It's a jungle out there. I love getting to spend so much time with Bella, but when I go back to work, I'll be happy to have that excuse to get out of some of this stuff."

Zoey deadpanned her.

"I'm not kidding. We are one sarcastic 'nailed it' comment away from becoming social pariahs. One frosting-nose-coming-out-looking-more-like-a-penis debacle away from being shunned."

Sensing Fawn was about to spiral like a contorted hazelnut plant, I stepped in. "Do you want pancakes?"

"Cupcakes, pancakes, what kind of cake is next?" Zoey asked, as Bella returned with the last grocery bag full of goodies.

"If you're making them anyway, sure." Fawn took a deep breath, successfully diverted from her meltdown, and smoothed out a crinkled paper recipe on the table with her palm.

"Mom's?" I asked.

"Yeah. She still makes a batch of them every now and then for the kids that come into the shop," Fawn said, and I smiled. Family Tree had always felt like a second home, but Mom worked hard to make it feel that way for everyone, not just us. The place was her own unique brand of magic.

"Which you'd know if you stopped by there more often," Zoey muttered in a gentle chide. Though they seemed to understand why I'd distanced myself from the store and respect it, they weren't above the occasional gentle reminders that it might be time to go back. I wasn't sure I was ready.

"May I please have pancakes too, Uncle Bear?" Bella asked.

I knelt and brushed some powdered pancake mix on her nose. My polite, sweet niece. She was so adorable when she wasn't running laps around her parents.

Bella giggled, swiping off the powder.

"You've got it, birthday girl. One Minnie Mouse pancake with sprinkles coming up." I winked at her and started the pancakes.

"What is a single, twenty-eight-year-old man doing with a stash of sprinkles?" Zoey eyed me with suspicion. "Are you sure you don't have a girlfriend you're hiding from us?"

"No girlfriend," I told her, yet again. We'd had this conversation more times than I could count. I went out with women now and then but tended not to make it past an evening or a few dates.

"About that . . ." Fawn said.

I shook my head and focused on my pancakes. "Not you too! I don't need a girlfriend."

"I know you don't need one, but you are at home or on a mostly male construction site all day. You never go out," Fawn said gently.

What was so wrong with wanting to stay home? I could be myself in peace and not feel like I had to uphold the version of a man that my birth father, Lyle, and the world wanted me to be. He had always thought living among so many women had made me "too soft" and couldn't stand my interest in mom's flower shop, Family Tree. He'd been rigid in trying to impress on me his own ideals of what masculinity should look like. I'd never agreed, but it had been easier not to set him off. Fawn wasn't done with me yet, though.

"If you'd let me help you with a dating profile—"

"No. *Hell* no."

"Please? You don't have to go on any dates unless you find someone you like." Fawn gave me a pouty face, and noticing her mom's pleading, Bella skipped to her side and gave me pouty eyes too.

"Keep out of this, tiny one. Eat your pancakes." I shoved a plate with the Minnie Mouse pancake in her direction, and her eyes lit up. She abandoned her mother's campaign and sat down to eat. "I'm not joining a dating site, and you are not doing it for me either, if you ever want to commandeer my stuff again." I had her with that threat. Fix-it Fawn regularly "borrowed" my tools to work on their fixer-upper home.

"If it's any consolation, he won't let me set him up either. I keep trying to take him clubbing with me so he can meet someone, but he won't go." Zoey heaved herself off the countertop to help Fawn measure out ingredients for the cupcakes.

"I. Don't. Need. A. Girlfriend," I said. The two exchanged smirks. "Quit meddling, you two."

"Oh, it's not just us. Lexie and Rose are in on it too," Zoey said.

Great, all four of my sisters joining forces against me. That was the last thing I needed. "They don't even live here anymore. What do they have to do with this?"

"We invited you to the weekly sibling conference calls. You declined. Said you didn't want to be outnumbered," Zoey reminded me. This was true, I had said that. I'd kind of thought they were joking. They really had weekly conference calls?

A knock sounded on my front door, and I cracked my neck in an effort to contain my frustration. What now? "At least someone knows how to knock."

"Hey, man. Up for a round of pool?" Ryan asked when I swung open the door.

I glanced at my sisters and niece in the kitchen, whispering conspiratorially. I knew better than to leave them unattended when they were so focused on manipulating my life. They'd ganged up on me since I was born. When I was six and afraid to ride a bike, they'd convinced me Lexie was hurt and needed my help and I'd have to ride my bike to get to her faster. At the time, it hadn't occurred to me that her younger brother was not the best person to rescue her, but the ploy worked. I'd been worried enough about her that I forgot the fear.

That was one of countless times before and since that they'd conspired against me, and no, they had not always been to my benefit. Usually they ended poorly. Deep down, I knew my sisters meant well. An irrational fondness swelled, blending with my suspicion and irritation.

"Yeah, sure. I'll be over in a minute," I said, waving Ryan away.

Ryan, however, ignored this, and craned his neck to see the sisters. He let out a low whistle. "Hello, ladies!"

Zoey blew him a kiss, which Ryan mimed catching as he fell against the doorframe as though stricken with love. Zoey rolled her eyes.

"No," I growled, and shoved Ryan's chest to push him back out of the house before slamming the door in his face.

"You know you gave me a spare key for emergencies, right?" he yelled through the door.

I pinched the bridge of my nose and sighed. "Is this an emergency?"

"Missed connections are a big deal, Bear. One could argue that a missed opportunity for love is important enough to qualify as an emergency."

The statement threw me off-balance. Missed connections. I'd spent the time till Zoey arrived regretting not asking the woman chasing the chicken for her phone number. Not just anyone would halt traffic for a chicken. Something about the way the woman moved had been entrancing. She was beautiful, and smiled like her life depended on it, even though she'd obviously been frazzled to the point of cracking when I'd walked up. Maybe Ryan was onto something, even if he'd seen Zoey here many times, and for them, a missed connection it was not. But there was nothing I could do about my own missed opportunity now. Still, I'd be remembering those sparkling blue eyes for weeks to come.

"Go, Ryan," I said.

"You've gotta learn to let your hair down, man," he shouted.

"Go!" I yelled. Finally, there were no sounds other than the thumping of his feet on my front steps. "Stay away from him," I scowled at Zoey.

"Yes, sir." Zoey mock saluted.

"And you"—I jabbed a finger in Fawn's direction—"I know you're the ringleader of this circus. Promise me you won't try to set me up on any dates or sign me up for a dating site."

Fawn returned my jab with a spatula speared in my direction. "I promise we won't set you up on any dates, nor sign you up for any dating sites."

I nodded, reassured, until I caught them exchanging a look that had trouble written all over it. I narrowed my eyes at the elder sister, who shrugged innocently before turning to pour batter into her cupcake tin.

"Later, kiddo." I fist-bumped Bella, then walked out the door, dreading the moment I'd find out what my sisters were scheming in the hurried whispers that came in my wake.

CHAPTER THREE
TRIXIE

"All right, Chick-Chick. Here's the deal. This is a stealth mission. That means no clucking. Do you think you can do that?" I asked.

She titled her head sideways.

Cluck.

I blew out a breath and rested my forehead on the steering wheel. We were doomed. Even if she didn't cluck, at the rate she was going, she'd probably poop all over me and give herself away. At least she'd survived the night and I'd been able to take her home with me, an overwhelming amount of medications in tow. In the two hours I'd been with her, she'd already gone five times. I felt like someone had just handed me a new game and set me up on expert level and I couldn't figure out how to do anything but keep walking straight into a wall. I needed an instruction manual.

Before we attempted this, I'd felt a need to give Chick-Chick and myself a pep talk, so we'd parked on the street around the corner from my apartment complex.

So far, my track record for sneaking pets past my landlord, Mrs. Girsham, was zero for five. I was pretty sure she'd liked me at first. On my move-in day, I'd started off well, delivering new-neighbor goodies to everyone in the building, but that favor wore off somewhere around my third infraction. I wasn't optimistic that the sixth time would be the charm, especially with an injured chicken that wasn't understanding the importance of staying under the radar.

My dance background made me good on my feet. I could move quietly. My animals had a track record of being less than understanding of the quiet rule, though, and it didn't help that Mrs. Girsham's favorite hobby appeared to be sitting with her nose pressed against the window, watching our lot for any misdeeds.

"Here goes nothing," I said to Chick-Chick, turning the key and pulling into the lot.

I glanced at Mrs. Girsham's window. Dark. No sign of the hawk-eyed landlord anywhere. We might be in luck.

I tossed a towel over the top of the recycling bin that I'd once again moved Chick-Chick into. It was less than the ideal home for her, but it was less obvious than the cage I'd bought. I'd have to bring that in collapsed and boxed up to avoid suspicion.

I'd taken only three steps across the lot when Mrs. Girsham blinked into existence in the window. I screamed and jumped, nearly dropping my precious cargo. She didn't even walk up to the window. It was like one minute, there was no one there, and poof! Suddenly, there she was, like something straight out of a horror movie. Not that I'd know. I did not do horror. For weeks after watching *Signs*, I'd gone to sleep with a squirt gun in my bed.

I blinked again, and she vanished. I almost wondered if I'd imagined her until her door flew open to reveal the old woman, in all four feet eleven of her glory, clad in a fluffy lavender bathrobe. She'd rounded off the look with hair curlers.

She waddled her way over to me like she was in a power-walking race. "Beatrix! Oh, Beatrix!"

I forced a smile, hoping I could somehow salvage this. If I was friendly and fast enough, maybe I could somehow make it to the door without her discovering the chicken. *Please stay quiet, Chick-Chick.*

"You can call me Trixie, Mrs. Girsham." I'd told her approximately seventeen times. It was particularly grating because Trixie isn't short for Beatrix. Never has been. My name at birth was Trixie, and I had no idea why she believed otherwise, but I couldn't convince her out of it.

"What have you got there?" she asked, eyeing my bin.

"Oh, just getting back from a run to the recycling center. Bringing my bin back home."

Her eyes narrowed. "And under the towel?"

"It's, um . . . what towel?" I winced. I was the world's worst liar.

Mrs. Girsham lunged for the blanket.

"No!" I yelped, yanking the bin out of her reach. "It's . . ." I racked my brain. Something, *anything*, to keep her from looking under the towel. "Porn!"

My face erupted with embarrassment, redness flowing over my cheeks like lava. A valid reason not to look, but not one I'd be able to look her in the eye after using. I was a woman with a healthy sexual appetite and enjoyed occasional visual stimulation, but it wasn't something I had any desire to talk to my elderly landlady about. At least the blush from talking about porn might make the lie more convincing.

Mrs. Girsham jerked back her hand as though stung, a blush creeping across her cheeks too. "Well then," she said, seemingly at a loss for words. Then she turned in disgust to return to her apartment. Holy cow, I was going to get away with it! At least my eternal mortification had earned me something. I hurried off toward my door, but before I could quite make it, the towel started moving.

Bawk, bawk, bawk!

Mrs. Girsham's pivot was instantaneous. "Lift the towel. Now."

Resigned, I hung my head and lifted the towel to reveal Chick-Chick.

"Again, Beatrix? And a chicken?" Now that she'd solved the mystery, her supersleuth face disappeared, replaced by a frown that screamed, *I'm not mad, I'm disappointed.* Dang, she could pull it off, too. She'd reduced me to feeling like a troublesome child.

"I know, ma'am. I'm sorry."

"You know the rules, dear. No pets allowed. That means no dogs, no cats, no fish, no parrots, no ferrets, no gerbils, no chickens. And none of whatever other random animal you'll come up with next. Bring it to the shelter!"

I sighed. Every time I'd tried to bring home an animal previously, I'd spent days scouring ads for pet-friendly places I could afford, and I'd tried again in between worrying last night. Apartments of any kind in the city were in short supply these days. Ones that were affordable *and* allowed pets were nonexistent.

"I tried, Mrs. Girsham. They won't let me bring anything other than a cat or dog. Certain animals could pose health risks for the existing animals, and our shelter isn't licensed for chickens. We can't risk losing our license. And even if we could, we don't have the right equipment to care for anything else."

"I don't know what to tell you, dear. The chicken is not allowed here either. You'll have to find another home for her."

It wasn't like I'd wanted another run-in like this with Mrs. Girsham. I'd already considered rehoming Chick-Chick. I was no stranger to rehoming animals. I regularly made dating profiles for the animals at the shelter to help them find their forever homes. But nobody was going to take an immobile, injured chicken that required special care in addition to a slew of expensive medications and vet bills. I was her only option, and I couldn't abandon her. I wouldn't. Being broken did not determine her worth. It didn't determine anyone's.

"Please, ma'am. I know the rules, but look at her. She needs help, and she needs special care that nobody else will give her. I know I've asked before, but I'm desperate this time. I'm all she's got. Will you please make an exception?" I gave her my best puppy eyes and flashed a hint of my lucky smile.

Maybe I still had some of that move-in-goodies favor, because her eyes and posture softened.

"I can't let you keep her forever. I don't want my building torn apart, and it wouldn't be fair to the other tenants. But you can keep her for a week. I'll give you one week to give you a chance to find her a new home."

It wouldn't be good enough, but I would take what I could get and worry about a permanent solution later. I sagged with relief.

"Thank you, Mrs. Girsham. I appreciate it."

She patted my hand, and then, pausing for me to nod my permission, petted the freshly cleaned and patched-up Chick-Chick.

"I'm not a monster, dear. You're a sweet girl, out there trying to save the world, one animal at a time. I knew something was up. You can't hide that bleeding heart of yours."

We said our good-byes, and once inside, I set Chick-Chick's bin on the ground and surveyed my tiny city apartment. Not exactly the ideal dwelling for a chicken.

I had one week to find a solution for Chick-Chick.

One week to accomplish something I'd failed to accomplish several times before.

What could go wrong?

Chicago Tribune Classified Ad

Room available in downtown Chicago home, owned by a city-dwelling lumberjack. Don't ask us what that means; we (his four sisters) are confused about what he's going for too. The good news is this lumberjack loves flapjacks. Move in, and pancakes will be yours for the taking morning, noon, and night.

Our surly brother, Bear (and yes, that's really his name—the Bear part, not the brother; we aren't the Berenstains), needs someone to tame his wild side, and by that we mean the opposite. We're not sure where his wild side is. He might have left it along the interstate a few years back, but we're hoping the right roommate will draw him from hibernation and remind him what life is about.

He's fairly domesticated for such a large animal, so don't fret, the place is tidy. If you're a slob, that's okay too. It will irritate the hell out of him, but we do that daily anyway, so a little more won't hurt.

In the event of a dispute, like you drank too many of the beers from his fully stocked fridge—which we encourage you to help yourself to—a friendly visit from us, his awesome sisters, is a text or phone call away.

We've been ganging up on him forever and can whip him into shape for you.

Utilities not included. Pet-friendly, because hello, a Bear is already living there.

Please contact 315-124-9876 if you are interested. Serious inquiries, from not so serious people, only.

CHAPTER FOUR
BEAR

I was drenching the bathroom floor. My phone rang for the third time in the last ten minutes. Each time it had been a different unknown number dragging me away from my attempts to cleanse myself. I was beginning to wonder if I'd entered some parallel universe where I was wildly popular. That was a universe I would not enjoy.

The phone rang for a fourth time, and I gritted my teeth. Whoever it was could give me two minutes to finish my shower in peace before I answered. I was rinsing the shampoo out of my hair when it rang a fifth time.

"You've got to be fucking kidding me," I muttered, switching off the water. I toweled off, then stepped out of the shower. I slid on the floor, wet with dripped water from my repeated checks to see who was calling. I caught myself on the counter just shy of learning how to do the splits by force.

"What?" I snapped, answering the phone.

"Oh, uh, I was calling about the room."

27

The room? What room? "I don't know what you're talking about. You've got the wrong number. Stop calling."

Thump, thump, thump.

Was that the door? My phone rang in my hand again. I sucked in a deep breath through my nose. "Man, I told you, you've got the wrong number. Stop calling me."

"This is the first time I've called you, though," a different voice said from the phone.

Thump, thump, thump.

"You haven't been calling me for the last ten minutes?" I asked.

"Nope. First call."

Thump, thump, thump.

"I've got to go." I hung up the phone.

After wrapping a coarse black towel around my waist, I stomped toward the front door. Not only was my phone blowing up, but nine AM on a Sunday and already one of my sisters was here to harass me. Could I never get some peace?

"I know I said you needed to learn to knock, but—" I pulled the door open to find not my sisters as I'd suspected, but three unfamiliar people standing on my doorstep.

Suddenly remembering my nudity, I threw the door closed and retreated to my bedroom to get dressed. The people on the porch had to be related to the calls; I didn't usually get visitors. But why?

"Bear! Bear, is that you?" muffled voices called through the door. They knew my name. The last thing I wanted to do was talk to a bunch of strangers. I liked my quiet and privacy, not that I got much with two of my sisters still in town. That hadn't changed since my childhood, when I'd had a habit of tucking myself in a corner of the shop, hidden under a large plant to do homework, and they'd come pull me into playing a game with them instead. *My sisters.*

I picked up my phone and dialed Fawn.

She answered on the second ring. "Hello, baby brother."

"What did you do?" I demanded.

"Whatever do you mean?" False innocence lilted in her voice.

"You know what I mean. Why are there people standing on my doorstep and others turning my ringtone into the song that never ends?"

"Not a clue," she says.

"What were you and Zoey scheming when I left the other day? I'm not kidding, Fawn."

The pounding on the door became more insistent, and my phone beeped to let me know I had another incoming call. Christ, I was going to have to change my number.

"All right, all right, don't get your panties in a twist."

"I don't wear panties," I grumbled.

"Boxers, whatever. I don't need to know my brother's undergarment preferences." She made a gagging sound.

"What did you do, Fawn?"

"You wouldn't let us add you to a dating site or set you up, and we know you've been struggling with money," she said.

I scrubbed at my face, hating that they'd figured me out. I only got paid for the jobs I worked, which were becoming fewer and farther between. The economy was down, and people weren't building. Still, I was getting by. I'd picked up a few odd jobs outside of work. Fixing things here, building shelves there. I didn't want my sisters taking pity on me or thinking I couldn't take care of myself. I was the man of the family, as my birth father had reminded me oh-so-many times in my life.

"Well, we thought of a way to solve both problems."

The pounding continued. "Dude! Can I look at the room? Did you know about the ad?" The voices came from outside. I looked around the house, considering the back door for escape, and saw eyes framed by cupped hands peering in through my kitchen window. Did these people have no limits?

I hung up on Fawn. I'd call my meddlesome siblings back later, but these people, whoever they were, had to go. My facial expression must have communicated that message to the one on my back porch, because they took off toward the front of the house at a run. One down.

I took a breath, then flung the front door open, causing a domino effect for the men and women standing on the front step. Served them right for invading my home like that.

"Why are you here?" I asked, in as calm a voice as I could muster.

They glanced at each other nervously before a woman edged back up the steps and handed me a copy of the *Chicago Tribune*. My eyes scanned the paper, and my nostrils flared as I read. I was going to kill my sisters. A guy held up his phone.

"Did you just take a picture of me?" I asked.

"Yeah, the ad is pretty funny. People are sharing it on social media. I bet I can get a few bucks for the picture for a follow-up piece on a local news site. The shirtless one will probably do better, though."

The shirtless one? I'd heard enough. These people had to go. "Get off my property! All of you." In the minute or two I'd been dressing and on the phone with Fawn, the number of people on the lawn had multiplied. Now a few wandered away, while others lingered. "Go!" I roared, standing up to my full six foot three and glaring down at the nearest intruder.

With that, the rest scampered away. As people packed up their things and retreated to their cars—parallel parked on our narrow street—a little blue hybrid pulled up to the curb. Another one? I couldn't believe a simple classified ad had gotten so much traction. My sisters were toast. I stomped down the steps to chase away the newcomer. I was prepared for battle. Then she stepped out of the car.

Wavy brown hair bounced on her shoulders as she stood.

I recognized her. Holy shit, it was the woman with the chicken from the other day. No way I had that kind of luck and would have a second chance at getting her number. The car did look familiar, now that I had her face to pair it with.

She rubbed her lips together like she'd put on Chap Stick, or lip gloss, or whatever. She glanced up, and a sweet blush spread over her cheeks. Did she recognize me? I mentally reached for my anger toward all the people I'd just sent away, but it slipped through my fingers and blew away on the wind.

She wore the damn perkiest yellow dress I'd ever seen, patterned with white polka dots. It hugged her curves, then flared out past her waist, revealing toned calves underneath and robin's-egg-blue Converse. The edge of my mouth curved up when I caught sight of the shoes. I'd been expecting heels but liked the unapologetically bright and casual shoes with the dress. It spoke to a measure of practicality and quirkiness.

Realizing I'd been staring too long at her body, I snapped my eyes back to her face. Her blue eyes met mine behind hooded lashes. Then she smiled the most dazzling, radiant smile. It nearly knocked me off my feet. Oh hell, I was in trouble.

I scratched my beard as she approached.

"Hi, are you Bear?" she asked. She hesitated, studying me further. "Oh! It's you!"

Her voice was as melodic as I'd remembered. It almost would have been nice if it had been annoying, to counteract the effect her appearance was having on me. No such luck.

I could lie and send her packing with the rest. My phone, now silenced, continued to buzz in my pocket. I probably should turn her away and figure out how to deal with the onslaught of calls and visitors, but my immediate attraction to her made that difficult.

"Are you okay?" A cute little wrinkle creased her forehead.

No way I was turning her away after how annoyed with myself I'd been for not getting her number the other day. "Yes, why?"

"Well, you didn't answer. You were staring at me for a long time. And you kind of look like you're in pain."

Damn it, Bear, get your shit together. At least I wouldn't have to fight an attraction for long. No chance at that number now. She'd ask her questions and be on her way and I'd never see her again. Staring like a fool was not the best first impression. An expression of pain didn't exactly scream *sexiest man alive*. At least, I didn't think it did. I'd grown up with a mom and four sisters and still didn't know what women were thinking most of the time.

"Sorry. I'm Bear."

Her blue eyes sparkled when she grinned in response. "Nice to meet you. I'm Trixie. Thanks again for the other day."

She held her hand out, and at least this time reflexes saved me from freezing up again. Her hand was so tiny and delicate, it felt like I was cradling a baby bird in my palms. Instinctively I loosened my grip in order to shake her hand as gently as possible.

The handshake tethered us together, and the connection electrified me as I stared into her eyes. Shit, I was staring too much, but I couldn't look away. Then again, she was staring back. That was different. Last time she'd been so distracted by the chicken, it seemed she'd hardly noticed me. That didn't seem to be the case now.

Her eyes flicked down to the side, maybe a show of flirtatious shyness. She dropped my hand and shifted, avoiding meeting my gaze again while a blush bloomed on her cheeks. That blush did things to me. I liked knowing I had that kind of effect on her.

I coughed to break the tension. "No problem. So what are you doing here?" Another internal grimace. *Way to make it sound like you want her here, Bear.*

"I was hoping to check out the room."

"You saw the ad?" I asked.

"Well, yeah. Me and probably half of Chicago have seen that ad. It was on my news feed like six times."

I groaned. This wouldn't be the end of people showing up and calling. "And you want to see the room?"

"Yeah. I have to move out of my apartment in three days. Kind of an unexpected thing. I'm looking for a place to live."

I blinked. My mind was moving as slow as molasses, but things weren't adding up. "And you want to live here?"

She nodded.

"With me?"

Another nod. Her smile slipped, but her eyes widened as she caught herself, and then it was back, so bright and brilliant.

She watched me, waiting for a response, and her right foot lifted to prop itself against her other leg. She didn't seem to notice she'd done it. Just your average girl, balancing on one foot on my lawn like a flamingo. I breathed out a laugh.

Her head tilted. "Is that . . . I mean, did your sisters tell you they printed that?"

"No."

Her grin slipped again, and this time she let it. "Oh . . . but you are looking for a roommate, aren't you?"

No. "Yes."

Where had that come from? I wasn't looking for a roommate. I stayed home for a reason. I liked spending my life alone, doing what I wanted with my time. Not only was I not looking for a roommate, I didn't *want* one. Although I could use the additional income, as much as I hated to admit it. My bills wouldn't pay themselves, and the second bedroom was unused anyway.

Still, living alone was great. I'd been awfully quick with my answer. Why had I said that?

A second later, the smile was back. I'd known this pixie of a woman for two minutes, if you didn't count glaring some asshole down for her the other day, and already I was hooked on that smile. I didn't want to think about the things I'd be willing to do to keep seeing it.

She shifted her flamingo stance to the other leg and looked around. "Well, that's good. I see not much changed in the last few days. Still not much of a conversationalist, are you, Bear? I like the name, by the way. It's cool. Is that your given name?"

My scrambled mind struggled to keep up with the barrage of questions and statements. She barely breathed between them. She was so animated and full of life. I liked it. "No, I'm not. And it's short for Barrett."

She nodded. "Okay, Bear, can I have a tour?"

I'd exited my home intending to chase people away, not invite them in. I did a quick mental inventory, trying to recall

how clean or dirty it might be and if I'd left anything embarrassing out. The house could never be described as spotless, but
I wasn't a slob. I didn't want to gross her out. Then again, how
much did I want her to like the house? If she liked it, she might
ask to move in, which, I reminded myself, I didn't want. Right?

I liked things the way they were—when Fawn wasn't bor-
rowing them, anyway. Beyond that, this woman was entrancing. Her quirky mannerisms and dress, and the way her wide
smile and electric eyes sparkled, pulled me in. Being platonic
roommates with her and not exploring the curves that her dress
proudly displayed, nor kissing those glossy lips, sounded like a
special kind of hell. And what had she said about three days?

"Okay." I turned to lead the way into the house, not looking to see if she followed. My mouth and body were doing their
own thing without the consent of my brain.

I dropped onto the recliner near the front door to pry off my
boots. Glancing over, instead of meeting her eyes, I found her
bent over, unlacing her shoes. It gave me a view straight down
her cleavage. Heat rushed through me. "Fuck," I cursed under
my breath, whipping my head around to pull my eyes off her
breasts.

Immediately, I started trying to think of things I could say
to drive her away. I could lie and say I was in a band that practiced in the living room, or that I did daily naked yoga. No, I
couldn't even pretend to be that skeevy.

"Hm?" There was a soft thud that I assumed to be her shoe
hitting the floor, free from her foot. Cautiously, I glanced her
way in my peripheral vision to make sure she had once again
resumed a safely upright position. With views like that, I needed
to get this woman out of my house or doom myself to a state of
permanent blue balls.

She was vertical and stood on the small rectangle of tile that served as the home's entryway in her mismatched socks. One was hot pink, with a print that looked like it was raining tacos. The other was even stranger, with some weird bug-eyed, goblin-like creature. I didn't want to find them endearing, but I did. Nor did I want to ask about them, but I sighed, resigned to the fact that it would nag me if I didn't.

"What the hell is that thing?"

She jumped. "What? Where?" She whirled around in search of the imminent threat, making me laugh. The spin made her dress flare up, exposing another inch of leg that got my blood pumping again. An inch of skin was going to make me lose my mind. I had to get a grip.

"Sorry." I held up a reassuring hand, then pointed at the goblin thing.

"Oh, you can't tell? It's Gollum!" Trixie ducked past me into the living room and launched herself onto my couch, lifting her feet to display the bottoms.

She certainly was making herself at home. I squinted at the text on the sock. "*My precious?*"

She smiled and nodded, before her jaw dropped as she registered my confusion.

"Seriously? Gollum, from *Lord of the Rings*? 'We wants it, we needs it, we must have the precious'?"

For that last bit, she bugged her eyes out, curled her fingers, and used a ridiculous-sounding creepy voice. I laughed again. When was the last time a relative stranger had made me laugh so much? Or anyone, for that matter. Was this woman real? I shook my head.

She continued to smile, but the way she slowly exhaled gave me the feeling I'd disappointed her, and I didn't like it. I hadn't disliked books when I was younger, but every time Lyle had seen me with a book, he'd shoved me out the door for more athletic endeavors. Not that he could be bothered to take the time to teach me how to catch or anything.

"Not much of a reader and never got around to the movies." I rubbed at my scruff, wary she'd have a negative reaction.

Her eyes flickered, but she otherwise didn't react. It was eerie how that smile stayed in place, but I was glad she hadn't pronounced me an illiterate caveman and stormed out the door.

"Well, if I end up living here, we can fix that." She winked. "You can borrow from my collection. I've got a little of everything."

I stared some more. God, the woman was going to think I was a creep if I didn't start talking more and staring less. Maybe that's what I wanted—to scare her off. Except it wasn't. She stood up from my gray couch and I winced, noticing for the first time how the section where I tended to sit was sunken in. The couch was a few years old and worn, but not in terrible shape. Still, giving her this clear visual of how I lived made me uncomfortable. If she moved in, she'd learn about all my habits and hobbies, whether or not I wanted her to. Not even my sisters had that much insight into me nowadays.

"Cable?" she asked, nodding at the TV.

"Yeah, and Netflix."

"Great! Can you show me the rest?"

I grunted my assent and led her to the kitchen.

Her eyes popped. She lifted onto her toes and flitted forward a few steps. "Wow!"

Again, my lips tugged, fighting to smile. My kitchen was my household pride and joy.

I hadn't been able to put the work and money into redoing the entire house yet, but I'd done the kitchen. Given my size, height, and muscle, I took in a lot of food before I filled up. Over the course of my life, I'd grown an appreciation for it, even if my culinary skills remained on par with the average college dorm dweller. Why expand the menu when I haven't had anyone else to cook for? Most days I resorted to pizzas or macaroni and cheese, but my kitchen was my happy place. Ironically, it was one of the only things I'd done in my life that might have made Lyle proud. Any doorway he darkened was my anti-happy place.

Trixie ran her hands over the granite counters and squealed at the tiled backsplash. The kitchen wasn't large, but I was proud of the painted cabinets that lined both sides, with stainless-steel appliances wedged in the middle of the cabinetry. My favorite piece was the dark wood of the high-top kitchen table. From the way Trixie admired it, she seemed to like it too.

"This kitchen is beautiful."

"Thanks." I felt a twitch of pride.

Trixie gave me a small smile, not her wide, brilliant one. Had she wanted to say more?

"I remodeled it last year."

And there it was. She lit up again, and my heart swelled with appreciation for her recognition of the work. "Impressive! As a hobby, or are you in that line of work?"

"I'm in construction."

She paused, then offered, "I work at an animal shelter."

"Okay." I knew I was being a terrible host. I was giving her nothing to work with in terms of conversation. I was out of practice. I'd long ago given up on conversing with the general public, when they'd taken the things I said and twisted them into things to bully me for.

I didn't talk much with anyone outside my family except Ryan. Grunting side by side over a video game with him didn't really prepare me for conversation with women, though, and he liked to hear himself talk. Still, I should have returned the question. I was coming off as a jerk. I knew it, and yet I couldn't seem to make myself do better.

We went out the back door so she could see the sandbox-sized backyard. It could have been bigger, but the already small space was mostly taken up by the deck, just large enough for the grill, and the small garden that lined the fence. She twirled on the deck, basking in the sunlight and the fresh garden air. It felt invasive to watch her, her arms thrown out to the side, spinning on the deck. Such an odd, impulsive thing to do. She was radiant, and I had to stop noticing it. This woman would not be my roommate. No one was going to be my roommate.

We went back inside, through the kitchen, and on to the living room, from which three unexplored doors remained.

I coughed and shut the door to my room. "That one's my room." There wasn't anything that would have been embarrassing for her to see. I didn't have posters from the swimsuit issue on the wall like a teenager or anything, but something about her seeing the place I slept felt too intimate.

I shoved the bathroom door open and stood aside so she could see. Thankfully, I'd hastily dried the floor with towels when I'd run back in to change earlier. "There's only one bathroom, so we'd be sharing."

Trixie walked into the bathroom and did a slow spin, her eyes taking things in. She nodded and walked back out.

"And this would be your room." I nodded at the second bedroom, adjacent to the bathroom. Her door was opposite mine, with the living room to separate us. And now I was mentally referring to it as her door. I was all over the place.

That face of hers remained stoically happy, but she tensed up a little. The room was mostly empty, but a small desk sat in the corner. A rack of weights that I rarely used stood against the wall nearest the door. Construction was usually enough physical activity for me. Overflowing from the closet were storage bins stacked upon storage bins. They were organized, but they took up a lot of space.

I tried to imagine seeing it through her eyes. Maybe she was worried she'd have to live among my junk and not be able to use the closet. "I would clean this stuff out of here. I would have before, but I didn't know about the ad."

Her shoulders relaxed, and she stepped into the room, wiggling her sock-covered toes in the carpet and inspecting the bare gray walls. What did they tell her? I felt so exposed, as naked as my decoration-free walls. This quirky girl who'd popped out of nowhere was whittling her way into my mind and my home, and I felt both terrified and excited by this prospect.

"Okay, let's talk specifics of the lease," she said, apparently having concluded her inspection.

A lease? Shit. I knew nothing about being a landlord. It should have occurred to me I'd have to talk about this. Had the ad already listed a price? Did I have to draw up a legal document? Was the fact that I was thinking about this an indication I was considering allowing her to live here? If she wanted to talk specifics, she was at least somewhat interested. That couldn't be right, though. Could it?

In what world would this woman have shown up, seen me, and thought *Yes, I want to live with him*? Surely we were both playing some kind of game, using the interest in the house as a stall tactic until one of us worked up the nerve to ask the other out. Maybe I was way off base, and this was only about the room.

Just in case, I ran some quick mental calculations on my expenses and gave her some numbers for rent and utilities. Beyond that, I didn't know what to say.

"Other than that, standard rental, I guess."

"Right." She smiled. "I put you on the spot. You only found out about the ad like five minutes before I showed up. You haven't had time to think this through."

"Yeah." I gritted my teeth. My sisters were done for. All right, killing them might be extreme, but I was *not* making them pancakes next time they came over. Then again, if they were hungry and I was cooking anyway, it'd be impractical not to share. But no sprinkles, except for Bella.

"I'd love to say take some time to figure it out," she said. "But I do need to move in three days, due to unforeseen circumstances. I'm not too worried about whatever paperwork you want to throw together. If you're game, I think I'll take the room!"

Something told me I should ask about those unforeseen circumstances, but I was so overwhelmed, I just wanted to nudge this tiny sunflower of a human being out the door so I could think straight again. My sisters had gotten me into this mess, but I still had the power to say no. Just because they'd taken out an ad didn't mean I had to let anyone live here. I could tell her I needed a day to think about it. If this morning was any indication, I'd have other options.

Who was I kidding? There would be no one I would choose over her, even if a neon sign in my mind was flashing *Bad Idea* on repeat.

Still, no need for rash decisions. I'd take the night to sleep on it. The whole idea was wild, and I ought to say no, but if I held off on a decision, I could review my finances. Yeah, an informed decision would be good.

"I need some time to think about it," I said. Her eyebrows sunk by a fraction. "I could let you know tomorrow."

"Oh, okay." She smiled reassuringly, or at least in a way that I thought was meant to be reassuring. It had too much teeth and looked forced. She really wanted to live here. "Sorry, I know this came at you out of nowhere."

"It's all good. Can I get your number?" I asked, and immediately wished it hadn't come out like I was trying to get a date, so I hastily added, "So I can contact you . . . about the room."

She gave a small laugh as she pulled out her phone. When her eyes met mine this time, she bore that megawatt smile, and I doubted there was any chance I'd do anything but agree.

CHAPTER FIVE
TRIXIE

"So," I started awkwardly, as Lindsey and I sorted through a bin of donations behind the long reception desk of the shelter. "I may need to update my address with you soon." I hoped so. I'd checked my phone for Bear's answer several times already today. So far, no luck.

"What? Why?" She stopped her sorting and swiveled in her chair, on high alert.

"Mrs. Girsham caught me sneaking in that chicken I called you about."

The very same chicken I had no idea what to do with if the room with Bear didn't pan out. I'd checked out a few other places both before and after I'd stopped by Bear's yesterday, and they were—to put it kindly—not viable options. At least, not unless I wanted to land in the hospital with complications from living in a mold-infested glorified janitor's closet.

"I'm not sure what to unpack first: that you're keeping a chicken in your studio apartment, or that you got caught trying to sneak in an animal again."

I avoided talking about my personal life too much at work, but since I usually tried begging Lindsey to let me bring my animal misfits here first, she was well versed in my contraband pet antics.

"Hey, they're tricky to smuggle. It's not like stealing a candy bar. They're big, and they move and make noises."

"Do you routinely steal candy bars?"

"No."

"Have you ever stolen candy bars?"

"No! I was making a point."

Lindsey scowled and, holding my gaze, dragged the glass candy bowl on our reception desk away from me.

"First of all, I'm allowed to have that candy. Second—"

"What did I miss?" Anastasia walked in the door with a beverage tray holding three coffee cups.

"Trixie is a thief," Lindsey said. "She's resorted to a life of crime. She's been living a double life all this time."

"It's always the ones you least suspect," Anastasia tutted.

"You two are impossible," I said. "I thought you were off today?"

Anastasia passed out the cups. "I am. I'm just popping in for a bit. I wanted to check on that Lab. Felix, right? He had me worried yesterday." The dog in question was a charming black Lab who had come to us malnourished and had been having trouble breathing yesterday.

"That's sweet of you. He's doing better today," I said.

I'd been worried about him too. I'd gone straight to check on him when I'd come in this morning and taken over for our night crew. He'd been found abandoned and in poor condition, much like Chick-Chick had. Unlike Chick-Chick, he was a dog, so we were able to take him at the shelter. I knew I couldn't personally take in all the animals I fell in love with, but it was nice to be able to help care for them at work.

I always tried my best to find amazing owners for our animals. I had an extra soft spot for the ones with rough histories like Felix, though. It was going to be my personal mission to find him an amazing forever home, as soon as possible. It was on my to-do list for the day to take some pictures for his dating profile on our website.

Anastasia left her things at the desk and disappeared down the hall to check on him. As soon as she was out of sight, Lindsey turned back to me.

"Okay, so apparently I'm getting you a criminal background check in addition to updating your address. Where are you moving?" Lindsey asked.

"Good question," I said.

"Still an apartment shortage?" she asked.

"Unless I want to cash in my life savings and maybe my soul too. How much do you think souls run for these days?"

"Heard it's a tough market for those. Supply and demand, you know. Lots of traded-in souls lately," Lindsey said, and I laughed. "Really, though, what are you going to do?"

I was itching to tell her about the apartment with the tall shy man with the plaid shirts that I wanted to rip off, but we were edging into territory I didn't usually share. Spilling a little more wouldn't hurt. I could tell her there was a place I was considering, and if she pried too much, I was an expert diverter. People usually liked talking about themselves, so most of the time people didn't even notice. I could spend all day, every day in friendly conversation with Lindsey without revealing much about myself at all.

"I may have a lead on something. I'm not sure if it'll come through, though."

"Oh?" Lindsey asked, propping her elbows on the counter and her chin in her hands. "Tell me more."

I bit my lip, feeling uneasy with more questions, but a person I might end up living with wasn't too personal, and I could think of nothing she could do with the information. And this was Lindsey. I'd known her for years now, even if I'd held her at arm's length.

"Funny story, actually. I'd been struggling to find a cheap place that allowed animals, and then Saturday I came across this ad in the newspaper—"

"That one that everyone's been sharing online?" The way Lindsey jumped, you would think I'd gone all Mario Fire Flower and spit flames at her.

"That's the one," I tried to sound more enthused about it than I was. I didn't have any qualms about the house, and I *definitely* didn't have any about the man living in it. I was actually kind of excited about those. I just wasn't prepared to live with anyone.

It had been a long time since I'd had a roommate. None since Julia. We'd shared a dorm in college, the kind of small space that left no room for secrets. I had to push it out of my mind, or I might break down. Revealing that sort of emotion in front of people wasn't a thing I did. After years of smiling like the judges were always present, I'd only shown my genuine feelings to Julia. I had thought we were best friends until she turned on me.

"You're moving in with that guy?" Lindsey shrieked. Mouth agape, she shook her head. "Do you even know him? You need to back up and give me the full story."

I winced. It was unsurprising to me that Lindsey had this reaction. She owned and managed the shelter. Lindsey was the house mom to the animals in our care, and to me, despite my best efforts not to allow her to "mom" me.

"I *might* be moving in with him," I corrected.

She was probably right about the rest. I'd thought I'd known Julia. I'd always been popular. With my sunny personality, I'd known many people on campus. One day, I attracted more attention than usual, and not in a good way.

People I didn't recognize were pointing and laughing. Finally, someone had taken pity on me and shown me why. Julia had posted a video on a site called Campus Gossip. The video captured me falling into hysterics after a call with my parents. It had been a truly vulnerable moment, where I'd ugly cried and wailed against their constant insistence that nothing I did was enough, no matter how I tried. I'd felt safe enough to fall apart in front of her, and she'd immediately exposed my vulnerability to the whole student body. She'd also shown the video to my then boyfriend, who dumped me to date her instead.

Ever since, I'd questioned how well I knew people and refused to let anyone see beyond my chipper exterior.

"No, I don't know him beyond meeting him when I went to look at the house."

"You went by yourself?" Her voice jumped octaves so quickly, soon only the dogs surrounding us would be able to hear her. "Did you see the follow-up article after the ad? It made him sound hostile, the way he drove people away. Although I didn't hate the shot of him in a towel."

I wouldn't mind an in-person view of him in a towel, something I very well might stumble across if he said yes. Chick-Chick and I were running out of time. I needed him to say yes.

"You'd probably tell people off if a mob of them showed up unannounced at your place too. He seemed all right to me. He didn't say much." His stoic silence hadn't been a turnoff either. He'd just seemed a little shy. He'd stared and stared, doing all the talking with his eyes. His thoughts flickered in them. It had been hard to leave; I'd wanted to crack that exterior and find out more about him. I wasn't about to tell Lindsey that, nor that he'd come to my rescue with the asshole when I'd found Chick-Chick.

"What do you mean, he didn't say much? You didn't interview him to make sure he wasn't a serial killer? Or talk through logistics or anything?" Her tone had left the dogs-only register and dropped to a wary stone-cold timbre. Stage two of the mama Lindsey freak-out.

"He's probably not a serial killer." I waved her off. I didn't need her to get me worked up about this. I'd decided I was keeping the chicken that reminded me so much of myself back when I was under my parents' thumb. Given that I was keeping her, my options were limited. The last thing I wanted was to share a place with someone again. It made me sick to my stomach. I'd agonized over the decision to make myself vulnerable like that again. I'd have to do my best to keep to myself. At least I had my own room this time—so long as he said yes. He'd say yes. He had to say yes.

"And yeah, we talked through the logistics, but his answers were mostly one word, and he didn't offer much about himself. But that's okay. If he agrees to let me live there, I can do enough talking for both of us. He mostly stared at me. He has a very intense stare."

"He stared at you," she said flatly.

"Yep."

"Like a serial killer would!" She threw her arms up, then went into stage three. Pacing.

Dogs yipped from the cages nearby, hoping her movement meant they'd be getting a walk soon, which, to be fair, they would. It was about time to switch shifts and let other dogs have playtime in our larger exercise room.

I laughed. "Lindsey, relax! He's not a serial killer. I got a good vibe from him."

She stuck a finger in my face. "Oh, no. Oh no, oh no, young miss. I know that look. It's the same one half the people who come in here give the puppies. You think he's cute, don't you?"

Guilty. Although *cute* was not the word to describe Bear. Yes, he was attractive, which is what Lindsey meant. Bear was an appropriate name for him. He towered over me and had a body thick with muscle, I assumed from a combination of his construction job and the weights I'd seen in his extra bedroom. Maybe my bedroom. He'd been wearing a red-and-black button-down with the sleeves rolled up when I'd gone to see the house. He'd left his top buttons undone and had a sexy three-day beard like he'd walked right out of the Brawny paper towel logo.

No, Bear wasn't cute. He was a scalding-hot mystery. I hadn't gotten a great read on him, but I could have sworn from his beard scratches, head tilts, and pauses that he found me intriguing too.

"He's not unattractive." I blushed.

"Christ, the serial killer is going to be in your pants day one."

"He's not a serial killer! And nobody is getting in my pants."

"I've got it. Invite him out. Let me meet him. Since you apparently didn't bother with the murderer questionnaire, I'll have to do it for you."

"Invite him out where?" I asked. "And there isn't time. He still hasn't agreed to it, and if he does, I move in two days."

"Why the rush?"

"Mrs. Girsham only gave me one week to clear out."

Lindsey grimaced. "Well, I guess that's better than her refusing to let you keep the chicken there at all. Still, someone needs to screen him before you get yourself killed. Marco and I are going to a Cubs game tomorrow night. He got tickets through work, and we have a bunch of extras. Come with us. He can bring a friend too."

"I don't know."

"If he's not sure, hanging out with him some more will help convince him. Call him. Text him. Whatever. Just get him there. Please? I'm worried about you."

She meant well. At least it would give me an excuse to nudge him for an answer on the room, and he probably wouldn't want to go. "I'll text him. No promises he'll come."

Lindsey tapped her fingers on the counter and stared.

"What?" I asked.

"So text him!"

"Right now?"

"No, tomorrow, so he only has an hour to prepare. Yes, now, sweetheart!"

I stared at my phone screen. I hadn't been planning on texting him immediately. I was going to work myself up to it. The thing was, I didn't want to get to know him. I was going to be living with a man I found attractive, and whom I wanted to keep at arm's length. If I had to keep a perfect face 100 percent of the time, I'd explode. It was going to be hard enough seeing him around the house. I didn't need to add socializing outside of it to the mix.

My heart drummed in my chest, and I shifted my feet. What if he said no to the room? Or was waiting to make a decision until it was too late? Lindsay was right, seeing him again might help force his decision. It was just a baseball game. Why was I making such a big deal about this? I was willing to move in with the man but not invite him to a sporting event?

A nagging in my brain reminded me I had only asked to move in with him with such a lack of nerves because I was blocking everything out. I wasn't letting myself think about roommates, and emotions, and betrayal, and how not moving wasn't an option. I'd decided to keep Chick-Chick, so this was something I had to do. My logic could overpower any worries I might have had. Nothing I could do about it, so no sense worrying.

The game was a whole different story. That felt like a date. Or did it only feel like that because I'd found the surly man oddly attractive? Or maybe not so oddly. Who wouldn't want a piece of that?

Hey, I typed, and hovered my finger over send. No, it was always irritating when people texted with a greeting rather than telling you what they were texting about. Delete, delete, delete. Better to come right out with it.

> Trixie: My friend has tickets to the Cubs game tomorrow. Want to come?

Oh no. I chewed my lip. What if it sounded like a date to him? It wasn't a date, it was a murderer screening event, but I couldn't exactly tell him that.

He wasn't responding. I'd messed it up. He'd think I was pushy and a creep and he'd say no. Chick-Chick and I wouldn't have a place to live. That would be awful. While the rest of the cells in my brain were running around screaming with their arms thrown up, not unlike Dwight's fire drill in *The Office*, a whisper of another worry brushed my mind. If I blew this, I'd never see him again.

My heart skipped a beat while I considered this, but then the panicky cells took control. I had to act. I needed to say something to fix it.

Trixie: You could bring a friend. Just to get to know each other a bit. Help you make your decision.
Trixie: Wouldn't want you stuck living with me without knowing what you're getting into.

My eyes felt too big for my face. They were probably as wide as saucers. I worked at a smile, then looked up at Lindsey.

"Okay, I texted him. Ball is in his court."

"That stuck-a-fork-in-an-electrical-socket look you've got going on right now is not exactly boosting my confidence about this whole scenario," Lindsey deadpanned.

"What? I'm fine. Everything's fine." Except my forced smile had stretched the edges of my mouth enough to make me experience pained flashbacks to dental equipment prying it open for X-rays.

"Uh-huh."

My phone vibrated, and I nearly dropped it.

CHAPTER SIX
BEAR

"What is your face doing?" Ryan asked, then pulled the caps off two beers.

I ignored him; my eyes focused on my phone screen.

Trixie: My friend has tickets to the Cubs game tomorrow. Want to come?

It had been one full day since she'd been in my house, and I hadn't given her an answer yet. I studied the two sentences for hidden clues. There was more to this invitation, I just wasn't sure what.

"Your mouth is doing this thing where the edges are tilting up. I think I saw some teeth in a nonsnarling way. Is that . . . Bear, is that a smile?"

"Fuck you," I said.

"Eloquently put, my friend." He handed me a beer and collapsed into the chair next to me.

He had a point. I wasn't the most articulate guy around. I'd grown up with a group of particularly chatty sisters who left no room for me in the conversation. Living with a houseful of women led to adopting their mannerisms as well, which led to years of bullying. Mimicking caveman conversational skills had been my bully avoidance system for years. It had seemed like the only solution to get the jerks at school, and my father, off my back.

I took a sip, and my taste buds protested the sour hops.

Trixie: You could bring a friend. Just to get to know each other a bit. Help you make your decision.
Trixie: Wouldn't want you stuck living with me without knowing what you're getting into.

I'd taken too long to respond, and she was clearly interpreting it as me having been scared off by what she'd asked. That wasn't the case; I just couldn't decide what I wanted to do.

No, that was absurd. I knew what I wanted to do. I wanted to go to the game. She radiated positive energy. I wanted to be in her orbit for even a short while. Doing that wouldn't help me decide, though. It would guarantee my answer would be yes. She'd cloud my decision-making.

"And now you're frowning like you're either about to let out a stubborn fart—in which case, get out of my house—or whatever is on your phone is messing with your head."

"It's the latter," I said.

"What is it?" he asked.

"It's from this girl that responded to the roommate ad."

Ryan straightened in his chair. "Oh? She gonna move in?"

"I don't know. Maybe."

"Do you want her to?"

That was the million-dollar question of the day, but wanting something didn't make it a good idea.

"Maybe," I repeated.

"I'm going to take that as a yes." Ryan took a long pull from his beer. I didn't bother to refute it. I could at least admit I wanted to see her again. Roommates I wasn't so sure about. Having to keep up the caveman act around the clock sounded exhausting. "Are you not sure if she's moving in because you've got your head up your ass, or because she hasn't decided?"

"My head is firmly outside of my ass, but the choice is in my hands, if that's what you mean," I said.

"Nah, it's intra-anal," Ryan said, nodding his head assuredly.

"Intra-anal? Remind me why I'm friends with you?" I asked.

"Because you're lazy, and I'm right next door. It's a friendship of convenience. Now really, what'd she say?"

I relayed her texts so far.

"Let me get this straight. Your big problem of the day is a free baseball game with a hot girl?" He slammed his empty beer on the coffee table, like that resolved it.

"Who says she's hot?"

He rolled his eyes. "I can see your face, man. Am I wrong?"

"No," I admitted.

"Great. Decision made. And she even has a ticket for a friend! If only you had a friend nearby who likes both baseball, and girls . . ."

"All right, fine. We'll go. What do I say?"

"What is this, fourth grade? I'm not helping you pass notes. Stop overthinking it, and text back the first thing that comes to your mind."

I reread her text for the dozenth time.

Trixie: Wouldn't want you stuck living with me without knowing what you're getting into.

I let my fingers tap out a response, no filter.

Bear: Stuck living with you? You make it sound like a bad thing. Should I be worried?

Immediately, typing ellipses appeared, making me picture her nibbling at a thumbnail, nervously staring at her screen, waiting for my response.

Trixie: Definitely not. I only snore a little.

I grinned, and out of the corner off my eye caught Ryan noticing my reaction to the text. He laughed, sank back into his chair, and focused on the TV.

Bear: I'm a sound sleeper, and we'd have a few walls between us.
Trixie: Then you're good. The game?
Bear: I'm in.

I exhaled a satisfied breath as I hit send.

"We in?" Ryan asked.

"We're in," I agreed. He raised his beer in my direction, and I tipped mine toward him. A baseball game with Trixie. Yeah, I'd cheers to that.

CHAPTER SEVEN
TRIXIE

The bar district surrounding Wrigley Field swarmed with people. Warm bodies bumped and collided as baseball fans fought their way down the crowded street. I laughed, half listening to the conversation of my friends, half hoping my eyes wouldn't betray my nerves.

What if Bear said no? Or if he failed Lindsey's serial killer detector? Sure, he'd said little and stared a lot, but that didn't make him murder-y. Surely her worries were misplaced. If he failed the test, though, I'd be a fool to move in with him. I didn't know what I'd do then.

My friends and I walked down the crowded streets toward the stadium. Lindsey's hands found my shoulders and steered me out of a stream of pedestrians moving the opposite direction.

"You all right? You totally spaced out," she said.

I worked my features into a smile. "All good. Just let my mind run off for a minute there."

She smirked. "You're nervous about this. You want him to make a good impression."

Of course I did! She clearly thought it was because of some crush, but that wasn't my concern. Earlier today I'd brought Chick-Chick to another vet appointment. Her diet had stabilized. The antibiotics were clearing up her infections, and the injuries we assumed were from a car were starting to heal, but she would have a long road. Odds were nil that I'd be able to find someone else willing to foot the bill or put in the effort required to take care of her.

There was no way I was giving up on her either. Her beady little eyes watched me with growing trust. I'd never betray that trust now that I'd won it. Since we'd gotten her on her first round of medications, the coloring on her comb and wattles—two terms I hadn't known a week ago—was deepening from a sickly pale pink to a healthier ruby red.

"Where are we supposed to meet them?" asked Lindsey's husband, Marco.

"Right up here, in front of Sluggers," I answered, nodding toward the bar.

Moving in with Bear was my only option. Otherwise I'd be back to square one with no time to develop a plan B. Then again, what if he passed the test and said yes? I hadn't had a roommate since my sophomore year in college. Sure, I'd always known that I'd live with someone when I got married someday, but I'd assumed I'd have time to get to know them. I could get comfortable with them first, and it would be someone I loved.

Despite what Lindsey seemed to think, that was not what was going on with Bear. As we waited, she grinned at me like she was in on some secret I wasn't privy to.

"What?" I asked.

"Nothing, you just look rattled. You're always so perfectly jolly—it's a new look for you. I'm dying to meet the man who has you so off-balance."

I laughed. "I think you're imagining things."

She wasn't, though, and I didn't like that she was reading me so well. My parents' insistence that I always carry my stage presence and never falter had translated into being the senior superlative winner of both best smile and most friendly. Maintaining that appearance through the rest of my life was exhausting. I thought I'd broken free from the need for it when I'd moved away from them, until the incident with Julia. Now I probably never would.

Being home alone and able to let myself relax and just *be* was so important to me. I was going to lose those private moments. I hated it, but every time I felt like chickening out, I was reminded of, well, my chicken. Because that's what she was: mine. I wouldn't let anything else happen to her. No matter how many difficult memories having a roommate might dig up. As far as being alone . . . well, I could always shut myself in my room. That's what I was telling myself, anyway.

Then I saw him. He wore a white cotton Cubs T-shirt that clung tight to his chest. A dark-blue button-down hung open over his shoulders, the sleeves rolled up on his muscled forearms. I hadn't known until that moment I had a thing for forearms. He nodded when he saw me.

"Hey there, grizzly bear," I said, aiming for a smile. All it got me was confused, furrowed brows. I tugged at the belt loops of my bright-red skinny jeans awkwardly.

"Hi, Trixie," he said, emphasizing my name, like he knew he was supposed to have some nickname comeback but had nothing. He stared me down until goose bumps formed on my skin from the intensity of his smoldering gaze. It felt like he watched me forever before he added, "This is my buddy Ryan. Our next-door neighbor."

"Ours?" I asked.

Bear's eyes widened. So, a slip. He hadn't decided, but the slip told me which way he was leaning, at least subconsciously.

"Well, maybe," he amended.

I could work with maybe.

"Nice to meet you!" I skipped forward to shake Ryan's hand.

"Hey there, beautiful. Bear didn't mention his potential new roomie was so gorgeous," Ryan said.

Mentally, I rolled my eyes. Externally, I flashed a winning grin. "Why thank you!"

Bear didn't seem to appreciate his comment either. He scowled at his friend. "Behave."

I wondered if he was saying it to protect me from unwanted advances out of chivalry, or if he was just worried Ryan would scare me out of the lease. I could hold my own. I wasn't concerned about some guy who thought he was a real ladies' man, but I didn't mind the protective instinct. Over-the-top flattery was not my bag. Still, to be polite, I brushed it off.

"Oh, it's all right." Behind me, the conversation had paused as my friends waited for their introduction.

After completing the ritual greetings and handshakes, Marco passed out the tickets, and we all made our way to the stadium.

Arms loaded with popcorn, a soft pretzel, and a giant plastic tube full of daiquiri, I turned from the concession stand at the same time that Bear turned away from a neighboring stand, carrying a beer. His eyes widened when he caught sight of me.

"Want help?" he asked.

"I've got it." I shuffled my snacks around, searching for a better grip.

"Let me help." He lunged forward just in time to catch my falling popcorn.

"Thanks," I said. "That would have gone everywhere. Popcorn explosion. The cleanup crew would have been pissed."

The edge of his mouth quirked up a bit. Not quite a laugh or full-blown grin. Tough crowd.

"Peanut shells," he said. It wasn't a complete thought, but given that we were at a baseball game and cleanup crews were used to those being dropped everywhere, I guess it was enough said. We needed to work on his conversational skills. Then again, maybe not. I was going to avoid him like I was back in eighth grade, he was Monica Maynard, and I was trying not to become her next fabricated gossip victim.

We walked in silence as I attempted to think of a new topic of conversation.

"So, you were hungry," he said, more statement than question, but we'd reached four whole words, so I was counting it as a win.

"Not particularly. I like the food and wanted to sample it all. If it wouldn't have cost me my first month's rent, I'd have gotten more. I figured you wouldn't have liked that much."

"Good call," he said, and his mouth spread in a genuine smile. Victory!

We reached the stairs, and I began my climb. "I'm so going to regret not getting the nachos," I turned to call over my shoulder.

Bear's head snapped up. Holy cracker jacks, he was checking me out! I grinned, flattered. Then I remembered I was supposed to be convincing him to be my roommate. My *platonic* roommate, and butt scoping was not to be permitted. Okay, I'd done a little scoping myself when he'd shown me the apartment. I'd liked what I'd seen. Some ogling was allowed, if it wasn't blatant. We'd only check each other out in secret. Look but don't touch. I could do that.

The others were already seated, and the only two seats they'd left open were on opposite sides of Lindsey. Her husband sat several seats down from her, talking with Ryan. So much for getting to know Bear. I wasn't sure whether to be grateful or annoyed.

With the look she gave Bear, she might as well have been sitting there with a notepad full of questions. "Subtle, Linds," I muttered, edging past her.

Bear handed me my popcorn and took his seat next to her.

"So," Lindsey said. "Bear is an interesting name. How'd you pick that up? Didn't go around mauling people, did you?" She honked out three forced laughs before cutting off and giving him the stink eye.

Bear was looking at her face, so I stomped on her foot in warning.

"Only on Tuesdays," he answered offhandedly, before quieting for the national anthem.

Once the game began, Lindsey continued her conspicuous grilling of Bear, with questions including, "Do you have any hobbies, or collect anything unusual that might need to be stored in a freezer?" I think she was referring to body parts. Geez. Also, "Is there enough storage space in your house for her stuff? Or do you have too many, I don't know, boxes, blunt objects, ugly dude furniture, weaponry . . ."

Later, when the umpire made a questionable call, the crowd erupted with boos and yelled criticisms.

Lindsey turned on Bear. "How do you feel about that call, Bear? Does it make you . . . angry?" The way she said *angry* ought to have been accompanied by a twitchy stare and a dramatic *Dun, dun, dun* track.

He shrugged. "It's just a game. They play like a hundred and fifty of them."

"One sixty-two," Ryan corrected.

Lindsey frowned. "What if it was a play-off game?"

"In that case, the ump should definitely be pushed off the Sears Tower." Sears, not Willis. Like a true Chicagoan. His answers were getting wordier the longer we were there. He seemed to be relaxing. Maybe it wouldn't be such a project to get him talking if we wound up living together.

Lindsey gasped.

"I'm messing with you. I'm not that into sports. It's one game, and if they lose them all, there's always next year." He took a casual sip of his beer and winked at me over the rim of his cup.

My eyebrows shot up. The surly man I'd deemed to have the verbal conversational skills of a mime was winking at me?

"I don't know . . ." Lindsey said.

"Lindsey, give the man a break," Marco said. "Sorry, dude."

Lindsey sighed. "All right. I need a bathroom break anyway."

"Seat shuffle?" I asked, as soon as she was out of earshot.

"Please," he said, and we swapped so Bear was safely wedged between Ryan and me, free from Lindsey's interrogation.

"You put her up to that?" Bear asked, his voice quiet. "If you're worried, you don't have to move in."

Though I was worried, it was less about him and more about having to bottle up my feelings even at home. I'd fail and have them broadcast to the world, only to lose friends, my living situation, and him. I met his eyes with a reassuring smile. "I still want to. And no, I didn't. It was all her, but thank you for so graciously putting up with it. Hopefully we can just enjoy the rest of the game."

He spent the next few innings talking to the guys and focusing on the game. He got up before the seventh inning for a concession run. I stood during the seventh-inning stretch and sang "Take Me out to the Ball Game" with gusto. When the song ended, I looked up to find him returned and scratching his beard with one hand, mouth hidden.

"Are you laughing at me behind that hand?" I asked.

"Nope."

I eyed him skeptically.

"I was merely appreciating your enthusiasm."

"Uh-huh." I sat back down, and he handed me a plate.

"Nachos?" he offered. "Couldn't have you regretting your snack choices."

"Are you trying to seduce me into moving in with you?" I asked.

His voice dropped to a husky whisper. "Is it working?"

Oh, holy hot sauce. That deep flirtation did things to my body that made me glad I still had alone time this evening.

"Maybe," I gasped.

"Was it the jalapeños?" he whispered, sending a brush of warm breath to tickle my neck.

I eased my head toward him to meet his dark eyes. The sexual tension between us was as thick as Tom Selleck's mustache. And I wanted to live with this man. If he agreed, I was going to have to buy new batteries. A lot of them with all the erotic twists my mind was taking.

Bear's posture shifted, like he'd come to a decision. Hope blossomed in my chest. He was going to say yes, I could feel it. It was strange to so desperately want something I was terrified of. He opened his mouth to say something.

"Oh my god!" Lindsey's voice sliced through the moment, severing the intense connection that had been there. It was between innings, and the teams were switching sides. Lindsey pointed at the giant TV in the outfield, which displayed bubbly letters spelling out *Kiss Cam*. Below it, a heart frame centered on Bear and me.

Oh no. Nope. Not happening. I might have been undressing him with my eyes five seconds ago, but I was not about to kiss him now. I wanted to be platonic roommates. I needed his house. I could not go messing up that situation with a hot romance destined for a short life-span. Even worse than a swift breakup leaving us with an awkward living situation would be growing attached to him. Attachment would inevitably lead to opening up to him, letting him see my emotions, the good and the bad, and that would only lead to him walking away.

Bear looked at me, a question in his eyes. So, he was down for it. Flattering, but not what I wanted. I gave my head the tiniest of shakes, not wanting to embarrass him in front of thousands of people. I watched him carefully for signs of a reaction. His face was unreadable. I worked to keep mine still, to mask the instant regret I'd felt after saying no, even if it was the right thing to do.

The stubborn camera refused to pan to someone else, and baseball fans roared their encouragement.

Bear lifted my hand to his lips. He glanced at me again, this time receiving a quick nod, and placed a delicate kiss there. My heart fluttered, and a tingle ran up through said hand and to my core. I gasped and stomped down the rush of pleasure that brief contact had brought. I hadn't known a kiss on the hand could be so sensual. Bear's eyes searched mine as he slowly lowered our hands.

Satisfied or bored, the screen finally shifted to another couple, who were already making out with impressive vigor.

"Sorry," he muttered, releasing my hand. "I thought the hand kiss would make the camera move on."

"Good thing you did. The crowd sounded like it was ready to morph into a voyeuristic mob, desperate to witness a kiss. Your plans are working out today."

"Two for two."

"Two for two," I agreed, shoving a chip, heavy with cheese sauce, into my mouth.

As the final innings progressed, the small space between us fizzed with electric tension. I couldn't help but fantasize about what it might have been like if Bear had kissed me. He was gentle in seeking permission, but I imagined that once he'd had it, his lips would have met mine with a tender ferocity. I could feel the prickle of his beard on my skin, sending chills along my spine. Fantasy public make-out sessions were not a good way to start a platonic relationship.

I shook myself from the daydream as the game ended, the Cubs winning by two. A swell of cheering people pushed our group with them toward the exits. Excited shouts and drunken hollers came from every direction. We exited the stadium and veered to the side, out of the flow of walking traffic.

Everyone said their good-byes. As Bear and Lindsey shook hands, she picked up her earlier line of interrogation. "One last question for you."

"Shoot," Bear said.

"What happened to the last roommate? You know, they're still alive, right?"

"Didn't have one. Only just decided to rent the room," he answered.

"All right, he passed. I'm eighty-three percent sure he's not a murderer." Lindsey patted me on the back.

"Eighty-three percent it is," I said. "I think that's an acceptable risk."

"In that case, the room is yours," Bear said.

"Really?" I squealed, unable to moderate my tone in my excitement and utter relief. Now I just had to figure out how to tell him I was bringing a chicken with me.

On the other hand, with some things, it was better to ask for forgiveness than permission.

I jumped at him for a hug. He tensed in surprise before softening and returning the hug. His arms were so warm and strong around me. It was the kind of hug I wouldn't mind feeling every day, and it was therefore exactly the thing I should not have. Platonic roommates. Chick-Chick and I needed the room and couldn't afford to lose it over a soured relationship. It was my turn to tense up, and I awkwardly pulled away.

"I'll just have to work hard to convince you of that other seventeen percent." His deep tone and flirtatiously hooded lashes were back. Was it my imagination, or had he emphasized the *work hard*? *Dear mind, do not wander to all the ways he might do that.* Heat rushed between my thighs at the implication. His words were full of promise.

CHAPTER EIGHT
BEAR

I wiped the dirt from my hands onto my jeans and tossed the handful of weeds I'd pulled into the bin. Trixie was moving in today, and I was stress gardening in anticipation.

My phone buzzed with a text warning that she was on her way. I'd gotten little sleep the night before, trying to block out images of her ass swaying in front of me as she climbed the stairs to our row at the game, or the way a pretty blush spread across her cheeks when I'd asked if my seduction was working.

It had been a joke. I hadn't consciously been seducing her or trying to win her over. The way she'd danced on her toes, balancing an armful of snacks, and the way she'd closed her eyes and moaned in delight with her first bite of each item in her selection . . . She'd mentioned the nachos, and when I'd gotten up to get a beer, my body had autopiloted to get them. It wasn't the kind of gesture I was used to making for a woman I barely knew.

I washed my hands, and through the open living room windows I heard a car pulling up and its engine shutting down. Game face. Platonic roommates. No kissing, no flirting, and most importantly, no boners. I forced myself not to think about how poorly this would go if these things required so much effort from day one.

I opened the front door to greet her. Trixie climbed out of the car and stretched. She wore a loose top, cut high, so a hint of skin showed beneath the fluttering fabric when she lifted her arms. Below that, she sported bright-purple yoga pants that hugged her curves in a way that made my throat constrict. I was so screwed.

She dropped her arms from her stretch and waved to me. *Focus on the task at hand, Bear. Help her get her shit inside, and then you can hide in your room where you can't be tortured with images like that.*

"The room's ready?" she asked.

"Take a look."

I followed her up the stairs into the house. She moved with an impossible grace, almost like she was floating. It was alluring as hell.

"It's perfect! Thanks for clearing that stuff out for me."

"Sure," I said.

"I can get most of my things, but would you mind giving me a hand with the bed?"

A rush of heat flooded my body. Christ, all she'd done was say the word *bed* and I was turned on. This was going to be a long day.

We got the bed inside. I'd have been a dick if I sat there and watched her carry in all the rest, so we worked in tandem. I tried to avert my eyes from the sweat dripping oh-so-slowly down her neck and disappearing between her cleavage as we unloaded box after box.

"I couldn't fit everything in my car. I've got a few things left at the apartment."

"Okay. I promised to help my sister fix her garage door today, so I'll be gone when you get back," I said.

"That's okay. It'll give me time to get settled." She held out her hand.

I dug in my pocket, then passed her a key. It was only a key, so why did it feel like I was handing over a lot more?

*　*　*

Four hours later I returned to the house, grimy from a day of work. Between gardening, helping Trixie, and helping Fawn, my shirt was caked in dry sweat. Hours-old sweat was not the impression I wanted to give Trixie of what to expect of her new living conditions.

I wasn't sure what the rules for interaction would be here. I'd never lived with anyone other than my family before. What was the etiquette? Better to tread carefully and avoid talking to her when it wasn't necessary. That I could do. I'd been doing it with most people for years. My plan was to go about my business as usual, minus casual around-the-house nudity, and follow her lead on interactions beyond that.

That plan went out the window when I got to our one bathroom and found the bathtub already occupied, and not by Trixie.

Trixie knelt on the floor in front of the tub.

"What the hell is that?" I asked.

"Oh, hi," she called over her shoulder. Then she looked all around the room except at the bathtub, deliberately avoiding it.

She definitely knew what I was talking about. "What, the new mat? Sorry, I didn't toss yours; you can change it back. Mine is squishy, though. Better for kneeling on."

I gave my head one stern *I know what game you're playing* type shake, banishing the image that other reasons she might kneel had conjured up. I didn't give a damn about the bath mat. Hers looked thick and far superior to mine. The purple was a nice pop of color too. Helping my mom in her floral shop as a kid had given me an appreciation for a bit of color. I liked having a woman in the house as an excuse for getting more of it while still being able to survive one of Lyle's unannounced father-son drop-ins.

I was talking about the bath's occupant: the chicken. How had this thought never occurred to me? How, in the last three days, had I never once thought, *Oh, I met her while she was chasing a chicken; that means she'll come with a chicken*, and vetoed this whole living-together thing?

"That was *your* chicken?" I asked. The way she'd chased the thing around and had looked afraid to pick her up hadn't exactly shouted, *I'm a chicken owner who catches chickens daily!* I might not have known Trixie at the time, but she'd looked very much out of her element, even if she had grinned through the whole fiasco.

"Well"—she laughed nervously—"she's mine *now*."

"Why is there a chicken in my bathtub?"

"Because she needed a bath. That's a silly question," she said. Oh, so she thought she was funny, did she? At least my current irritation was working wonders to nullify my attraction to her.

"Trixie—"

"She's got injuries and health issues, so she needs lots of baths to keep her wounds clean."

"Why is there a chicken in my house?"

"The ad said pet-friendly, and it didn't limit the types of pets." She focused on scrubbing the chicken, keeping her face hidden from me and toward the tub.

"You're kidding."

"Nope. There's a copy of the ad on the coffee table if you want to check."

I rushed over to the table, where, sure enough, dead center, was a copy of the ad. *Pet-friendly.* The line was highlighted. The conniving woman had deliberately failed to mention she had a pet chicken and was prepared for me to have this reaction.

I cursed my meddling sisters yet again. Clenching the now crinkled newspaper clipping in my fist, I stormed back to the bathroom.

"You can't have a chicken here."

Trixie stroked the chicken's feathers. The bird clucked in response, and she cooed affectionate noises back at her.

"Yet I do," she finally said.

"All right, Mrs. Jefferson, you *may* not keep a chicken in my house."

"But her health is too fragile for the yard. And who is Mrs. Jefferson?"

"Mrs. Jefferson is a pain-in-the-ass teacher I had that used to correct my grammar like that," I growled.

"I didn't correct you."

"Fine, you used grammar to manipulate the discussion in your favor. Quit changing the subject."

"I'm not the one that brought up Mrs. Jefferson," she teased. She bent to pull the plug and start the water draining. *Don't look, don't look, don't look. Cling to that anger.* Her ass was beautifully round against the taut fabric. It was going to be seared into my brain. Not the distraction I needed for this argument.

"Since when do you talk so much?" she asked.

It grated on me that she'd so quickly caught the stark contrast between how I acted with others and how I behaved in my own home. Maybe I didn't think it was any of her business. Or maybe it felt like she was disappointed that I was talking more. I hoped she didn't prefer to think of me as some brainless grunt.

Evidently giving up on a response, she lifted the chicken up into a fluffy purple towel that matched the bath mat.

"You'll hardly notice she's here." Trixie ducked her head to avoid my eyes as she glided past me to her bedroom, closing and locking the door behind her.

I stood, feet rooted to the white linoleum that was speckled with water droplets that Trixie and the chicken had left in their wake. *She ran and hid!* And I'd barely notice her? In the first five minutes, I'd very much noticed her. I tugged at my beard as though trying to wring from it a decision on whether to pursue the argument.

Finally, I sighed. It seemed I lived with a pet chicken now. But I wasn't letting a chicken live here permanently. Trixie was afraid of that outcome, if she was running from it, and I didn't have it in me to press the issue at the moment. We'd save that for another day. All I wanted was to wash away the day's filth, have a drink, watch TV, and relax.

Resigned, I shut the bathroom door behind me and returned to the shower. A stray white feather clung to the wall of the tub, alongside a strand of long brown hair. My life summed up on the wall of a tub: girl hair and chicken feathers.

CHAPTER NINE
TRIXIE

A screech of the metal handle turning and the pitter-patter of water hitting the shower walls told me he wouldn't barge in here and throw me out. Not now, anyway. I held my position a moment longer to be sure, then peeled myself off the door before my ear molded to it.

My heart thundered in my chest.

"That was a close one," I said, eyeing Chick-Chick with my hands on my hips.

I dried her off and spent the next fifteen minutes doing her medication routine. By the time I'd finished, the shower had stopped running.

I held her on my lap, petting her tiny head, and read aloud to her. I had no idea what kind of books chickens typically went for, but she was getting a dose of fantasy for now. My reading layered over the garbled sounds of the TV in the other room.

My eyes kept darting to the door in the expectation that Bear would come bursting through and insist I take my chicken and go. I hadn't exactly been forthcoming about the fact that I'd be bringing any pets, let alone a chicken with major health issues. As glad as I might be that he hadn't kicked us out yet, I wasn't relaxing either. He'd gone from *No, you're absolutely not keeping a chicken in this house* to silence and ignoring us with surprising ease. Suspicious ease.

I wasn't pushing my luck. I'd stay cooped up in this room, pun intended, with my chicken, and just hope he'd forget long enough to come to terms with having her here.

We continued reading our story, and when I was all read out, I moved to conversation.

"Cluck, cluck, cluck?" I asked.

Cluck, cluck, cluck, she replied, giving me a dissertation on her opinion of foreshadowing as a literary device in our current read . . . or something. I clucked a few more times in response.

Evening fell. The TV still murmured in the adjacent room, trapping me in mine. I crossed and uncrossed my legs, trying to increase the size of my bladder by sheer force of will. The more I tried to avoid thinking about how badly I needed to go, the worse my need became. My traitorous body said, *Oh, you're ignoring your bladder with relative success? Allow me to alert you to a few other things.* Before I knew it, my stomach was rumbling. My eyes kept flicking to the empty glass on my nightstand as I tried to work up some saliva in my chalky, dry mouth.

My body was waging war to force me into confronting Bear, and I was losing the battle. I crossed my legs yet again, and the beating of my heart became a thrumming loud in my ear until I couldn't take it anymore. I'd have to go out there.

After returning Chick-Chick to her crate, I stood facing the door. I passed my hand in front of my face like a mime, wiping away my anxious expression to reveal my trademark smile. Time to face the judges. Everyone liked cheerful people. Happy people didn't get themselves and their pets kicked out of their new houses. *Get that wretched frown off your face. You won't even place like that.* The voice in my head sounded like my mother's.

I cracked the door open and peeked around it.

Bear sat on the couch, seemingly relaxed, with his feet propped on an ottoman. He gave me a quick nod before returning his attention to the TV. I darted across the living room to the bathroom to do my business. Hands washed and dried, I again stood behind a door, working up the courage to exit.

Okay, so he hadn't launched into an argument as soon as I'd popped my head out. He'd barely even looked up. *Be cool, Trixie.* Just a trip to the kitchen for snacks. I had brought a few things over from my apartment, but a grocery trip would be required soon.

Again, I poked my head around the door.

"Do you always peer around corners like that before moving between rooms, or is this special treatment?"

Fluffernutter, I hadn't thought about how obvious my wariness would be. I stepped into the living room in response, wearing a tentative, guilty smile.

His focus remained on the screen. "I'm not going to kick you out. Not tonight, anyway. You can relax."

The effect of his words was immediate. The tension released from my shoulders as I exhaled.

"Thanks." I turned toward the kitchen, ready to relieve my hunger now that my stress and bladder had both been taken care of.

"I made myself mac 'n' cheese. Help yourself to the leftovers."

Mac 'n' cheese, yum. Way more appealing than the bag of salad I'd placed in the fridge in my ritualistic optimism about eating healthy. The amount of browned lettuce I contributed to the garbage can was a disgrace, and a source of great shame. Yet the practice continued. I was a human work in progress.

If he wasn't going to kick me out, no sense in hiding anymore. I joined him on the couch with a bowl of mac. "Wine?" I nodded toward the glass of red he held in his hand. I'd had him pegged as more of a beer drinker.

"Something wrong with that?" he asked, taking a sip. "I'm not much for beer."

He'd drunk it at the baseball game, but I guess baseball games aren't a wine kind of venue. This was going well. *Nice conversation starter, Trixie.* I wasn't sure how pointing out his beverage choice was insulting, but he seemed to think so. "Just an observation. Who's winning?"

He scratched his beard. When the score popped back onto the screen, he answered, "Cubs."

"I can see that now," I said wryly. "It didn't sound like baseball before. Sounded more like a drama . . ."

He grunted. I had a feeling I'd get very good at interpreting grunts living with this man.

We watched the game in a silence that teetered on the edge between comfortable and not. The quiet was fine, except it made my skin tingle with the realization of his closeness. My body was on a roll with its betrayals tonight, as it ached for me to move closer to him. My mind was winning this one. No way was I scooting closer. Getting involved with my roommate/landlord would be a bad idea.

The game cut away to a commercial for a male enhancement product. I maturely stifled a laugh when Bear hastily changed the channel. He clicked up a few channels, landing on a *Grey's Anatomy* rerun, and set the remote down.

"During commercials," he clarified.

"Okay," I said.

We watched for way longer than the duration of a commercial. Holy Cheerios, was Bear a *Grey's Anatomy* fan? I decided to test my theory.

"Oh, Alex. He's my favorite. He's so cute."

"That's Jackson," Bear said reflexively. Then his eyes widened as he realized his mistake.

I itched to yell, *I knew it!* but cut him a break and held my silence, allowing myself only a small, knowing smile.

We watched two full episodes back to back in a now companionable silence, without exchanging words. I took his remaining on the channel as admission that he liked the show, something he hadn't wanted to divulge to begin with. Good. Pleasure should never be guilty. It felt like a new line had been crossed. My stomach flipped with a mix of delight at his trust and anxiety that his openness with me would lead to my openness with him.

Bear stood to refill his wineglass. "Want anything while I'm up?" he asked.

I froze, and the room spun around me for a minute. Such an innocent question, yet not one you often heard if you weren't living with someone. As soon as the words left his mouth, they began echoing through my mind in Julia's voice, a voice I could still hear clearly all these years later. A voice asking that question and later mocking me, betraying my trust, and stealing my boyfriend, scraping the dust off my barely buried issues about displaying my emotions.

"Are you okay?" he asked. He took a hesitant step toward me, realizing I was reeling but trying not to overstep.

I was far from okay. My chest was tight. I focused on taking slow, steady breaths so I didn't hyperventilate and launch myself into a full-blown panic attack. Bear was not Julia. Just because I'd shared a living space with Julia too did not make them the same, but logic was having trouble regaining control over my emotions. I forced a smile and a nod. "Yeah. I think I'm going to head to bed, though. Good night."

"Good night," he called after me. Though I avoided his eyes, I could hear the question in his voice.

There was a difference between admitting to a "guilty pleasure" show and talking about an event that had shredded me, even if I only ever let myself think about it when I was alone. For years I'd been reprimanded at the first sign of a scowl. If my smile slipped in a performance and I ended up losing, my dinner was withheld. After all that, I'd been betrayed by the first person I'd allowed to see behind that mask. How could I move past that kind of trauma?

I lay in bed, hearing the soft clang of dishes against the sink and the thump of footsteps on the ground. My gut twisted at the remembered sounds, more prominent than they'd ever been from neighbors in an apartment building. I hadn't experienced hearing another person moving around in my space after dark since Julia, and before that, my parents. I'd only ever lived with toxic people, and every reminder turned into echoing taunts and spinning faces. I yanked my pillow over my head, clenching it over my ears. A door shut; water ran. My pulse beat against my brain. *Thrum, thrum, thrum.* I couldn't block any of it out. I tossed the pillow back down and sat up, rolling my fingers to drum them on the mattress.

The light under the door winked out, and another door shut as Bear retreated to his room. Free from any chance of a witness, I caved to the emotion and let out a quiet sob as tears streamed down my face.

CHAPTER TEN

BEAR

Trixie was naked in my shower. She'd been living here for two weeks, and I still hadn't gotten used to this, just as I hadn't gotten used to her abrupt disappearances. Most of the time she exuded such pure joy, I couldn't help but be drawn to her. She was always quick with a laugh. From the way she offered her help around the house and her stories about the animals at her work, it was clear she cared deeply about everyone around her. I couldn't get enough.

Trixie's voice echoed off the shower tile as, in true Trixie form, she belted out *Walkin' on Sunshine*.

Despite her usual effervescence, every once in a while she'd seem agitated by something I'd done or said, though I'd yet to figure out what was setting her off. The corners of her lips would tremble as though fighting to frown. She'd keep her smile plastered on and retreat to her room. I was determined to understand why.

Still trying to forget that she was naked mere feet away, I ground my teeth and ignored my throbbing pulse as I shoved my breakfast burrito into the toaster oven.

The first night had been torturous as I wondered what amount of clothing she slept in. I was a boxers sleeper myself, and imagining her in a similar state of undress nearby had kept me up most of the night. That and the clattering and clucking of a chicken would take serious getting used to. I needed to talk to her about it, but every time I thought to, I remembered her hiding that first night. Given the choice between seeing her lock herself away in her room and spending time with her, I couldn't help but pick the latter.

"Damn it," I cursed, burning my finger on the burrito as I pulled it out, having been distracted by continued thoughts of a naked Trixie with water flowing over her skin.

That first morning she had stumbled out of her room in a pair of shorts so small they were surely designed to torture me. Her thin tank top also left little to the imagination. Not that my imagination hadn't run wild with it anyway. She'd trudged into the kitchen in her rainbow bunny slippers, her hair a wild mess, proclaiming that she needed coffee.

Trixie was the damn cutest hot mess I'd ever seen. In the following days, I'd had to resist the temptation to set my alarm earlier than necessary, just to be sure I'd witness the scantily clad zombie walk.

It was day fourteen of the agony of her tempting proximity, coupled with my wild imagination, and I was losing it. I had to get out of there. Plate in hand, I slammed the door behind me and stomped over to Ryan's house.

"I'm finishing my breakfast here," I announced when he answered the door.

Ryan shrugged and stepped aside to let me in. "That bad, huh?"

"She's showering. You've seen her." I tore off a bite of my bagel.

"She's showering and you are over here with me? Why didn't you join her?"

"Because it's a platonic house-sharing situation. We're not hooking up."

"I give that about another week," Ryan said.

"No, I'm not going there. Too messy when it goes wrong."

"So can I give it a go, then?" he asked.

"Hell no."

He shrugged. "Your sister's more my type anyway."

I shot him the dirtiest glare I could muster. He'd been eyeing my sisters since the day I'd moved in and they'd started showing up unannounced on the regular.

"All right, all right." He chuckled. "I still don't see why you don't go for it with Trixie, though. It's your house. If it goes to shit, kick her out."

He made a valid argument, but I couldn't even pretend to myself that kicking her out was a genuine option at this point. I'd been living with a chicken for two weeks. If that hadn't been enough to make me boot her, not much was likely to be. I had to calm down and get used to Trixie's nearness.

We'd formed a rhythm, taking turns cooking. We didn't even require much discussion about it. She'd caught me with my *Grey's Anatomy* fixation and hadn't even called me out. Her amiable smile had morphed into a knowing little smirk toward the TV. I knew I'd been caught, but she didn't say a word, just kept watching it with me. Since, watching reruns together had become something of a nightly ritual.

I huddled by Ryan's window, peering through the blinds like a child afraid of some monster down the road. Only I was a grown man, and I was afraid of my roommate turning me on. Again.

"Not to complain, but are you planning on leaving soon?" Ryan asked. "Because I need to get to work eventually."

"One minute. There she is."

Trixie exited the house, locking the door behind her. She walked on her toes to her car. I wondered if she knew she did that. She had all these quirky little mannerisms, like the flamingo stance she always did, and the way she squatted to eye level when she poured any drink, as if watching the lines on a measuring cup. They added up to make her the most fascinating creature I'd ever met.

And she was a creature. She was alien to me, but I was determined to learn the real meaning of each of her smiles and get to know what made her tick.

She drove off to work. Ryan was out the door and on his way before I even made it to my front steps. I walked up to the front door and tried the handle.

Locked.

I'd even seen her do it. In my haste to flee from an impending tight-jeans situation, I'd run out the door without keys. Hell, I didn't even have my phone. Now *I* was going to be late, not that I cared all that much. My job paid the bills, but with the jobs my company was earning becoming fewer and farther between, losing it wouldn't be so great a loss. Even if I found some shitty other job, I couldn't make much less.

I jogged around the house and tried the back door. No dice. My bedroom window, the kitchen window, all locked. Fawn and Zoey both had spares, but I had no phone to call them.

Knowing them, one of them would show up at some point today, but I didn't have all day to sit around and hope for that. I needed to call in or get to work.

There was one other chance for salvation: Trixie's window. I got a ladder out and propped it against the side of the house where her room was. It was unlocked.

I hesitated. Was this an invasion of her privacy? I hadn't set foot in her room since helping her carry things in. She left her door open most the time, so I'd seen it from the outside, but it felt weird to let myself in.

She'd understand. This was an emergency. If she didn't, to hell with it. It was my house, my room. She was just temporarily living in it.

I heaved the window open. My broad shoulders got wedged between the panes. I twisted to force myself through. I pushed against the ladder for extra force. My body didn't move, but the ladder did. It fell away from my feet and left me hanging, head and shoulders in the house, the rest dangling out the window. Not good.

Chick-Chick cocked her head at me from her perch on the newspaper bed Trixie had laid out for her.

"All right, you loud, smelly bird. If you can figure out a way to help me out of this mess, I promise not to kick you out."

Chick-Chick only continued to stare, unmoving.

"Come on, that's a good deal."

She stuck her beak into her feathers and groomed, done with me.

"Need help with that, big brother?" Zoey asked, from somewhere around the region of my feet. Of all my sisters, Zoey was the worst to have found me like this. I'd never hear the end of it. Still, I'd never been happier to hear her voice.

"Zo! The ladder!" I shouted.

"One sec, I'm documenting this. You never know when you're going to need blackmail. It's important to take advantage of these kinds of opportunities."

I ground my teeth.

"Oh, look! Another like on my selfie from this morning. Hashtag Monday vibes."

"Zoey!" I yelled.

"Oh, fine, fine. You're no fun. Don't get your boxers in a bunch. Here's the ladder." The solid step of the ladder pressed up under my feet, and I sighed in relief.

"What now? I draw the line at touching my brother's butt. I'm not pushing you."

"Did you bring your key?" I asked.

"What's going on?" Trixie asked.

My face flamed. Not only was I stuck in a window, my ass hanging out of it, but it was the window to her bedroom. What was she doing back here?

"I thought you were at work," I said.

"What did he say?" Trixie asked.

"I don't know. He seems to have forgotten we're talking to his rear end and not his face," Zoey said. "Speak up!"

"I said, I thought you were at work!" I yelled.

"I was on my way, but I realized I'd forgotten to give Chick-Chick her medicine."

"Who's Chick-Chick?" Zoey asked.

"My pet chicken!" Trixie squealed. "She's so sweet. Do you want to come meet her?"

"You're living here with a pet chicken? Oh, I cannot wait to tell everyone about this. Heck yeah, I want to meet her," Zoey said.

"Zo, a little help?" I shouted. "Any day now."

"I told you, I draw the line at sibling butt groping. We'll go in and push you from the inside," Zoey said.

Their voices disappeared, and a minute later they strolled into the room with a serious lack of urgency, chatting away about Chick-Chick.

"What's the plan here?" Zoey asked. "On a scale of one to need to grease you up with butter, how stuck are you?"

"Please don't grease me up with butter," I said. "What are you doing here, anyway?"

"If you'd prefer I leave . . ." Zoey turned on her heels.

Laughing, Trixie turned to follow.

"Zoey," I growled.

"All right. Mom had a lot of orders to fill, so I helped out last night."

I felt a twinge of guilt. It ought to have been me helping Mom out. I'd always been the one who loved it there the most, running my fingers over the knickknacks she sold and inhaling the sweet fragrances. I'd loved the bouquet assembly lines we'd put together on busy wedding weekends, which had felt like a game. Each mention made me miss it more. A visit couldn't hurt. Maybe I'd finally stop in there next weekend.

"She had some extras and knew you were on my way, so she asked me to drop off these on my way to work." She carefully set a vase on Trixie's nightstand.

Zoey and Trixie each took a shoulder and pushed. I popped free and fell past the ladder, landing hard on the ground.

"Oh shit," Zoey said, in a calm tone that did not express the same alarm that the words did.

"Bear!" Trixie shouted in genuine concern. "Are you okay?"

"Fine," I groaned. I ran inside and shot off a quick text to my boss to say I was running late, then flew into the bathroom to brush my teeth.

When I came out, Trixie capped the lid on some medicine and gave Zoey a quick hug. Not a good sign. She was getting too close to my sister way too quickly.

"So I'll see you Friday night?" Zoey asked.

"See you then," Trixie agreed.

"Later, bro. I left your drill on the kitchen table." Zoey waved and headed out the door. I watched her go like the last remnants of my sanity were walking out with her. I wasn't sure what had just transpired, but I was confident I wouldn't like it.

"What's Friday night?" I asked, warily.

"First, tell me what you were doing in my window," she teased.

"Technically, it's my window," I grunted.

"Not an answer," she singsonged. "You know, you could have just gone in through my bedroom door. It was open."

"I didn't want to go in your room. I locked myself out. Yours was the only unlocked window."

"Well, that's an anticlimactic story behind such an interesting event. I might have to make up a better one."

I groaned. "Did Zoey take pictures?"

"Loads." She grinned.

"What's Friday night?"

"Oh!" Trixie lit up at the reminder, as if we hadn't just been talking about it. "She invited me to go out to a club with her. She seems nice. You're coming, right?" She was standing on one leg again. That damned flamingo stance was so adorably distracting.

"Uh-huh." I grunted my vague agreement to whatever the last thing she'd said was. How did she not topple over? It seemed like an absurdly long time to be balanced.

"Really? Awesome. It'll be so fun. I can't wait," she cheered.

"Wait, what?" I glanced back up at her, trying to replay the conversation in my mind. Oh shit, I'd agreed to go clubbing. I hated clubbing! I was going to be miserable every second, but backing out would mean leaving Zoey alone with Trixie for an entire evening to play matchmaker and talk me up to her. I had to go with them or doom myself to Zoey's relationship meddling. That would put at risk a living situation that, despite its frustrations, I was growing accustomed to rather quickly.

"Zoey said you never come. I guess there's a first for everything, right? Better run. I'm late already. See you tonight!" She tiptoed past me and out the door.

Just like that, the woman had gotten me clubbing. I'd gone from leaving my home strictly for work, errands, and Ryan's to going to baseball games and clubs. I was lost without a lifeboat, drowning in a sea of brightly colored polka-dot confusion.

CHAPTER ELEVEN
TRIXIE

"You getting some extra Felix snuggles in before you head out for the night?" Kimmy asked when she found me for our shift-change handoff chat.

"Yep." I gave the sweet dog a few final head scratches and a hug. He'd been so shy and terrified of people when we'd taken him in. He still was uneasy around strangers, but he'd gotten used to the staff and was just the sweetest thing. Under Anastasia's expert care, he was getting much healthier too, but I kept an extra close eye on him.

I grinned as I stood to walk with Kimmy and give her the rundown on where things stood with all the animals, what needed to be done, and any special watches.

"You're in a good mood tonight," she commented, when I'd finished giving my update.

I supposed my mood could have been worse. I was looking forward to hanging out with Bear once I got home, a sentiment I probably ought to be worried about. I didn't think Kimmy was picking up that eagerness to see him, though.

"Yeah, I guess so," I said. "Anything else you need?"

I'd given her my usual bright act: the wide smile, the chipper tone. That's all she saw. Inside, my stomach was a twisty mess, because before I could spend time with my sexy—I mean adequate—roommate, I had to do one other thing first.

"No, I think I'm good. Have a good night!" Kimmy said, then turned back to feed the cats who were due for their dinner.

I grabbed my purse and got in the car. The city might be beautiful, but its traffic was not. This was one time I wouldn't mind the awful Chicago rush hour while I got my task over with. It wasn't a conversation I wanted to have in front of Bear. It was one of the days of the year that I absolutely dreaded: my mother's birthday. I dialed her number and put the phone on speaker, then pulled out of the lot.

"Hello, Trixie," she said.

I was grateful this was an audio only call and she couldn't see me flinch at the sound of her voice.

"Hi, Mom. Happy birthday," I said.

After not speaking to either of my parents through most of college and a few years after, I'd finally confronted them a year ago about the trauma they'd put me through as a kid. The apology I'd gotten had been one of those nonapologies that starts with "I'm sorry *you feel* . . ." The lack of sincerity in that kind of statement hadn't done much to help me move on. Despite that, I did think they were starting to see just how messed up the way they'd treated me had been. Since I'd called them out, Mom actually paused to think before she spoke, and her tone held none of its former malice, each word coming out as more of a gentle, exploratory prod.

"Thank you," she said, and that was where level-ten awkwardness began. The birthday wish had been the purpose of the call. That complete, neither of us knew where to go, but speaking as infrequently as we did, we both felt obligated to stay on the phone at least a little while longer.

"How's Dad?" I asked.

"He's fine. Should be home from work soon, and we'll go out for dinner for my birthday."

"Where are you headed?"

"A new sushi place."

I nodded, as if she could see me, because any logic I possessed was out the window. All efforts went to putting one metaphorical foot in front of the other here. "So . . . what's new?"

In the silence that followed, I imagined my mother holding back a sigh, both of us just doing our best to get through this conversation. I might have forgiven, but I wasn't sure that forgiveness was complete, and I certainly hadn't forgotten. I was still fighting the impact their actions had had on my behavior—heck, on my personality.

"Not too much. We bought a new refrigerator." This was why we didn't talk. All we had to share was news about appliances. The pinnacle of adulting.

"Well, that's . . . riveting." I felt a little bad for saying it, but my parents were the few people who had an inkling of what I was without my joyful mask, since they were the original enforcers of it. At least now I could be honest with them, even if sarcasm was not in the spirit of moving on.

Maybe we'd get there eventually, but it'd be a long time before our relationship resembled anything like what a parent/

child relationship ought to be. Rebuilding those bridges wasn't going to happen in a day.

"Trixie—" she chided. My heart rate picked up in anticipation of one of the lectures I'd grown so accustomed to hearing throughout my life, and had been so relieved to be without for the last few years. It didn't come, though. She just sighed.

But I couldn't get my heart rate down. This call needed to end. I forced out a quick update on my life. How work was going, that I'd adopted a chicken, and about Bear. I'd known talking about Chick-Chick would make me feel better, but I was surprised at just how much more at ease talking about Bear made me feel. With each word, the tension in my body slowly relaxed until I was a swoony, melty puddle of feelings behind the steering wheel.

"Well, a chicken is certainly an interesting choice," Mom said, bringing all my anxiety right back to the surface.

"Yep," I said through gritted teeth, daring her to say anything more. She didn't press it, but I was out of both updates and ducks to give. "Well, I'm almost home. Have a good dinner."

"Okay, thanks for calling."

"Yeah, sure," I said.

"Bye."

"Bye." I hung up and rested my wrists on the steering wheel, flexing my hand to release the tension. Another phone call down, and the unspoken tradition of talking only on special occasions continued.

I pulled into the driveway, still in a bit of a funk. I needed something to wake me up and shake me out of it. Something to make it a little easier to hold my smile in the call's aftermath.

I swung the front door open, and Bear looked up from the couch.

I tossed my bag to the floor, and while trying to keep the drain off my face, I did my best to tell him—with my mind—that tonight I needed some saving. "Let's do something fun for dinner."

CHAPTER TWELVE
BEAR

"Let me get this straight," Ryan said. "You're over here because you needed a second kitchen for dinner with your roommate?"

"Yes." I carefully sliced the jalapeño from our garden and laid it across the cheese slices.

"And this elaborate dinner requiring two kitchens is grilled cheese?"

"I didn't say it was an elaborate dinner, I said I needed a second kitchen."

"You and that girl have a weird vibe going on. If you keep coming over here to hide, I'm going to have to charge you rent." All of this was shouted from the next room, where he was slumped in a La-Z-Boy, watching TV. "Hey, you want to make me one of those while you're at it?"

"I would, if I wasn't on a time limit," I said.

I'd explained this to him many times already, but he wasn't listening. Trixie had burst in the door after work and announced she'd wanted to do something fun for dinner. I'd asked her what she meant by that, and she'd seemed stumped. She didn't know, but she wanted it to be fun. No pressure.

We'd been talking more and more. At least, I was. Her enthusiastic responses to nearly everything I said had me conversing more with her than I did with anyone. She'd spoken a lot too, but I noticed she talked about things—books, movies, TV shows, what was going on at her work—but never herself.

Despite my annoyance about her chicken, which made all sorts of noises at all hours, we'd formed a truce. Maybe even a friendship.

Whatever it was, I felt enough of an emotional connection to her to want to fulfill her request for a "fun" dinner. Even when it was just the two of us sitting on the couch together, I'd been having more fun with her than I had in a long time. She was such a ray of light that it was impossible not to have fun around her.

I'd thought about it, and my mind had gone back to an old family tradition. Growing up, after Lyle had left, every other month we'd have expiration day. Mom would pull everything that was near its best-before date out of the fridge and pantry. Our big family would break into teams and compete to see who could devise the best meals from the hodgepodge of food items before their expiration.

I'd explained the concept to Trixie.

"That sounds like lots of fun! There's only one problem."

"What?" I asked.

"We hardly have any food."

I considered this, and she was right. Aside from frozen preprepared meals, I had only a few basic staples, plus the garden.

"Oh! I've got it. A grilled cheese contest," she suggested. A good idea, because though the fridge was empty, the cheese drawer was stuffed full to overflowing. I liked cheese.

And so we were having a contest to make the best grilled cheese with the items we had around the house, fifteen-minute time limit, and separate kitchens so we couldn't copy each other's work. I pulled my sandwiches off the pan, thanked Ryan, and carried them back to our house.

Our house. I hadn't realized I'd started thinking of it that way. She'd been there only about two and a half weeks. It wasn't surprising to me, though. She took up a lot of real estate, not only in the house itself but in my mind. She'd sneaked in, and I hadn't noticed her until she was everywhere.

I knocked on the back door, balancing my plates on my arm. "You ready?"

"Ummmmm," Trixie said, not answering the question. I took that as a no and sat down on the deck to give her another minute. This wasn't exactly *Top Chef*; I'd allow a little flexibility on the time limit. There was an awful lot of clanking coming from the kitchen, considering we were making grilled cheese.

Then the smoke detector went off.

I abandoned my plates and bolted to the kitchen. Trixie stood at the stove, two items that resembled square hockey pucks more than sandwiches on the counter. I held the door open to wave the smoke out. She clicked off the stove, glanced up at me bug-eyed, then started laughing.

I hesitated, frozen on the spot, unsure if this was a *Let's laugh together* kind of laughter or an *I'm laughing because if I don't, I'll cry, but if you laugh, you're dead* kind of laughter. She glanced at me between laughs, and I couldn't help it. A laugh choked out of me.

This launched her into another fit, which was interrupted by a high-pitched squeal/hiccup kind of laugh that she seemed unable to control. She doubled over, tears at the corner of her eyes as she dumped the failed sandwiches into the garbage.

"I think you win the contest," she said, catching her breath.

"I hope you like spicy food." I retrieved the pepper jack and jalapeño grilled cheese sandwiches I'd made and set them on the table.

"My parents never taught me to cook," she said in mock defense. "I doubt they even know how to cook. I had nannies who did the cooking when I was younger," she said between bites. "My parents didn't care about much other than my dancing."

The last was added as a quiet afterthought. She shook it away, the smile never leaving her face. When she peered up at me, it widened. "These are some darn good sandwiches."

It had been the first insight she'd given me into her life, other than some details of her job. I wanted to know more, but I took my hint from the subject change that she didn't want to elaborate.

Sandwich talk it was. "The secret is using mayo instead of butter. It doesn't smoke as quickly," I said.

"Genius." She finished the last of her sandwich and eyed the other half of mine. I liked that she wasn't afraid to eat in front of me.

"Want another one?" I asked, placing a protective hand over my other half. Hey, I was hungry too.

"May—" she started, but then she sat bolt upright, like a dog who'd heard a rustle in the bushes and was on high alert. "Did you hear that?"

I strained my hearing. The click of the air conditioning, birds. That was it. "No?"

"Ice cream truck!" she yelled, and shot out of her seat, as though she were an eight-year-old hit with that same revelation. Her spirit was infectious. I grinned and followed her.

She ran on her toes the whole way, bouncing on them in place once she reached the sidewalk. I came up behind her, still not hearing the truck. A minute later, the tune of *The Entertainer* being played on a loop reached my ears. Did she have supersonic hearing? She usually asked me to turn up the sound on the TV.

"How did you hear that?" I asked.

"Specialized hearing. I can hear an ice cream truck miles away." She already had her wallet in hand.

"You're lucky it was headed down our street."

It felt like it was moving in slow motion, since she'd heard it when it was so far away. We watched as it stopped to make sales to a couple groups of kids on its way.

"We should have run down there," she said.

"I don't do running," I said.

"Me either. Unless it's after ice cream. Or away from something deadly. Ice cream and mortal peril are my only motivators strong enough to run."

"Sounds about right."

We talked more as the truck continued its crawl toward us. That foot of hers slid up her calf, and she stood there in her flamingo pose.

"This is torture," she said.

"The two of us talking? Yeah, I know."

Her foot dropped to brace her, and she gave me a playful shove. The spot where her hands touched me radiated a phantom warmth. I'd say I liked this playful side of her, but it was too much of her to be considered a side. She was this playful and chipper most the time, or at least she was from what I'd seen in the last few weeks.

When I'd agreed to let her move in, I'd expected we wouldn't see much of each other. We'd share a house and pass each other occasionally in the shared spaces, but that would be about it. I hadn't imagined we'd be spending every evening together, or that it could—or would—be so fun. I couldn't remember the last time I'd consistently enjoyed myself so much.

The truck finally arrived, and we placed our orders. Trixie ordered the Tweety Bird and announced that it had gum ball eyes. The adult thing to do seemed to be to order a plain bar, but this ice cream truck experience, and Trixie getting her Tweety Bird, was giving me a wave of nostalgia.

"Go on, get a fun one," she said, apparently now capable of reading my mind. "You know you want to."

"I'll get the Ninja Turtle," I said, handing over my money.

"Cowabunga, dude," Trixie said. "Wait, did they say that?"

"I think so?" I wasn't sure. My memories of the show were vague.

We sat on the back deck and ate our ice cream. My heart tugged for her in a way that was surprising me less each time I felt it. She was becoming far more than a roommate to me. I really cared about her, and as we ate, I watched her and grinned like a fool.

Trixie stared at the lilies, transfixed. It wasn't the first time I'd caught her doing this. We had a decent garden, given the small size of our yard, with a variety of vegetables and flowers, but she always seemed to stare at the lilies in particular.

"You like lilies?" I asked.

She froze midlick, which sent my mind off in a direction I immediately had to call it back from before it became a problem.

Aside from the picture being too tempting and provocative, something told me watching her would startle her into a subject change, so I ate my ice cream with the focus of someone trying to use chopsticks for the first time.

The silence dragged out until finally she laid her empty stick on the deck. "I've always liked them."

"They're pretty." I finished my ice cream, which was as good as I remembered.

"Mm-hmm," she agreed, noncommittal. I sensed more, so I waited. "My parents got them for me for my second dance recital. I loved the flowers so much, it became our tradition. Every recital after that, they brought me lilies. I've got mixed feelings about the parents, but I still love the lilies."

And there it was. The comment about her feelings toward her parents and the fact that she'd specified her *second* dance recital nagged at me. There was more to that story, but maybe she'd sensed this near revelation and line of questioning coming, because she made an excuse to check on Chick-Chick and ducked inside.

Except for wine refills and restroom breaks, I didn't see her the rest of the night.

A torrent of clucking punctuated the evening. I tried to summon my irritation, or the previous urge to tell her the chicken had to go. I couldn't find it.

CHAPTER THIRTEEN
TRIXIE

"I can't believe you're going to stay up late enough to go clubbing with us," Zoey said to Fawn's reflection in the mirror as she swiped on mascara in our bathroom the following night.

"I can't either, but I wasn't about to miss Bear at a nightclub. How'd you do it?" Fawn asked, squeezing the handle of a curling iron.

"I asked." I'd been pleasantly surprised when he'd said yes. Clubbing didn't seem like his scene, but he'd surprised me with his TV habits already, so I'd figured this was another case of Bear's preferences seeming at odds with his character.

Bear sat on the couch, stress playing with Play-Doh. I kept a bowlful of the stuff on the coffee table for nervous fidgeting. He'd laughed at the idea, but after only a few days had taken to playing with it while we sat and watched TV together. As we prepared for the evening out, he stretched and shredded that Doh like he was practicing for the pizza-tossing world championships.

I almost wished they hadn't told me it was an odd thing for him to agree to, so I wouldn't spend the whole night over-analyzing it. Zoey said she'd invited him many times before and always gotten a quick no. What did it mean that the first time I asked, he'd agreed right away? He hadn't sounded enthusiastic. "Uh-huh" wasn't the most overwhelmingly positive of responses, but he had agreed.

"You just asked." Zoey laughed. "I should have known." Her eyes danced with suggestion, though what they were suggesting I didn't know.

Bear drove and insisted his sisters leave me the front seat, not that he needed to do much insisting. The sisters had been headed for the back seat anyway, where they spent most of the ride with their heads bent together, whispering.

The club wasn't one I was familiar with, but it was a popular one, apparently. A long line spiraled around stanchioned ropes, but Zoey marched right past it.

"Zoey!" The bouncer pulled her into a hug.

"Hi, Wayne. These three are with me," Zoey said.

"Come on in," he said, waving us past, to the annoyed groans of those at the front of the line.

I raised an eyebrow at Fawn, and she leaned in conspiratorially.

"This club seems to be Zoey's designated dating pool. I think she has three former partners who all work here."

"And amicable breakups too, apparently," I said.

We walked in and were blasted with the urgent pounding of the bass as we walked down the hall to the main room of the club. It was dark, with flashing strobes and smoke pouring onto the dance floor. Major sensory overload.

Zoey started dancing while she walked as soon as we entered the room. With a look of wonderment on her face, Fawn gazed around the room at the vast dance floor, ringed by seating nooks with black couches, and two huge bars. She'd heard about the club but apparently had never been. Bear looked lost, faced with the sea of sequined and scantily clad twentysomethings. I wasn't sure how I felt yet.

"I'm going to need a drink," Bear shouted in my ear to be heard over the music.

I nodded and headed toward the bar. As we wove through the sardine-packed crowd, his hand grazed the small of my back. It sent a tingling rush up my spine. *Don't read into it, Trixie; it's just so he doesn't lose you in the crowd.* I shouldn't be excited about his touch. I didn't want his touch. He was my roommate, and we were not going there. Still, all my focus homed in on that spot where his hand had touched me, and it was not an unpleasant sensation.

I ordered myself a cocktail and started a tab. I watched Bear as he leaned over the bar, waiting for the bartender to finish mixing my drink. I stared at his scruff, fighting the powerful urge to run a hand through it. Biscuits and gravy. I wasn't even drunk yet and was having inappropriate urges toward Bear. Better take it easy on the alcohol.

Zoey was already sitting in a corner with Fawn and a handful of people Zoey appeared to know. I retrieved my drink from the bartender.

"For you?" he asked Bear.

"A Bud Light," Bear called over the thrumming music. Interesting. Beer at the baseball game and the club. He drank it often for someone who didn't like beer.

"What?" he asked. "I can feel you staring at me."

"Nothing." I shook my head.

"Trixie!" A woman with a miniscule black skirt and sparkly top came running over and pulled me into a hug. "How are you?"

"So good!" I answered. I had no idea who she was. "Living the dream."

We shout-talked for a few minutes, Bear swigging his beer and watching me. I made a polite excuse about needing to get back to my group and said good-bye.

"No introduction?" he asked, with what might have been a hint of disappointment. I wondered if it was because he'd been interested in her or because he felt slighted by me.

"I couldn't! I had no clue who she was."

Bear frowned. "She acted like you were best friends."

"Trixie!" Another woman, this time one I recognized, pulled me into a fly-by hug as a friend of hers dragged her in another direction.

"And her?" he asked.

"Annika, the barista at the coffee shop by our house," I said. "She's a sweetheart."

"Do you habitually hug everyone?"

"Yep," I answered. It was true. I gave out hugs and smiles like I was handing out beads at a Mardi Gras parade.

He shifted and worked his mouth like he was about to say something but thought better of it.

"Let's go find your sisters," I said.

He raised a hand and pointed at the crowd in the corner, where Zoey was perched on the end of the bar.

"How is she not getting kicked off there?" I asked.

He pointed again, this time to the ponytailed bartender who was flirting with Zoey.

"That explains it," I laughed, and we walked in their direction.

"I think she's one of Zoey's exes. Or past hookups. Or whatever," he explained.

"Baby brother!" Fawn stumbled over. "Zoey gave me shots."

Bear's response was an expression of pain.

"A lot," she giggled.

"Two!" Zoey shouted over the shoulders of the others in her group. "She's had *two* drinks." Zoey gave the bartender a finger wave, then hopped down to join us. "She's such a lightweight."

"I have kids! I don't get out often enough to drink," Fawn said.

"That's funny. My kids are the reason I drink so much," said Sarah, another of Zoey's friends. "Trixie! Hey, girl. How do you know Zoey?"

We exchanged pleasantries before the sisters excused themselves to the restroom and Sarah retreated back to the circle of Zoey's friends by the bar.

Bear folded his arms and stared at me.

I laughed. "She adopted a dog from the shelter."

"Do you know everyone here?" he asked.

"Of course not!" Though I had spied other people I knew. I pressed my lips together, but the edges of my mouth quirked up.

"Shit, you do," he said.

"Not *everyone*." I returned the wave of one of my old neighbors from across the room. Big city in a small world. As much as I enjoyed the game and was tempted to show him how many people I knew, most were acquaintances that I didn't have a burning desire to talk to, and his unreadable reaction was weirding me out. It almost felt like my knowing a lot of people was a bad thing.

We stood in our group a while longer, Zoey plying us with more drinks. I was feeling a decent buzz when Fawn, moving like a blur, flew into me and looped her arm with mine. "Let's dance!"

Zoey appeared out of nowhere, grabbing Bear's arm and pulling him out to the dance floor. Fawn and Zoey dove right in, wiggling their hips in time with the music. I stared at Bear, and he stared back at me, his posture rigid, like a stone.

My body swayed of its own volition, a temptation I'd never been able to resist around music. Even though my training was in a variety of classical styles, I moved no matter the music. I loved to dance and considered it nothing short of a miracle that it hadn't been ruined by my parents.

Dancing always brought me back to the day my life changed and my parents took notice of me, a blessing mixed with a curse if ever there was one. I was glad for the different style of dance tonight. I could enjoy myself and move my body, as my muscles often itched to do, without betraying my classical skills. That would lead to questions, and questions led to things like talking about my parents' soulless detachment from me before that recital. Mother's utter disgust at anything that wasn't a display of total happiness and put-togetherness once they became fixated on my dance "career." Her ferocious insistence that I be the best, look the best, and win.

On the dance floor, though, I could sway to the beat and let myself be free. I flung my head back and raised my arms. My legs carried me, and a true ease washed over me. I didn't have to work to maintain my cheerful air when dancing. It made me feel alive.

A song later, Zoey and Fawn pecked at Bear to get him to dance. He did that scratch-at-his-beard thing that seemed more like a thoughtful reflex than an actual itch. Fawn hip-checked him, and he stepped from side to side with militaristic form, not at all like any kind of dance.

"Hopeless," Zoey chided, then took off to refill her drink.

Fawn spun back into her own rhythm, having lost any sense of the beat and doing her own thing on the dance floor. Bear watched me, and something in his eyes gave me the sense that he wanted to dance but was holding himself back.

Alcohol coursed through my veins, making me brave. On an impulse, I took his hand. I raised his arm and spun myself under it to the music. With surprising ease, he spun me back and caught me with his other hand. His large arms engulfed me, solid and warm.

I glanced up at him with a flirtatious smirk.

He pulled me in close to speak into my ear over the techno beat. "If you keep looking at me like that, my sisters might get the wrong idea about us."

"Oh?" I feigned innocence, tugging his rough hands down to my hips. "What might that wrong idea be?" What was I doing? Body pressed against his, I moved. I buried my face in his chest to hide the flush in my cheeks from my arousal.

Bear tensed at the contact, then relaxed back into motion, splaying his hands on my side. "Are you trying to kill me?"

"And have to make my own pancakes?" I teased, running my hand down his chest. My mind was screaming *bad idea, bad idea*, but the music and liquid courage made me bold. I was never braver or more comfortable than with a rhythm moving through me.

Okay, a little dancing with Bear. What harm could come from that? I allowed myself to get lost in the sounds, and in this giant of a man who danced well when he let himself.

We danced to song after song. The sometimes gentle, sometimes rough brushes of our bodies were making my breathing heavy in a way that had nothing to do with the exertion. The song changed, and the tempo quickened. My skin tingled all over as I moved, and my legs wobbled. Bear's hand, gently caressing my hip as we writhed together, seared my skin.

I tipped my face up, and he looked down to meet my eyes. The loud music became an echo, almost as though we were underwater, and all I could see and all I could feel was Bear. I slowly leaned forward, tilting my mouth up toward him. His eyes darted to my lips, then back to my eyes with a question. I leaned further, and he tilted his mouth down toward mine.

Suddenly, a train of people pushing to the middle of the floor crashed into us, breaking the moment. I nearly moved back in, but out of the corner of my eyes, I saw the sisters huddled together. They grinned widely as they watched us. On second thought, maybe he was right. They definitely looked like they were getting *Send my brother down the aisle* vibes.

Hooking up with Bear would make our living situation—something that was already a challenge for me—even more awkward. I had to keep reminding myself it was bound to end poorly. I took a step back and threaded my hand into his. He spun me out effortlessly, and I broke the contact, throwing my hands up in the air to dance on my own.

Bear followed my lead, angling his body to open ourselves up for others to join our dance circle. Zoey looked annoyed, and Fawn smiled knowingly—more astute than I'd have thought her capable of being in her current state—and twirled her way into our circle.

Not long after, we paid our tabs, which were surprisingly inexpensive, something that probably had a lot to do with Zoey's over-the-bar good-bye kiss with the bartender.

"I'm surprised you didn't stay and wait for her to be off work," I teased Zoey from the front seat.

Zoey shrugged. "She'll have to clean up even after they close. She's a few hours from being done, and she'll be tired. She's got my number."

"Playin' it cool," Fawn said between hiccups. Not a chance she was driving herself home. She was the biggest lightweight I'd seen in a long time. As we pulled into the driveway, Fawn felt around in the dark. "Who moved the handle?"

"Nobody moved it, you're just drunk." Zoey opened her own door, bathing the car in the dome light's glow.

Fawn was too busy gaping at being called drunk to notice that she could now see the elusive handle. Bear and I climbed out and helped wrangle a stumbling and now outraged Fawn over to Zoey's car.

"Put her in the back seat. She'll pass out before we reach the end of your street," Zoey said.

Fawn hiccupped. "That's true. It's way past my bedtime." *Hiccup.* "You're a bad influence." She jabbed a finger in my direction.

"Who, me?" I laughed.

"Yup," Fawn said. "But it's okay, because I like you."

"I think your sister is the bad influence, but I like you too," I said.

We rolled her into the back seat. Zoey retrieved a sweater from among the discarded energy drink cans, receipts, shoes, and other miscellaneous items that crowded the floor. She folded it up like a pillow, and Fawn cooed as she laid her head down on it.

"You good with her?" Bear asked.

"Yeah. Owen will help me get her inside. He'll think it's hilarious," Zoey said.

As her taillights disappeared around the corner, Bear and I retreated into the house.

I flung my purse down on the couch. Bear and I stood in the living room, staring at each other. Silence hung heavily between us. The air was syrupy with it. My body remembered the feel of his and was replaying each touch in excruciating, vivid detail. I needed to cool things down. We stepped in unison toward the kitchen. I needed to avoid contact at all costs if I was to have any success at not jumping his bones tonight. When our arms came close in the doorway, I leaped back as though they were opposing magnets, repelling each other.

"Go ahead," we both said at once. "No, you."

We laughed.

"I'm going to take a step now," I said.

Bear held out his hand in an *after you* gesture.

Playing for time, I traced the edges of a glittery pink blob magnet of no discernible shape that was stuck to the fridge, likely a creation of Bear's niece, Bella. My spine tingled, sensing his stare. Finally, I poured myself water. "Want one?"

"Please," he said, behind me. He was close. Too close. Was this kitchen always this small? It didn't usually feel so small. It wasn't normally this hot in here. Maybe we needed to turn on the air conditioner . . .

As I handed him a glass, our fingers brushed, and my eyes widened. He turned away, scratching his beard.

My feet took over. I darted to the far side of the kitchen table. In my panic, I slammed my glass onto it far harder than I intended to. Even that minute contact with his hand had my entire body back on edge. I was squirming where I stood. I leaned over the table, pressing my palms firmly onto it to keep from touching him.

He watched me and warily set his own glass down. "What are you doing?"

"Putting a barrier between us," I gasped, inwardly cursing the betrayal of my breathy tone.

He spread his arms and placed his palms on the table, mimicking my stance.

"And why are you doing that?" His voice was a deep rumble, and I fought back the moan that began in my throat. Was his voice always so deep? No. I was like 93 percent sure it wasn't. I was affecting him too.

"Because I don't trust myself right now."

He let out a low chuckle. "At least it isn't me you mistrust."

"I didn't say that." Despite myself, I grinned. "I just mistrust myself more at the moment."

"I see," he growled. Actually growled.

My voice rose a quivery octave. "I think we need to set ground rules."

He lifted his palms and rubbed at his face again, even more than normal. His hands swung around with a kind of nervous energy. He didn't appear to know what to do with them.

"Ground rules like, keep a table between us at all times?" he asked.

"Dragging a table around could be tedious, but you're on the right track."

He stared me down, waiting for me to continue.

"You know what I mean. Don't tell me it isn't taking all you've got to keep your hands off me." My face flushed in surprise at my own boldness. I suddenly panicked that I'd read him all wrong and my implied admission of struggling to contain my own hands was about to be very embarrassing.

"I won't," he said. So, not a misread then. I wasn't sure if that was a relief or not. Less embarrassing, yes, but not exactly making it easier to resist him.

"And do you agree that us hooking up would be a bad idea, given that we live together?"

His hands returned to the table, this time gripping the edges. Dang, it was taking all his strength to resist. He tipped his head in a single resolute nod.

"So, obviously, dancing together again is out of the question, given the effect it's currently having on us."

Bear hesitated, then gave another nod.

"What else?" I asked.

He shrugged. Helpful. Apparently, this was the silent Bear, generally reserved for public settings. The mildly talkative Bear that usually came out in private was nowhere to be seen.

I straightened. My pulse returned to a more normal level as we talked it out. His eyes flicked down to my foot, pressed against my calf, then back up to my face.

"The suggestion is good, but maybe not with a table," I ventured. "We need some social distancing up in here."

"I don't think there's room in the house to be six feet apart at all times," Bear said.

"Okay, how about three?"

His eyes darkened. "And are you going to carry around a measuring tape?"

"It was just a suggestion," I said defensively.

"Three feet," he growled. "No dancing."

"Actually, the three-feet thing should take care of most of it. With three feet distance, we can't dance or—" I hesitated, my pulse throbbing in my neck under the heat of his stare.

"Or?" he prompted, his voice that gravelly rumble that told me he knew exactly what *or* meant, and he wanted to do all the *ors* right now.

"Or touch," I whispered, swallowing hard, those eyes boring into me. His fingers twitched on the table.

"Or?"

My core clenched in reaction. Oh Pikachu, he was going to make me say more. No, he couldn't make me stay here and play this out. This conversation could end here and now. Internally, I whimpered. I didn't want it to.

I was having to carefully wrangle my breathing to a normal pace. At the moment, I felt more inclined to pant. My chest heaved as I forced a slow, steady breath. His eyes shot to my cleavage. He'd definitely noticed. His eyes narrowed as he forced them back up to my face, his hands raking his chin through his scruff. I'd have done dangerous things to be the one raking fingers through that scruff right now.

"Kiss," I said.

His jaw worked back and forth, those wandering eyes trained on my lips. I wanted to taste his, feel them on mine. The lack of sensation there threatened to burn me up. I bit my lip to assuage the ache.

He buckled at the sight, then leaned on the table, his face inching toward me. I was already beginning to question the logic of this three-foot rule. The table would make a better canvas for heavy petting than it was a barrier.

"Or?" he whispered.

A damp heat rose between my thighs, and my legs trembled. Even though the table kept our bodies distanced, our faces were only a breath apart, our eyes fixed on each other's.

"Sex?" My voice pitched an octave higher in nerves and heady anticipation. In such close quarters, the dilation of his pupils in response was clear.

"Three feet?" he asked again.

I nodded. If I tried to speak, my voice might have risen high enough that only dogs could hear it.

"You've got it, roomie." He shoved off the table and walked off to his room.

His sudden departure and stark reminder of our living situation were a bucket of cold water, poured over me and rushing through my veins. It crashed me back to reality. The ultimate buzzkill.

I fled to my room and slammed the door behind me. On second thought, I turned back to lock it, not that I thought Bear would let himself in. What I needed was for someone to lock me in from the outside, so I didn't accidentally-on-purpose wind up in his bed.

"I'm in for more than I'd bargained for with that one, Chick-Chick," I said, filling up her little bowl with food.

She clucked at me happily.

Physical attraction aside, I needed to put a stop to whatever was happening between Bear and me. I'd allowed myself to get close to a roommate before, and it had come back to bite me. Hard. I hadn't been careful about that here. I'd come in with every *intention* of being careful, and yet I was going to need an action plan to keep Bear away, and to keep myself from him.

CHAPTER FOURTEEN
BEAR

I was learning a new lesson: hangovers were even more unpleasant when they followed a night of zero sleep because of a raging case of blue balls. Trixie had been more intoxicating than the beer I'd choked down.

This was a job for mass quantities of caffeine. My phone vibrated on the counter as I pressed start on the brewer.

Fawn: Had fun last night. Was great to meet Trixie.

That was a pry if ever there was one, and I wasn't biting. Although I was curious what she thought. I huffed out a breath. No. Asking would turn it into a whole big thing. But maybe Fawn could give me some perspective to cool my jets, because I couldn't function with more unsatisfied, sleepless nights.

Bear: What did you think of her?

There. Question asked. I put my phone back in my pocket where it belonged and impatiently waited for the coffee. Only seconds passed before the familiar buzz had me fishing it back out again.

Fawn: You already know Zoey and I loved her.
Bear: Do you think Mom and Dad would like her?

There I went, acting before thinking. If the initial question would open up a can of worms, this would open up a whole aquarium of eels. Proving the point, my phone rang immediately. I hurried to answer it and run outside before I woke Trixie.

"Zoey and I thought you'd make a great couple, but I expected it'd take longer than this for you to see it. If you want our parents' opinion, though, it must be serious," she said, jumping straight to the point.

"I don't want to get their opinion. I was just using it as a barometer for yours. Strictly for curiosity's sake."

"If you want their opinion, introduce them to her."

No. Absolutely not. That would not be happening. If my sisters were ready to shove me down the aisle, my parents would conjure one of those airport-moving sidewalks to expedite it.

"Did I lose you?" Fawn asked.

"No."

"Hmm . . ."

I'd been *hmm*'d by sisters many times before, and it always meant trouble. "Fawn."

"What?" She attempted to sound innocent and came across as anything but.

"You know what. Stay out of it. No meddling."

"Oh, what's that, Bella sweetie? You need Mommy?" she asked in a tone that made it clear Bella was not actually calling for her. "Sorry, Bear, must go."

The line went dead, and I shook my head. Without Fawn to distract me, my mind quickly returned to thoughts of Trixie pressed against my chest, moving to the music. As soon as I'd inhaled a cup of coffee, I went straight for the shower.

I tried to summon the energy to scrub my body as the water beat down on my skin, washing away the toxins leaking from my pores.

From the moment she'd set foot on the dance floor, I hadn't been able to take my eyes off her. She moved with hypnotizing grace and practiced ease. I had new insight into the enigma that was the woman I was living with. When she'd first let the music take control, she'd thrown her head back. The lines on her face had vanished, her mouth curving up into what I now was certain was her true smile. That had been the sexiest thing about her, even more than the easy sway of her hips.

I turned off the water and toweled myself dry, smiling at the little signs of Trixie around the room: her bottles of products on the shower ledge, her hot-pink toothbrush balanced in a purple cup.

I'd known I was done for before she even touched me at the club. She'd grabbed my hand, and I'd shut off the part of my brain that was trying to remind me she was my roommate and let my body take over. Then she'd looked up at me with those hooded lashes, and fuck. I was going to need a second cold shower if I didn't get my mind off her soon.

I pulled on my boxers and a pair of shorts.

Trixie was right. We needed boundaries, or things would go to hell quickly. That didn't make her rules grate on me any less. After feeling her skin on mine the night before, the last thing I wanted was three feet between us. Three damn feet. Not even "a reasonable distance" or "no touching." She had to put a three-foot label on it. I didn't like it.

After throwing my shirt on, I exited the bathroom. Her door was still shut.

No waking sounds came from her room, so I stormed out to the garage. My joke from last night now seemed a perfect, if petty, way to stop the three-feet nonsense. We were adults and could keep a respectable distance without having to measure out an approximation of three feet. I retrieved my tape measure. If she was so specific, then I would take her literally.

I wanted to knock on that door and climb into bed with her. I needed to get her off my mind, and fast. Pancakes. I'd make pancakes. Pancakes were the answer to everything. I poured the batter into the pan and hesitated. Trixie wore frilly, brightly colored, polka-dot dresses and mismatched her socks with a frequency that had to be intentional. I snatched Bella's sprinkles out of the cabinet and shook some onto half the pancakes before I could second-guess myself.

I heard her bedroom door creak and a yawn, then the bathroom door shutting. A minute or two later, Trixie zombie-walked into the kitchen in one of those miniscule outfits she called pajamas. Her hair stuck out at wild angles, and she was wearing fuzzy slippers. I was getting turned on by a grown woman in bunny slippers who looked like she'd stuck a fork in an electrical socket. It was all very confusing. She was wildly hot even as a mess, and I was coming to adore her quirks. Damn it.

"Good morning!" She smiled, despite her tired eyes. "Oooh, pancakes."

She moved to grab her plate off the counter.

"Wait," I cautioned her, then pulled out the tape measure, extending it three feet. "You better step back and let me put your plate on the table. I'll have to eat at the counter."

Her ever-present smile remained, but extra crinkles appeared around the edges, and her eyes were full of fire. Oh yeah, she was pissed.

The tape measure cracked and flopped limply to the ground.

"Don't be ridiculous." Her tone was high and bright but rigid. "You can sit at the table."

I was so glad she was giving me permission to sit at my own table in my own house. It was grating on me to be so drawn to her and so irritated by her at the same time. I knew her rules were for the best, and I also wanted to do everything I could to convince her to discard them.

"And break one of the rules five minutes into the day?" I asked.

She rolled her eyes at me with an annoyed smirk. "Point taken." She lunged within my radius of space to grab the plate. My skin crackled from the nearness, proving the validity of her rule, but hell if I'd ever admit that.

Trixie stared down at her plate, a wide smile spreading. "Bear."

"Yeah?"

"Did you put sprinkles on my pancakes?"

I had. As far as I knew, sprinkles didn't spontaneously will themselves into existence just because pancakes were being presented to a unicorn of a woman. I hid my face behind my coffee mug.

"Oh Bea-ear," she sang.

"It seemed like something you'd like," I admitted.

She squeezed a Buddy the Elf–sized portion of syrup out. "I very much do. Thank you."

I nodded and leaned against the counter, eating my own pancakes. We ate quietly, if not entirely comfortably. Tension remained in the air. The bubble of it had been popped by the sprinkles, but it dispersed and floated around us, ready to strike. I was making bubble analogies for reading the room. Shit, she was getting into my head.

"I'll get the dishes," she said, holding out her hand for my plate. She washed, humming to herself, and I dried. Side by side, we stood in unspoken agreement to ignore the ridiculous three-foot rule.

As she handed me the last plate, I broke the silence. "Can I meet her?"

"Meet who?" she asked.

I flushed. Was this a weird thing to ask? If I was going to live with her, there was no point ignoring her. "The chicken."

Trixie's eyes lit up. "You want to formally meet Chick-Chick?"

"Yeah," I said. "Despite what you said, keeping her in your room does not make her silent and scentless. I definitely notice her. Might as well get to know her."

She placed her hand on my arm, causing the hair on it to jolt to attention, and met my eyes. "Thank you."

Her alluring gaze pulled me in until I forgot what we'd been talking about.

Trixie tiptoed out of the room. "Come on!"

I waited outside her door as she retrieved Chick-Chick, then placed her into my unprepared hands. I fumbled to find the right grip, paranoid I was either holding her too loosely and would drop her or too tightly and would crush her tiny frame. I was clueless.

Her talons pressed into my arm, and I stared at them. As a man of my size whose job required manual labor, my forearms were not small, yet her talons covered them. I couldn't remember ever being in such close quarters with a chicken before, let alone holding one. I'd never realized how huge their feet were.

Trixie sank to the ground cross-legged and tugged on my pant leg, encouraging me to follow. She motioned to the floor, and I carefully set Chick-Chick down. I hovered my hands over her awkwardly, unsure how to engage now that I wasn't holding her.

Sensing my hesitation, Trixie smiled and reached for my hand. "May I?"

I nodded, and she guided me to stroke Chick-Chick's feathers. Trixie released my hand, and gradually it felt less awkward. I startled when the chicken flapped and hobbled a step away.

"Is she still sick?" I asked.

"She's healthier than she was. See how her coloring is getting redder here?"

I nodded. "She has a limp."

"Yeah, we think she got hit by a car before I picked her up. I kept her from walking around at first so she could heal, but she's allowed to now. I've tried, but she hasn't been interested, and there wasn't much room to experiment."

Guilt immediately rushed through me. It was my fault this gentle bird who had now scrambled over to Trixie wasn't thriving. I rubbed at my face. I did not want a chicken roaming my house. Then I looked at Trixie and saw how she worked to maintain her positivity. I couldn't take that away from her. I'd yet to see her let out a frown. I didn't want to be the one to put one there. The worst I'd seen was her smile slipping to more of a neutral expression.

It wasn't that I disliked animals; I just had no desire to care for one. It might be fun to have one around that I wasn't responsible for.

"She can roam," I said at last.

There it was. The real one. The smile that made the whole room brighter. I'd deal with a hundred chickens to see her that happy.

Chick-Chick pooped on the floor. Okay, maybe not a hundred.

Trixie's eyes widened, and her face flushed. "I'll get that."

I sighed and stood to retrieve cleaning supplies. "Don't bother. I'll get it. You can help her get acclimated."

I felt her eyes on me as I went.

When I returned with paper towels and cleaning spray to mop up the mess, Trixie was cooing softly and stroking Chick-Chick, who had panicked when Trixie had moved her farther away, encouraging her to explore.

"It's okay, sweetheart. I've got you. It's a good thing, I promise."

I stood in the doorway, watching her calm the chicken. She hummed a lullaby. Chick-Chick's frantic movement slowed, and her panicked screeches became more of a confused warble.

"You're good at that," I commented.

"There, there," Trixie cooed. "You're all right."

She tried again, moving Chick-Chick away with deliberate slowness. This time, the reluctant chicken stayed calm, but she froze to the spot and refused to move.

"She trusts you," I said.

"I'm surprised she does. I take her to vet appointment after vet appointment where she gets poked and prodded, and I have to give her all these medicines she hates. It's a wonder she tolerates me at all." Seeing Chick-Chick wasn't going anywhere, Trixie edged next to her.

I studied the beautiful woman in front of me, with the constant smile. The good humor and the bleeding heart. I couldn't imagine anyone using the word *tolerate* to describe being around her. She was so much more than tolerable. She brightened my days and made me want to brighten hers. She made me agree to get out of the house just to spend more time soaking up her brilliance. But if I said all that, it'd lead down a road we couldn't take in our platonic-roommates agreement, so instead I settled for, "She knows you saved her."

Trixie was silent for a moment, absently petting Chick-Chick's feathers. "Maybe. I hope she knows I'm trying to help."

"I think she does."

Trixie's lip quivered, and she stood abruptly. "Be right back." She sprinted to her bedroom and slammed the door behind her.

Had I said something wrong? I didn't think so. What was she running away from?

I strained my ears and heard a sniffle.

"Trixie?" I asked.

"One minute!" she shouted, a little shake to her voice.

Chick-Chick cocked her head at me.

"Don't look at me. I didn't do it. At least, I don't think I did." Years of living with many women might not have helped me understand their emotions, but I knew how to deal with them. I didn't know Trixie well enough yet to know if she was a cry-on-your-shoulder type girl or a *Leave me alone to cry it out; attention will only make me cry more* kind of girl.

From the way she'd run off and shut the door, and given that she wouldn't so much as crack a frown generally, I was leaning toward the latter. Just in case, I armed myself with tissues and chocolate before I knocked. "Are you okay?"

"Fine! I'll be out in a bit." Her voice continued to waver, but she showed no signs of letting me in. I was placing her firmly in the second category. Still, I placed the candy and tissues in easy reach, on the shelf near the door to her room, should they be a necessity when she opened up. Music turned on, likely to cover the sounds of her muffled tears. I wasn't fooled.

"Guess it's you and me," I told Chick-Chick. "Ready to explore?"

I moved her to the hard surface of the entryway. Any accident cleanups would be much easier on tile than carpet. *Work smarter, not harder* and all that.

Chick-Chick made no effort to move around. She stared. She clucked. She shook out her feathers.

I knelt down and tried calling to her. No dice.

I could try to bribe her with food, except that her food was locked in the room with Trixie, and despite living in the same building as Chick-Chick for the past three weeks, I had no idea what chickens ate.

"Your mama is in the other room crying, and I have no idea why," I whispered. "But I'm pretty sure seeing you walking around, living your best life, would cheer her up, so it'd be great if you'd give this a try."

Chick-Chick stared, bent her head, and pecked at her plumage.

Well, this wasn't working. I tried everything, including quietly singing and dancing like Farmer Hoggett in *Babe* when he cheered up the little pig. Nothing.

I abandoned Chick-Chick near the table. I pulled a stemless wineglass out of the cabinet to pour myself a drink.

Behind my back, I heard a faint click. I froze.

Tap, tap came the clicks again.

I turned and looked down to see Chick-Chick hobbling into the room, flapping her wings for balance.

"Trixie!" I shouted.

She came flying into the room, panic on her face, and I had a moment of guilt for stirring fear in her.

"What's wrong?" She spun about, looking for the danger, then her eyes fell on Chick-Chick and widened.

"Nothing's wrong. Sorry, I didn't mean to scare you. But look!" I pointed needlessly. She was already kneeling on the floor.

"You're doing it! You're doing it, girl! Look at you go!"

Chick-Chick turned toward Trixie and clucked excitedly. Her pace quickened, and she ran, or came as close to a run as she was capable of, toward Trixie. Any remnants of the panic Trixie had felt relaxed away, and she shone with pride.

My eyes teared up, and I was glad my father was probably in another state somewhere and not around to tell me to "man up." Looking down at the joy emanating from Trixie and the happy chattering of Chick-Chick, I decided not to fight it and allowed the tears to flow. I'd only just met Chick-Chick, but I was proud. Mostly, though, I was reacting to Trixie. She grinned. If she was all cried out from whatever had upset her before, I'd do the happy crying for her.

I wiped my eyes. The motion caught her attention, and she saw my tears. Her lips parted as though to speak, then instead, she stood and barreled into me. Her slight frame pressed against me. Head low on my chest, she wrapped her thin arms around me. I enveloped her in mine.

The feeling that ran through me was far from the lust I'd experienced previously when we'd been in close proximity. This time, the emotion was a gentler one that left no room for any rules she might develop. It was a feeling I didn't dare name.

I wanted to know her. I wanted to see that joy on her face over and over again, but I wanted her sorrow as well. I wanted to see the real her, the one behind all the smiles, real and fake. I didn't think I cared how long it would take. As we hugged, the dynamic between us shifted with the force of an earthquake. I knew there was no turning back.

CHAPTER FIFTEEN
TRIXIE

Bear was holding me. Those strong arms of his were squeezing me tightly but oh-so-gently to him, and I didn't want it to end. At least, not until the tick of the wall clock called attention to the length of our embrace. Somehow the ticking made it awkward. I panicked as my mind began a frantic loop of *What now? What now? What now?* My body tensed with anxiety. Sensing this, Bear relaxed his hold on me, his arms falling to his sides.

I sucked in a deep breath, the physical distance giving me the emotional room to breathe. So much for my rules. Not only did we not have three feet of separation, I'd gone running straight into his arms.

I'd made the rules for a reason.

Don't get a roommate. Roommates, like family, see behind walls better left solid, and everything falls apart. It was my ultimate rule, and I'd broken it weeks ago. I'd given myself a new rule in its place: don't get close to him. When that failed, I'd voiced limitations to him, and those hadn't even lasted a day. I hardly blamed Bear for that. I'd been the one to push past the boundaries.

Why had I hugged him? Because I loved Chick-Chick. I saw so much of myself in her, and caring for her brought me so much joy. Bear had cleaned up after her without question and eased my guilt over how I might make her feel. He'd shed those silent tears, which looked out of place on such a mountain of a man, all because she'd walked. He'd so freely and easily shown that emotion, something I couldn't do. He got her, and by association, he got me.

"You okay?" he asked for the third time today. No, I wasn't okay. I was having an emotional crisis, and because we shared a home, I didn't have the privacy I needed to vent those emotions. I wanted to share them with him so much it hurt. It was the first time since Julia I'd felt comfortable enough with someone that I might open up. Maybe I could let go instead of falling back on the same mechanics that had been forced onto me by my parents and that had become a fundamental piece of how I operated. Every time I came close, though, Julia sprang back into my mind—passing around that video, abandoning me and stealing away my boyfriend, proving my horrible parents right.

Bear might be different, but I still couldn't get past it. I wasn't ready to open myself up to him, no matter how much he called to me or how much I longed to be with him. I might never be, but I knew it was too late for rules to do me any good. I was attached, and now I'd gone and hugged him. Pandora's box had broken open.

"I'm good," I lied. He'd probably heard me crying through my door, and that was more insight into my emotions than I was comfortable with.

He watched me. Still my move, then. "I could use some air. I think I'll make a grocery run."

"All right." Bear's fingers found his scruff. He looked away. I looked away. We were two people intently looking at things that weren't each other, so not looking at anything at all. How very productive.

He'd acknowledged that I was leaving. That was my cue to go, and yet my feet were stuck to the floor like particularly determined barnacles.

Turn around and leave. Get some space. Clear your head.

My feet continued to refuse. Bear kept staring, and I knew I was taking too long to do or say something. This was a solo shopping trip. I was getting breathing room from him, time in the car to feel the feels.

"Do you want to come?" I blurted.

"Sure." His answer was immediate, but his face remained expressionless.

So we went on our first joint shopping trip. There was mild, awkward confusion as we sorted out whether to share a cart or get our own. We opted for a shared cart and walked around the store side by side. The easy small talk about the week's meal plan and favorite snacks and a teasing argument over which cookie was superior to the others helped relieve the awkward tension between us.

We were in unfamiliar territory, explorers on an alien planet. Our . . . dynamic? *Relationship* didn't feel like the right word. Whatever it was between us was changing faster than Lindsey coming up with an excuse to avoid poop patrol at work. I didn't know what it meant or how to proceed. He didn't seem to, either, so I was grateful for some semblance of the easy balance we'd had over the last two weeks.

*   *   *

Later that evening, Bear, Chick-Chick, and I crashed on the couch, eating a frozen pizza, fresh out of the oven, with a fresh bowl of popcorn and watching *Family Feud*.

On-screen, Steve Harvey approached the last member of the Alvarez family. "What is one thing you will never forget to pack for a trip?"

I paused the TV for deliberation.

"It's gotta be a cell phone," I said. "Everyone is so attached to their phones, there's no way they're forgetting that."

"You've been here three weeks and I've seen you lose your phone six times, and that's only when I've been home."

Heat crept up my cheeks, and I shoved him.

"All right, smarty-pants. What's your guess?"

"Toothbrush," he said, and sank back into the couch, smug.

"Want to bet?"

"Loser does dishes." We both reached into the popcorn bowl, and our hands grazed each other's. It had all the new and forbidden excitement of holding hands for the first time with a boy in high school. He made me giddy, and this was exactly what I'd been trying to avoid. We both snapped our hands back, and I jumped.

"You go ahead," I said, letting him grab a handful first and opting not to acknowledge the moment. "What if neither of us is right?"

He paused to finish his bite and swallow. "I wash, you dry?"

"Deal," I said, and resumed the show. The last Alvarez guessed "shoes" incorrectly. The Garlinger family had a chance to steal and opted for "swimsuit."

"Survey says?" Steve stepped back and looked up at the giant board.

"Cell phone, cell phone, cell phone," I whisper-chanted as Bear watched in silence.

"Toothbrush!"

I chucked a piece of popcorn at the screen. "Are you kidding me? I can't believe you got that."

"I've seen this episode before," he said casually, fighting not to smile.

My jaw dropped. "You rat!" I flung another fistful at him.

"Hey!" He chucked some back at me, and it turned into an all-out popcorn war, which morphed into throwing so the other person could try to catch it in their mouth, a game we both sucked at.

"Can chickens eat popcorn?" he asked. "We could use a cleanup crew."

"I have no idea," I admitted. I'd Google it later. For now, I wanted some buttery goodness for myself.

As we teased, I inched closer and retrieved some of my ammunition from his pant leg. My eyes reflexively met his as I ate the popcorn, and I realized belatedly that I was leaning over him, staring into his eyes and seductively eating a piece.

"Careful, Trixie," he cautioned.

The warning only made me want to push him further. I stared straight at him, not saying a word, and licked the butter from my fingertips.

"Fuck," he said, shifting himself under me.

Before I could respond to that, the front door burst open, and a stream of people flooded in. I sprang back like I'd seen a snake, an actual one, and not the euphemistic kind. We both stuffed our hands under our legs, as if they'd been doing something they shouldn't be.

"Didn't mean to interrupt." Zoey's smile was knowing and wicked.

"We could come back later," Fawn suggested. "Bella, don't touch that. Owen, can you get her?"

Owen, Fawn's husband, whom I'd heard about but not yet met, chased after the little girl, who had grabbed the remote and run into the other room. An older couple, presumably Bear's parents, followed them in.

"You didn't interrupt anything." Bear stood and extended a hand to help me up. "Hi, Mom. Hi, Dad. This is Trixie."

Some sort of silent conversation occurred between Bear and Fawn. I'd have to ask him about it later.

"So you're the girl I've heard so much about," his mom said.

My eyebrows nearly jumped off my face. Heard so much about? What would he have said about me? If he was telling his mom about me, maybe I'd already let this go too far.

"From Zoey and Fawn, dear," she clarified. "Don't look so alarmed."

Okay, so not the best job at concealing my reaction on that one.

"What's everyone doing here?" Bear asked. "You're a little late for dinner."

"Family meeting," his dad said.

"Call me Carrie." His mother shook my hand. "Sorry to invade, sweetheart. We gave up on getting him to leave the house a long time ago. It's easier if we come to him."

His sisters had said the same previously. On one hand, I could tell Bear was a bit of a homebody. On the other, it hadn't taken much convincing to get him to the baseball game and club with me. Far less than it took his family to get him to come over or Zoey to get him to a club. I slid that little tidbit into the mental filing cabinet under Bear-isms to consider later.

"Still could knock," Bear grumbled, as his family rained down on the house like a plague of friendly locusts. Bella was still being chased around by her father. Bear's stepfather scooped up a slice of pizza and plopped down on the chair adjacent to the couch. His mother shook her head, inspecting the ruins of the great living room popcorn war.

Zoey rummaged in the fridge. "Don't you have any beer?"

"No," Bear and I answered in unison.

"Trixie, meet the Ross clan. We're just missing Rose and Lexie," Bear said.

"Present and accounted for," came a muffled voice from near Fawn.

Fawn held up a tablet that displayed a split-screen video chat with two women bearing the trademark green eyes and round nose that Bear's family members all had in common.

"Hey," Bear said, frowning. He zeroed in on Carrie. "Mom, what's going on? It must be serious if you've got them on the line too."

"Russ, dear, will you call the meeting?"

"Butts in seats!" Russell roared.

Bella squealed out a giggle and came tearing out of Bear's bedroom. Owen's face contorted with determination before he dove, tackling his daughter to the ground. She landed gently. His face skid across the carpet. Rug burn. That was going to hurt later.

Fawn bent to retrieve the remote as Owen breathed hard on the floor.

"Why is the carpet wet?" he moaned. He looked so defeated. Poor guy. I wouldn't tell him I'd cleaned up chicken poop only a half hour earlier in the exact spot his face was lying.

"Routine steam cleaning," I said.

Fawn put on a kids' show for Bella, and the rest of the family retreated to the kitchen. Bear grabbed my hand and gave it a gentle squeeze. "Sorry about this."

"No worries. I'll hang out with Bella."

"Don't be silly," Fawn said, "You live here. That makes you practically family."

Practically family seemed like a stretch, but they seemed the type of chaotic family whose home was always open. The way they let themselves into our house, I'd bet that when the siblings were growing up, their house had been a revolving door of neighborhood kids. I could see their holidays including anyone they heard had no one to spend it with. I already knew and liked Fawn and Zoey, but I liked the others immediately.

Bear shrugged. "It's up to you."

Refusing would have felt rude, so I joined them in the kitchen. As everyone got settled, I made myself useful and passed out wine.

The room was mayhem. Fawn was inspecting the rug burn on her husband's face. Zoey was chatting away with the virtual sisters, while Bear and Owen leaned against the counter, talking about a renovation Owen was planning for their bathroom. Russell gnawed on a giant hunk of cheese he must have retrieved from the fridge in the time it took for us to move from the living room to here.

Carrie cleared her throat, and the room went silent. "I called this family meeting because I have an announcement to make."

She met the eyes of everyone in the room, on-screen and off. The woman was an effective speaker, I'd give her that. When she was sure she had everyone's attention, she continued. "I'm going to retire. I haven't made any decisions yet, but a developer is interested in buying the space."

The words hung in the air like a balloon that was slowly losing its helium, right at eye level and impossible to ignore.

When the silence broke, it wasn't a mere pop, it was an eruption. Everyone began talking at once, leaving the speakers indistinguishable, at least for someone who had only just met half of them. Mouths were moving, Fawn was crying, and rather than Bear's usual beard scratch, it looked like he might pull the hair right off his face.

"But what about the shop?"

"A developer? They'll destroy everything you've built!"

"When?"

"I'm not taking it over."

Carrie's face crumbled, and I could feel her heart shattering to see her family torn up by this decision. Russell saw it too and escorted her out the back door for fresh air.

Wanting to give the family space, I checked on Bella and found her entranced by a TV show, oblivious to the turmoil in the next room. Returning to the kitchen, I came face-to-face with Fawn, who was sucking breaths in and out at an alarming rate and swaying on her feet.

"Here." I towed her to my room and sat her on my bed, then shut the door so we could talk in private. "You okay?"

She shook her head so fast and so much, it was more of a vibration.

"The store. It's so much. It's everything to this family. It's her life's work. We grew up there. We can't let it go. Some developer can't just come in and tear it down. That place is home. It would destroy us."

"She said she hasn't made any decisions yet." I rubbed her back, and she shook a little less.

"But what's the alternative? It's my responsibility. I'm the eldest that lives around here, and I'm not working right now. I always planned to go back to work, but Bella still needs me, and I had a career I always figured I'd go back to. I was good at it too. I never wanted to take over the shop, but I wanted its warmth and comfort. It's the perfect family home base. It somehow never occurred to me that this day would come and that if I didn't step up, it would be gone."

"This is a lot for you to take in," I said. "It'll be a big change for everyone, no matter what she decides. But I don't think it'll happen tomorrow. You have this amazing family, and I know you can make it through this together. Why don't we go back in there and hear what else she has to say? You can sleep on it, and when it's not so much of a shock, you can look at it with fresh eyes. I'm always here to talk."

Fawn leaned into me, and I wrapped my arms around her.

"Thanks, Trixie. I'm just going to clean myself up a bit first." She excused herself to the restroom, and I bent to give Chick-Chick a quick pet.

Before I got up, the bedroom door slammed shut, and a wild-eyed Zoey leaned against it.

"It's a jungle out there," she said.

"Big news," I agree. "You all right?"

"Nope," she said. "Owen took the iPad away from me before I hung up on Lexie and Rose. Rose has it in her head that I should take over the store and has no problem sharing that opinion with everyone else. I love Family Tree just as much as the rest of the family, and I've always been happy to help when Mom's needed extra hands, but I have my own businesses already. Plural. Because it's a collection of smaller operations rather than a brick-and-mortar store that they can see, none of my family seems to understand that."

"That must be really frustrating."

"It is." She rolled her neck. "Okay. I'm recharged. I just needed a moment. Thanks. You coming?"

I followed Zoey before my bedroom became any more of a merry-go-round of Ross siblings in crisis. We entered the kitchen to find everyone else had returned.

Carrie lifted an open hand, and the room was silent once again. She might be retiring, but she must have missed her calling as a managerial speaker. Her crowd control was impressive. Probably she'd learned it from years of wrangling this wild family.

"I'm going to work through the end of October to get through the busy season," she said calmly. "I'm going to hold off on a decision for a few more weeks, but I can't push it further than that, or I'll risk losing the developer's offer. They've been . . . aggressive in their requests."

She wove her words with a soothing, hypnotic tone. The panicked family breathed in her ease and relaxed in perfect sync, like a well-practiced and choreographed dance troop.

I was riveted but felt like an intruder. It didn't feel right that I was a part of this conversation or that any of them would be coming to me for advice, yet here I was.

"I want my children to live their own lives. I don't want my decisions to dictate what any of you do." She paused, making another round of eye contact. "That said, you all know that this store means a lot to me and has meant a lot to our whole family."

Russell took his wife's hands in his and nodded at her. I sensed an impending need for tissues and slipped out of the room to retrieve some.

From the living room, I heard Carrie continue, over the sounds of Bella singing quietly along with the music emanating from the TV. "You all were practically raised there. Your games, peeking through the flowers, pretending you were in the jungle. I remember pairs of you curled up in the back room, helping each other with your homework." Her voice wavered. "We were there so often, sometimes that place felt more like home than our house did."

A tear trickled down her face as I reentered the room. I made my best effort to be discreet as I slid the tissue box onto the table and glided deeper into the kitchen, toward the fridge.

"I don't want to leave it, but my arthritis has made the work difficult, and the developers made an offer that is difficult to refuse. It's time. Your father and I want to travel. As much as I've always loved my job, we only get one life, and I don't want to spend it all working." She squeezed her husband's hand, like she was hanging over a cliff and he was the only thing keeping her from falling. "I'd prefer to keep the shop in the family. But if none of you feel called to that, then I understand."

Even as an outsider, or perhaps because I was one, I knew that she would understand, but it would hurt her. She'd put her heart and soul into that store. Anyone with eyes and ears would have known that. Her five children all looked at each other, in person and via tablet screen, before once again the cup overflowed and everyone was talking at once.

At least, the four sisters and Owen were all talking. Carrie and Russell were staring into each other's eyes. Not only had he been her lifeline for that speech, but this stare was communicating so much. I envied them. My heart swelled as they radiated emotion. Even as a spectator, I felt the pain this decision brought them, but also the relief that it was out in the open, and their hope and excitement for their next adventure.

Carrie didn't control or moderate the tornado of thoughts and emotions being hurled around the room. She held on to her husband and let the sisters say their piece.

I listened as the sisters flung out questions like *Are you sure?* and *But you're doing okay, right?* Carrie ignored all of them. They bickered among themselves, about how they would take it over if only they lived closer, or if they hadn't gotten that promotion at work, or whatever other reason they had. Nobody wanted to lose the shop, but nobody wanted to take it either.

They were all a flurry of anxiety and concern. Except Bear. I listened to the others, but once I'd torn my eyes from his parents, they stayed on him. His eyes never left the wall. He fixated on a section of the wall, a slight imperfection in the paint where it met the ceiling, and didn't say a peep.

The sisters' concern turned to anger as each argued her reasons the others should step up and why they couldn't let the place go. Zoey looked like she was about to smash the tablet in frustration, and then—

Tap, tap.

Tap, tap.

Tap, tap.

The room once again went silent. This time not a result of Carrie's stern leadership, but because a chicken had ambled its way into the room.

Bella popped her head around the corner. "I found a chicken!"

CHAPTER SIXTEEN
BEAR

Nothing breaks up a family feud like a good chicken. After Chick-Chick wandered into the kitchen last night, the meeting had fallen apart with no resolution. There isn't any coming back from a chicken interruption. Unexpected chickens tend to derail a conversation. Yet, a solid fourteen hours later, the conversation wasn't done ricocheting around my mind.

Mom had three months to determine the store's future. Three months until my childhood slipped away. That shop was the epitome of family to me. I couldn't believe my sisters were so willing to let it go. We'd all spent so much time there growing up, though none of them had taken to helping Mom out like me, at least not until I'd been bullied into abandoning it. Maybe if I hadn't been so afraid to go back, she wouldn't be considering this right now. Maybe if I'd been there recently, we wouldn't be in this position, but I hadn't, and it filled me with deep shame.

The fresh scent of florals had attached itself to my skin as a child, thanks to the long hours I'd spent among the brilliant and varied blossoms. Every time we'd gotten a new variety or made a unique arrangement with something quirky like thistle and fern curl, I'd dropped everything to help Mom, and begged for extras for my room.

My thoughts were on the shop as I went around the house collecting trash, which was not as delightful smelling as the remembered flowers. Trixie was out and about, so I was doing garbage day cleanup. The trash filled up much faster with two humans and a chicken than it had when it was only me. My mind continued to drift back to the previous night as I cleaned.

None of the sisters wanted the shop. But I did. Not that anyone had asked or would ever directly ask. When each sister had been trying to pin it on the others the night before, not once did any of them consider suggesting I do it. It wasn't their responsibility to do so. If I wanted it, I knew I'd have to speak up and say it myself.

It wasn't their fault they didn't think of me. I enjoyed the aromatic scents of the shop and the challenge of creating something beautiful, but once word had gotten around at school that I liked "playing with flowers," the teasing had started. The bullying got worse, and my oh-so-sympathetic biological father would tell me to toughen up. Be a man. It was still his favorite topic when he occasionally breezed through to mess with our lives.

I dropped an armload of glasses off at the sink—Trixie tended to leave them everywhere. I wouldn't put it past her to be practicing water-glass music. That would be a Trixie thing to do, if ever there was one. Alternately, she might have a fear of dehydration requiring that she always have a glass nearby, or a specific aversion to cleaning up water glasses, even though she was relatively tidy besides that.

I lugged a trash bag from the kitchen out to the bin by the garage, then rolled it out toward the street for pickup. My mind raced with internal debate. My construction job wasn't terrible, but I didn't love it, and I wasn't getting as much work as I needed. Could I take over the shop?

I feared losing the solitude and privacy I'd grown accustomed to, necessitated by my need to maintain the so-called "masculine" image my dad had forced on me. I wasn't sure if I could handle the constant exchanges with people that a role in retail would require.

I couldn't keep my focus, which is also why I didn't notice my peril until it was too late.

A cacophony of barking broke through my thought bubble. I sought the source and found a mass of fur hurtling toward me at an alarming rate—a pack of dogs so large it was indecipherable where one dog ended and another began. In the middle, eyes bugging out of her head, arms straining as she struggled to keep up, was Trixie.

The tornado of pooches plowed into me. Unprepared for the hit, my ankle rolled, and I was knocked to the ground. I batted away dog butts, sharp nails, and whipping tails, curling up to protect my vital organs as the canine tsunami whipped over me.

"Oh my god! Bear!" Trixie yelled. A patch of light shone through the fur. It was either my salvation or the light at the end of the tunnel that you're supposed to stay away from. The angelic face peering down at me made me fear it was the latter.

"Trixie?" I groaned, finally regaining my senses after the initial shock and muscling the dogs off me.

"Are you okay? I'm so sorry, they just took off!"

"Whose dogs are these?" I asked. "Why are there so many?"

"Mrs. Nelson asked me to dog-sit today, and she has four dogs. Honestly, she'd probably have more if it were legal."

"And the fifth?" A black Lab was doing his best to shove his way past my arm to slobber all over my face with enthusiasm, and he was succeeding. A thick sheen of saliva coated my cheek and dripped from my beard. I shifted my legs to stand and get my face out of his range.

"No idea. Picked him up three blocks back. No tag. I circled the block three times trying to find an owner, and he won't stop following me."

I moved to put weight on my left foot and only barely managed to contain a scream, which came out as a groan. Pain shot through my ankle and radiated through my foot and leg. My hands flew to clutch it out of reflex, and the additional touch to the sensitive spot sent a second wave of agony ripping through me.

"What was that?" she asked, her arms relaxing as the dogs realized they weren't going anywhere and calmed down.

"What?" I asked, half listening and half staring in frustration at my ankle that didn't want to support any of my weight.

"That groan. And that wince. You squished up your face like you were in pain. Are you hurt? Oh god, where does it hurt?"

"I'm fine." I waved her off and held my breath to brace myself for the pain as I again attempted to stand. Searing agony stabbed into my ankle, and it gave out, failing to support me again. No use pretending anymore. I frowned up at Trixie from the driveway.

"Well?" she asked.

"Ankle."

"Oh pumpernickel. How bad?"

"I can't stand up," I growled in frustration. I was going to need X-rays. I eyed my car, wondering if I could drive with a broken ankle. My driving foot was fine, but with the level of pain I was in, it wasn't worth veering off and winding up in an accident. Could I have Trixie take me? I wasn't sure if we had a favor-asking type of relationship. I knew she wouldn't say no, but I didn't want to make things more uncomfortable than they already seemed at times.

Then again, it was her fault I was hurt. Before I talked myself out of it, I asked, "Do you think you could give me a ride?"

"Of course," she answered without hesitation. "To the ER?"

"Hell no, that shit's too expensive. Urgent care."

She inspected my ankle. The sight of her bent over in skinny jeans and a turquoise shirt with daisies on it in the middle of a horde of dogs was almost distracting enough to make me forget the throbbing pain in my ankle. Almost.

"Let's get you out of here." She stood next to me and squatted to ease her shoulder under my arm. I draped it over her, keenly aware that if I weren't in excruciating pain, I'd be celebrating her allowing me to drape an arm over her in public.

One dog chose that moment to hump her leg. I mean, I appreciated the sentiment, but read the room, little buddy.

"What about them?" I asked.

"I guess they'll have to come with us," she said.

I froze. "All of them? Can't you just drop them back off at their house?"

"I promised not to leave them alone. She said they tear the house apart. That's why she needed a dog-sitter."

A few minutes later, with enough fur flying around to make our driveway appear carpeted, Trixie had all the dogs crammed into her car. It was laughably small for all of us but a better option than the small cab of my truck, since she was opposed to putting the dogs in the flatbed.

"I can't believe I'm riding to urgent care with four dogs," I muttered, having counted them through the windows.

"There's five. The stray jumped in too."

"I only see four," I said.

"The Chihuahua probably can't get up to the window. Sorry, you might have to share a seat."

She made sure I had my balance before ducking out from under my arm to open the door. I turned around and crashed backward onto the seat. A large Lab mix clambered over the center console and began slobbering all over my face again.

"Well, Jelly likes you," Trixie noted, waiting for me to get my legs inside before shutting the car door after me.

As Trixie got in, I located the Chihuahua, who promptly bit the foot attached to my injured ankle. "Ow!" I yelled.

"Sorry," Trixie laughed, failing to hide it. "I forgot to warn you, Nacho likes to hide, and he's got a bit of a mean streak."

"No kidding." I pulled my feet as far away from him as I could. "Are they all named after food?"

"No, the bulldog is Sir Woofington."

* * *

Trixie pulled in front of the urgent care center's entrance. The small parking lot was mostly full, so she idled the car to come around and help me. I closed my eyes and sucked in a deep breath to brace myself for the impending pain when I had to stand up. I took Trixie's hand and hobbled. Before I could shut the door behind me, Jelly took advantage of the opening and bolted.

"Oh snickerdoodles!" Trixie yelled, glancing with panic between me and the dog.

I slammed the car door closed before another dog escaped. "Go! I'll be fine."

"Sorry!" she shouted over her shoulder, taking off after Jelly, who was now barking at a squirrel taunting him from a tree on the edge of the neighboring parking lot.

I felt guilty leaving her alone to chase the dog, but on this ankle, I wasn't catching up to a dog anytime soon. I figured the best thing to do was get inside so she wouldn't be worried about trying to tend to me as well.

I hopped to the door and got myself checked in, and thankfully was provided with a wheelchair. Fortunately, there wasn't a wait, so I was ushered to a room. The exam room was on the outside of the building, its small window facing the parking lot.

There was no sign of Trixie. I hoped she'd retrieved Jelly and was hanging out in the car, waiting for me. The doctor looked at my ankle and ran me through the pain scale routine. I resisted the tough-guy standards of a lower rating and went with an honest seven.

The radiologist wheeled me back for an X-ray to check for a break. After returning to the exam room, I scrolled through news articles on my phone while I waited.

A knock sounded on the door.

"Come in," I called.

The doctor reentered the room in her lab coat and jumped back when she looked up.

"What the . . ." She trailed off.

I turned to the window to see what had caught her attention. There was Trixie, squared off against a squirrel and Jelly, like Chris Pratt in the cage with the velociraptors. She made a flying leap for Jelly, who evaded her grasp with a flying leap of his own for the squirrel, who in turn leapt for the tree. Oprah was giving out flying leaps today—you get a flying leap, and you get a flying leap! Trixie landed hard on the ground.

"Crap. That's my roommate. She's going to wind up needing an appointment too."

Trixie stood and brushed off her jeans. She went into sumo stance and rounded on Jelly. Jelly hopped back and forth, facing off with her. Trixie lunged again and got a second faceful of grass. She knelt on the ground, giving up on chasing the dog and resorting to pleading. Her hands were clasped as though in prayer, and her lips—oh those lips—begged the dog to come to her.

Jelly jumped from side to side in a play bow with no intention of obedience. Trixie threw her hands up in frustration and stormed off toward her car, which was parked in the shade, where a row of dog noses stuck out the cracked windows. It didn't look like an intentional tactic, but it worked. The second Trixie's back was turned, Jelly took off after her and pounced, knocking her again to the ground, this time with his paws on her back. She rolled over and tackled him, transitioning to a belly rub. She laughed openly, her eyes crinkling with brightness as she played with the dog.

The doctor snapped me back to reality when she spoke. "Well, that livened up my day."

I jerked my head away from the window.

Her grin widened. "Oh, I see. That's how it is. Don't worry, if she comes in for those scrapes, I won't say a word."

Hell, I was so damned transparent, but the way Trixie glowed—I couldn't help myself. Roommate or not, I'd developed feelings for her. I ignored the doctor's comment.

"Moving on," she said. "I've got your scans back. You're looking at a break," she continued. "I'll give you a temporary splint and a referral to an orthopedic doctor. They'll probably put you in a cast for several weeks, then switch to a walking boot."

I finished up with the doctor and crutched my way out front. Trixie had pulled into a space near the entrance, all five dogs accounted for.

"What happened here?" I asked, eyeing the shredded foam strewn across the back seat.

"Exhibit A for why Mrs. Nelson didn't want them left at the house unsupervised. It's broken?" she asked, as I plopped into my seat, checking first for the Chihuahua. "Don't worry, I've got Nacho," she added.

"Yep."

Trixie bared her teeth in as close as her smile ever got to a grimace. "I'm so sorry, I can't believe this happened. It's all my fault."

"True," I agreed. "But it is what it is. Don't worry about it. Do you need me to watch the dogs while you get your wounds tended?" I gestured at the grass stains on her knees and elbows.

Her face reddened. "Tell me you didn't see that."

"I didn't see that," I said.

"Oh sugar, you saw."

"The doctor did too," I agreed.

"Lovely. You ready to go?"

I nodded, and she glanced down at Nacho.

"I can't drive with him on my lap."

"You can't put him in back?" I asked. She raised an eyebrow at me. "Fine." Warily, I reached toward Nacho. I offered him the back of my hand to sniff, which he did. After a thorough, suspicious eyeing, he allowed himself to be handed off. He glared at me one last time, then curled up on my lap.

"He's sleeping on your lap? He trusts you! Nacho is an excellent judge of character."

"He also bit me," I pointed out.

"I think he'd have bitten Mother Teresa on first meeting. I still say you're in the clear."

"Glad I've got the rat dog's approval," I said.

"I've got to drop them back off at their—"

"Yes, you do," I interrupted.

She grinned. "So that's a no to bringing home five dogs, then?"

"Yes. The chicken is more than enough."

"Dogs don't poop nearly as much as chickens."

"Trixie," I warned.

"I'm kidding. I'm dropping them off, and I'll do another loop to look for the lost one's owners. Do you want to pick up anything to eat on the way home?"

I glanced at the bat-eared dog named after Mexican food on my lap. "Taco Bell?"

Trixie laughed. "I see why he likes you. Taco Bell it is."

CHAPTER SEVENTEEN
BEAR

I took off work on medical leave. Trixie still worked days at the shelter but spent evenings playing nurse to both Chick-Chick and me. Chick-Chick required her normal care, and Trixie kept me supplied with ice packs and whatever else I needed so I didn't have to hobble to get it.

I spent my days with Chick-Chick, both impressed and annoyed by how often she defecated. Despite the obnoxious amount of time I spent on cleanup duty, she was all right. We snuggled on the couch, an old towel underneath her to keep me safe from her accidents. I clucked my way through conversations with her, much like Trixie did.

Chick-Chick seemed to be doing better. Sometimes I'd set her on the floor and give her free rein of the house while I watched TV. She still didn't move well, and I cringed every time she smacked her wings on something in an effort to balance, but her quality of life seemed to have improved. She had more energy, and it had to be better than being cooped up in

Trixie's room. She'd stroll around the house, and when she got tired, I'd pick her up and snuggle.

When Trixie walked in one day after work and found us curled up together on the couch, it earned me a genuine smile and made all the cleanup worth it. I can't say I minded the chicken's presence either. The call-and-response game she played with her warbles was comical.

One day while Trixie was out, I was refreshing the newspaper that covered the ground in Chick-Chick's pen. As I cleaned, I noticed the circles in bright-pink ink that Trixie had drawn around various classified ads. They were all for temporary odd jobs. Helping serve at a dinner party, lawn work, event staffing. I rewound my memory, looking back over the last couple weeks. Trixie had been home far less than she had at first. I'd assumed she'd been out and about with her never-ending supply of friends and acquaintances, but maybe not. Perhaps the dog-walking fiasco wasn't something she'd done on a whim for extra spending cash, if she was this intensely seeking side hustles to supplement her job at the shelter. Come to think of it, she'd been scrolling through Craigslist the other day too, probably looking at more of the same. I glanced around the room, and my eyes fell on a stack of opened mail sitting on her nightstand. No, I shouldn't snoop.

I glanced at the glowing red digits on the alarm clock next to the stack of papers. Four thirty. She wouldn't be home for a while yet. One little peek wouldn't be horrible. I was only doing it because I was worried about her. Chick-Chick clucked.

"You won't tell on me, will you?"

She tilted her head to the side, then sank down into herself, looking tired, poor girl.

She wouldn't be snitching on me anytime soon.

I stood and walked to the nightstand, taking a mental picture of how everything sat so I could return it to its place and hide the evidence of my search. The first was a denied application for a pet care credit card. Below that, a vet bill. I picked it up. There was no total, because the whole first page was full of line items. Exams, treatments, and medications, all from a few weeks ago.

I flipped to the next page, also full of line items. The bill continued on a third and fourth page, summing at the bottom of the fourth. When I read the subtotal, my stomach dropped. Despite several payments, Trixie owed over $3,000 for Chick-Chick's medical care. She still took her to regular appointments and was constantly restocking on medicine. The bills would only keep growing. No wonder she was looking for odd jobs.

I arranged the papers back in their original places, or at least what I hoped were the right spots, not that Trixie struck me as one who would notice something slightly out of place. I backed out of her room and into the kitchen for water.

I needed to figure out how to talk to her about this, and how to help. I wasn't rolling in money, but especially with her sharing recent bills, things were a little less tight for me. I could cut back her rent, or let her have a month or two free, but she was so proud, I didn't see her accepting a handout without a fight.

I could make a payment for her, but she wasn't likely to be paying off the full balance for a while. And being the smart woman she was, she'd figure out what I'd done. No, I had to get her to talk about it and offer help without it feeling like charity.

My phone rang, and Trixie's name popped onto the screen. I jumped and glanced around. Had she somehow known I'd been going through her things?

"Hello?" I answered.

"Hey, are you home?" she asked.

"Yes, you okay?"

"Yeah, but I'm running late and forgot my makeup bag, and I really need it. Is there any chance you could meet me somewhere?"

Maybe I'd get a chance to see what she was up to and offer some help after all. "Sure, no problem."

She gave me the address, and I crutched my way out the door. We both pulled up to the house at about the same time. I flung open my door to bring her the makeup bag.

"Oh no! Don't get up. I'll come to you." She locked her car behind her and ran over to me. "Thanks for this. You're a lifesaver."

"Oh, good, you're both here," a woman said, exiting the house we were parked in front of. I glanced at Trixie, and she shrugged.

"Both?" she asked.

"Yes, please come inside before the children start to arrive and see you." She waved frantically.

"Mrs. Lawson, I think there's a misunderstanding. This is my roommate. He was just bringing me something from home. It's just me helping out today."

"Oh no, that won't do," she said. "This is little Jayden's seventh birthday, and it must be perfect. This will be a special core memory for him. He *must* have both of you. I'm sure I mentioned that we wanted the duo on the phone."

Trixie's smile remained, but it was a very fake customer service version. "I don't think you did. I'm sorry, he can't—"

"It's okay, I'll do it," I said. I didn't know what I was signing myself up for, but I'd been looking for a way to help Trixie, and with this lady making demands, it was an easy way for me to step in without it looking like too much of a handout.

"There, you see? Problem solved." The woman was wringing her hands and kept glancing into the house behind her. "Kyle! No, don't put that there; it's like you're deliberately ruining this for me." She turned back to us. "I have to take care of everything myself. Let yourselves in. Second door on the left." Then she disappeared, and poor Kyle, whoever he was, was probably getting an earful.

CHAPTER EIGHTEEN
TRIXIE

I found my voice. "Thank you. But you shouldn't agree to things without knowing what you're getting into."

"You dragged me into living with a chicken. How much worse could it be?" he asked.

I bit my lip. There were plenty of people in this world who wouldn't mind terribly what I was about to do, or rather what we were about to do, but I didn't think Bear was one of those people. It could go either way, but that coin toss would largely depend on the uniforms Marsha had in mind.

I laughed anxiously. "Oh, you'd be surprised," I warned.

Bear's eyes narrowed. "Well, I've agreed anyway. Let's go before that lady finishes up with Kyle and turns her wrath on us."

"Good point." I ran around to the other side of his car to retrieve his crutches for him, then back to help him up.

We slowly made our way into the large home. In terms of the scale of decorations, the place looked more like it was decorated for a wedding than for a seven-year-old's birthday party, if that elaborate wedding were superhero themed.

"Is that . . . ?" Bear asked, apparently so stunned he was unable to finish the sentence. He gaped at the blue-and-yellow masked monstrosity in front of him.

"A champagne fountain pouring from the hands of cardboard cutout Hydroboy? Yep, it would appear it is." The spandex-clad superhero had a gloved hand outstretched, and champagne streamed out from behind it. No wonder these people had been willing to pay so much. They had no concept of reasonable spending. As much as I felt terrible for what I was getting Bear into, he'd volunteered, and this was too big a paycheck to pass on. Besides, it would be too late for Marsha to hire someone else, and I didn't want the birthday boy to suffer for his parent's failure to mention she wanted the full duo and not just me.

Recovering from our awe, we proceeded down the hall to the second door on the left, following Marsha's instructions. Curtains covered the inside of the glass doors to what was usually a study. It was the size of our living room and lined with bookshelves. The desk probably cost as much as all of Chick-Chick's vet bills combined. Marsha had set up a vanity, and two garment bags hung on hangers in the corner.

"What exactly are we getting ready for?" Bear asked.

"For a birthday party," I said nonchalantly, peeking into the garment bags to survey the damage.

"I gathered that much, but what are we doing for the party? Are we serving food or something?"

Oh sweet, innocent Bear. Hang on to that precious ignorance a moment longer. "Or something."

"I don't know how I'll carry a tray, but we can figure something out."

"You know it's too late to back out, right?" I asked.

"I'm not liking the sound of this."

"And I didn't actually ask you to do this. You volunteered." Oh man, he was going to be so pissed.

"Okay . . ."

"It isn't my fault you didn't ask questions first. You really should gather more information before agreeing to things. So, it's a good life lesson!"

"Spit it out, Trixie."

"We're the superheroes," I blurted in a rush, then attempted a *Haha, isn't this funny? Surely you see the humor in this* smile.

He blinked. "That doesn't sound so bad."

No, it didn't. I sighed, unzipped the garment bags, and peeled back the sides. "And these are the costumes."

"No." He pivoted on his crutches and back toward the door to the study.

"Wait! Too late to back out, remember?"

"Not like they can do anything other than refuse to pay me," he said.

"Right," I said, catching him and pulling at his arm. My gentle tug stopped the mountain. Bear tensed up and hung his head. His jaw worked.

He heaved a deep breath. "Fine. I'll do it."

My heart skipped a beat. "You'll what?"

"I said I'll do it. You chased me to get me to, didn't you?"

"Well, yeah, but I didn't think you'd—"

"You're pushing your luck, Trixie," he grumbled.

"Right. Shutting up."

"That's a whole lot of spandex," he said.

"Yup." Oh pumpkin spice, stuff was about to get real.

CHAPTER NINETEEN
BEAR

I was the biggest sucker alive.

I'd thought, *Oh, she just needs another set of hands for a simple odd job. I'll volunteer. I'll have to hop, but we'll figure it out. I'll make her keep all the money to help pay her bills.* A simple, foolproof plan that turned out to be foolhardy instead.

Be a good roommate, I'd thought. Help the gorgeous woman with the quirks you can't get enough of and keep a chicken alive at the same time. I can't come right out and ask her about the bills, so I'll show up at one of her odd jobs and offer to help that way.

Brilliant fucking plan, Bear.

"If it makes you feel any better, I don't want to do this either." She picked at her own spandex costume and shuddered. Hers was a violet full-body suit, with some sections of black, heeled black boots, gloves, and a thin mask that tied around the eyes. It looked like there was a cape as well.

"So you don't often play superheroes?" I asked.

Trixie's brows furrowed. "Nope."

"Then why are we doing this?" If I was going to have to go through with it, I might as well make the most of it and nudge her about her financial issues. That way, we could work together, moving forward on finding a solution. One that didn't involve—I glanced at the offending article of clothing—that.

Trixie took her time in responding, studying the books on the shelves.

"I'm a little tight on cash," she whispered.

I glared at her.

Trixie turned her back to me, her shoulders tensed. Her tone was hard when she next spoke. "Okay, fine. I'm a lot tight on cash. I bit off more than I could chew with Chick-Chick's vet bills, but I'm not giving up on her."

I contemplated acting surprised, but what was the point in that? I already knew that staying platonic roommates was unlikely to happen. She'd broken my ankle, and I'd still only come to like her more. If there was any chance of something growing between us, it ought to start with honesty.

"I know," I admitted. "I saw the circled ads and the vet bill when I was changing out Chick-Chick's cage."

"You were snooping?" Her voice was accusatory. From the strain in her shoulders, I was fairly certain that if she were to turn and face me, I'd not be treated to one of her usual smiles. I'd get a rare sighting of a Trixie scowl, or whatever her face did in private. She made no move to turn.

"No, I was grabbing newspaper for the floor of her cage and stumbled across it." The newspaper ads hadn't been snooping. I couldn't claim the same for the vet bill, but my honesty policy had its limits.

"I can't believe you were digging through my things," she said.

I knew a moment of indignation. Fine, I'd snooped, but wasn't that a small wrong compared to what I was about to do for her? I'd never worn spandex in my life that I could recall. Let alone a lime-green suit with a lemon-yellow Speedo-like piece to go over it.

"And I can't believe I'm about to throw on this costume and parade around in front of a bunch of kids and their parents, so we're all full of surprises today." The suit wasn't even just a body suit. No, it continued up to include a mask, leaving only thin holes for my eyes and mouth.

Trixie was silent for a beat. "Point taken," she muttered. "Speaking of, we probably need to get ready."

I closed my eyes for a resigned sigh. "Okay."

We agreed to face away from each other while we changed. I did my best to hurry, given the added challenge of dealing with my cast, which I barely managed to pry the stretchy fabric over. Keeping my thoughts off the fact that she was undressing behind me was no easy task either. Eventually our respective rustling came to a stop.

"All set?" she asked tentatively.

I grunted my assent. "You owe me big-time."

We both turned to face each other, and I fought the urge to clutch my chest when my heart rate went through the roof. I tugged at the fabric on my neck, which suddenly felt even tighter. Holy fuck, did she rock that spandex. If she were the superhero coming to my rescue, I'd have no problem maiming myself on the daily. Someone drop a safe on me or something, Acme style, as long as she's on duty.

Then she started laughing.

161

I was busy admiring how stunning and sexy she looked, and she was *laughing*.

"It's *so* bright. Why is it so shiny? My eyes are burning."

She was the queen of brightly colored cheery outfits. If she thought it was bright, it really was bad.

"Can you breathe? How is your voice not an octave higher right now? That thing is like ten sizes too small for you."

"I'm tall," I said, by way of explanation, my cheeks flushing, thankfully hidden by a mask.

"And the beard. Oh my god, the beard tucked into the mask." Tears sprang from her eyes and she doubled over.

"You're doing wonders for my self-confidence," I said.

"Whew!" She heaved a breath, holding her side. "I'm sorry. You're right. I'll pull myself together. Just give me a minute."

I glared at her, and she started laughing again.

"I can leave you know."

She held up a hand. "No, no, no. Don't leave. I've got it. I'm good now, I swear. And for what it's worth, your body looks hella good, but your, um"—she waved in the general direction of my crotch—"is a bit obscene for a children's party. And the beard, and the cast just make it wholly ridiculous. But it's fine. It'll be fun. A quick two hours, and we can forget this ever happened."

"Two hours?"

Trixie's phone buzzed, and she glanced at it.

"Ope, that's our cue."

"Uh-oh, who could that be?" Marsha said dramatically and far louder than necessary from the other room, and I braced myself for the impending wave of embarrassment. "It's Awesome Guy and Amazing Lady!" she shouted.

"Those aren't seriously our names," I muttered to Trixie as we rounded the corner.

"I know," she whispered. "We sound like off-brand super-heroes, but apparently it's a popular new kids' show. I checked."

Trixie crouched, then leapt out from behind the wall, thrusting her hand into the air as if she were flying. "Prepare to be—" she shouted.

"Amazed!" The children shouted back, filling in the rest of the apparent catchphrase. Did I have a catchphrase? I hadn't exactly had time to read up on my character. I hadn't even known his name until two seconds before rounding the corner.

I set my crutches and swung myself forward, in the best impression of Trixie's flying leap as I was capable of with my injury. "Awesome!" I yelled.

"Sauce!" the kids yelled back. Huh. I'd managed to stumble on the catchphrase anyway.

Marsha's eyes locked on my crutches and my cast and widened, and her face darkened to an unhealthy-looking deep rose red. Despite the color, if she was any part of a rose at the moment, it was the thorns.

"We received a call from the chief to inform us it was some-body's birthday!" Trixie said.

"Why is his face all lumpy?" a kid in the front asked. I scratched at my beard through the fabric.

"Awesome Guy, I thought you couldn't get hurt," another child to the right observed.

"Yes," Marsha said through gritted teeth. "How did the man of tungsten break an ankle?"

"I—" I had nothing, so I stopped talking and looked at Trixie desperately. She'd gotten us into this mess; she could get us out of it.

"Awesome Guy wanted to be the best superhero ever, but in order to fully relate to the people he helps, he wanted to see what it was like to be injured like this, so he's vowed to wear a cast and use crutches for a few weeks!" she said with admirable enthusiasm. Clutch.

A boy up front wearing a crown, presumably Jayden, frowned. He was not buying it.

"So who wants to play a game?" Trixie asked, pulling their attention.

She led the party through a handful of games, me quietly tagging along beside her.

While the kids ate cake, we posed for photos. I did my best to avoid answering questions, but the children were relentless.

"And that was when the, uh, bad guy—"

"Evil Man?" a little girl asked, eyes wide with amazement.

"Yeah, that's the one. That's when he, uh, threw a tractor at the building."

"But his power is laser eyes," one of the kids protested.

I ground my teeth. "Yes, so that's when I knew it was really his evil twin brother."

"Evil Man has a twin?" the girl asked, now less amazed and more suspicious.

I nodded.

"What's his name?"

His name? What's a name, pick a name . . . "Larry."

The kids blinked at me, and a brief silence descended. The trickle of the champagne fountain might have been crickets.

"That's not a supervillain name. That's just . . . a guy," the little girl said, and all the other kids nodded along.

"He hasn't passed his villain test yet, so the council of bad guys hasn't given him one."

I could see more questions building. I had to get out of here.

"So that's when I trapped him and put him in jail." Awesome Guy and Amazing Lady had some new backstories and subplots that were unlikely to be accurate to the comic book, or show, or whatever. "Hey, Amazing Lady, I think I heard the alarm. The chief needs us!" I shouted, and Trixie nodded at me from across the room.

"It's present time, kids!" she shouted.

While the kids were distracted with presents, we made our escape to the study to change. When Trixie peered out the door to make sure no kids were around, a man was standing in the hall. He had bags under his eyes and his hair was mussed, but his outfit was pristine.

"Kyle, I presume?" Trixie asked.

"Yeah. Here's your check. Better get going before Marsha is able to step away for a minute. She's kind of pissed."

"Sorry about that. Had only planned on it being me."

"No worries. I thought it was hilarious. Sorry, man. But yeah, she mentioned something about speaking to the agency. You don't want to be here when she gets going."

I didn't doubt that. "Ready when you are," I told Trixie.

"Let's skedaddle."

CHAPTER TWENTY
TRIXIE

"Somehow I don't think she's going to leave us a positive review," I said as I slathered on my nightly skin care routine.

"Nope," Bear said. "She said something about calling the agency. Is that going to be a problem for you?"

I snorted. "No. I wasn't there through any agency. Her husband hired me through a Craigslist ad and had me talk to her about the details. Just wait till she figures that out."

"Poor Kyle."

"Poor Kyle," I agreed. Bear lifted his wine cup, and I solemnly lifted my empty rinse cup in a toast to him. We held a moment of silence for him, before I started laughing again. "The look on her face when she saw you, though."

"The man of tungsten?" he asked. "That can't be real."

"It's a thing! Man of steel was taken."

"Tungsten is stronger anyway."

"I'm sorry that was such a chaotic mess. Thank you for doing that, though. At least it paid well. I needed the money,"

I admitted. I'd been trying to keep my money troubles hidden, but now that he knew, I might as well clearly express the depths of my gratitude.

"I know." Bear cleared his throat. "Which is why you're taking my half for her bills too," he said.

My head shot up. What had he just said?

"Look, I know what you'll say, but I want to help. You're not taking any of my money. All I did was volunteer to help you, so that's what this is."

It was another one of his unexpectedly long-winded speeches. I was growing accustomed to them. He'd go from using the fewest words possible to suddenly having a lot to say, all for me. But I couldn't take his money.

"You already helped me enough by moving in here," he added. "You definitely earned that money. You were great with the kids. You should keep it."

Images of unpaid bills folding around me in a giant paper airplane and flying me off, never to be seen or heard from again, taunted me. The money would help, but no. He'd done more than enough. I remembered the way he was frozen in place, standing still like a terrified, lumpy god.

"You need it," he said. In the other room, Chick-Chick clucked loudly, impatient for her dinner. "She needs it."

She did need it. At her last visit, the receptionist had apologetically told me if I didn't start making more payments soon, they'd no longer be able to provide care, and the inner city didn't have many options for veterinarians that could treat farm animals.

It wasn't just my pride that made me want to refuse him. Casual acquaintances didn't give each other money, especially not when it was so hard earned. Landlords didn't give their tenants money either. We were leaving easy roommate territory and venturing into something beyond that. We were moving toward friendship and, the way my blood heated around him, maybe something more.

I had friends. Lots of them. Even before I'd started filling my calendar with odd jobs, it had rarely been empty, and was usually booked by different friends each day. I didn't let anybody reach the "more" category, though. Not since Julia had reached best-friend status and then ripped my heart out.

I ached to have that type of relationship with Bear, but it was better to bottle things up. I liked the new home I'd found for myself and Chick-Chick. I liked him. Maybe the yearning for more was worth enduring to have a friendship with him. What if he saw behind my walls and didn't like what he found?

People liked people who smiled. It was that simple. It had been proven to me by judges, my parents' persistent reminders, auditions, and through a roommate's betrayal. A smile and a brave face led to opportunities and friends. Frowns lead to failure, loss, and loneliness. I just wished the friendships didn't feel so lonely too.

My mind worked to push past the need for him and instead build an argument against his charity. Bear flipped through the TV, only half-attentive. "If you say no, I'll charge you less for rent to make up for it."

"I already know what to put on the check." I was half teasing, half making a feeble argument. His head tilted in my direction, his eyes saying, *Really?* Somewhere, though, the annoyed look got lost. His pupils dilated, and his breath hitched as he watched me. I swallowed hard the extra saliva that appeared under his scrutiny. He actually had me salivating. I remembered the tension of knowing he was nearly naked behind me while we changed, and the way he filled out his costume. He had nothing to be self-conscious about there. I wanted to take it for a ride.

No! Letting anything more happen with him was too risky. I immediately broke our eye contact, looking away. Whatever he'd been thinking about—and let's be real, I don't think it was self-centered to assume it was me in spandex—seemed to shatter in his mind, and he returned to the subject at hand.

"You're taking the money."

If I didn't accept this, I had a feeling he'd tell me I owed less than I did when our utility bill came around. I smiled. Now that I'd decided not to fight it, I might as well show my gratitude.

"Okay. Thank you." I let the words hang in the air, hoping he understood how much I meant it. The money we'd earned was not enough to bail me out of the gaping financial crater I was in, but every little bit helped.

"Trixie?" he asked.

"Yeah?"

"You don't have to hide things from me. I'm your friend. Even with my mobility limited at the moment, if I can't do much physically to raise money, I can at least keep my eye out for opportunities. Let me help."

I was inclined to argue. This wasn't his problem to solve, and I didn't want to be more of a burden than I already was, but his eyes were too sincere. Instead, I just nodded.

"Do we need to talk about—" He waved in my direction and down at himself. Giving up, he scratched his beard.

That glorious bulge, I thought. "What we saw in there?"

Bear nodded.

"It's not like you haven't seen me in less," I said. "My skin was covered head to toe."

He gave me a look.

"Okay, so your outfit was a bit more revealing, by way of outlines," I admitted. "It was professional, nothing more."

I had tried not to look when we'd turned around, or all throughout the party, really. I'd made a valiant effort but failed miserably, and since then hadn't been able to shake the image of the taut outlines of his body. Who knew men could have such beautiful backsides?

I walked on my toes to the kitchen, then poured myself and Bear very generous glasses of wine and brought them to the sofa.

"So we forget about it. Deal?" I asked.

"Deal," he agreed, accepting his glass and lifting it in a toasting gesture before taking a sip.

Yep, everything would go right back to normal.

We'd move on and pretend he hadn't thrown on an outfit he'd been mortified to wear and dived into a public-speaking situation with zero preparation. Somehow I'd have to move on with him as my landlord and friend and try to forget that he was my literal and figurative hero.

CHAPTER TWENTY-ONE
TRIXIE

Bear was as good as his word in helping me brainstorm other things to do for money. I'd done some personal shopping, poured beer at a festival, and done market research on the weekends. I'd also offered to babysit for Fawn, and she had jumped at the opportunity for a sitter while she was attending a friend's baby shower. That hadn't been Bear's suggestion, but he'd helped me with it anyway, whether he knew it or not.

The only problem was, Bear was going to be at the doctor's most of the day, and Chick-Chick needed medicine midday. Fortunately, Fawn agreed to let her tag along.

"You've got our numbers. Don't give her any candy. She'll tell you we always give her some, but don't fall for it. She's a tiny manipulator," Fawn said.

"No candy. Got it."

"Oh, and hey, since you're looking to make extra money, aside from what we're paying you, feel free to use her for a lemonade stand and split the profit. You'd be surprised how much she rakes in. Everyone wants their own kids' fund raisers to get attention, so they go out of the way when they see a lemonade stand. And you've got your own little mascot."

Fawn headed out, and Bella and I were left to it. We leapt across pillows playing the floor was lava, and she gave me a checkup with her play doctor kit. While I made her mac 'n' cheese for lunch, I proposed the lemonade stand for the afternoon. "And Chick-Chick can be our mascot."

"She'll be the best mascot!" Bella said. "None of my friends had chickens at their lemonade stands. I'll have the coolest lemonade stand ever!"

Bella shifted in her seat, all business. I grinned at the little cutie. I loved this kid.

"I've got a sign from my last stand, and a table in the garage."

Perfect. The supplies were already worked out. Then she hopped down from her chair and took off at a run.

"Hey, Bella, where are you going?"

"One minute, Aunt Trixie!" Oh boy. Had Fawn asked her to call me that? The way the sisters had looked at me and Bear at the club, I wouldn't doubt it.

The thing was, I liked the sound of it. I wanted kids of my own someday, but having a pseudo-niece was fun in the meantime, and Bella was adorable. The implications of the title had my heart pounding though. Bear. I wasn't freaked out by being with him, specifically. The way he was so patient and gentle with me, the ease of living with him, the way he made me laugh when he wasn't trying and swooped in to help me whenever I needed him—it all made my body go wobbly with desire every time I was near him.

"You coming back, kiddo, or do I need to come chase you?"

"Just a minute!" she shouted.

It wasn't about him. I was freaked out about not being freaked out. I knew being called *Aunt* should have alarmed me, and the fact that it didn't concerned me. I was allowing myself to get too close. I needed his house as a place to live. I couldn't afford to have an imploding relationship make me homeless. I'd come to respect him and appreciate his presence too much to want that relationship tainted by him seeing me as anything but happy, and if we got any closer, that would be inevitable. Nothing good ever came of that.

Bella skidded into the room, tearing me away from my thoughts. She extended a My Little Pony notebook out to me. I flipped it open to find a lemonade recipe.

"Mama and I tried different recipes. People like this one the best." The mini business woman had it all figured out.

One hour and two bellies full of mac later, we were out in the sun with our stand, attempting to make lemonade. Emphasis on attempt. Chick-Chick was making things difficult.

Every time Bella picked up a lemon to squeeze it, Chick-Chick started flapping at her face. Sweet, gentle Chick-Chick had suddenly turned into an attack bird.

"Eek!" Bella shouted, and ran across the yard.

Chick-Chick gave chase, but it was a rather anticlimactic chase, given her limp.

"What do I do?" Bella asked.

"She's never done this before! I can put her inside." I moved toward Chick-Chick.

"No! She's our mascot!"

"Mascot or not, I can't have her claw you up."

"Why is she only coming after me?"

"I think it might be the lemons. Throw it here!" I said, before remembering she was five and didn't have the best coordination yet. The throw was wild and spun off several feet away from me. Moving with a speed I'd never seen out of her, Chick-Chick pulled her wings back and started running. Jousting jelly beans, she was making herself aerodynamic. She was serious about this lemon.

I bolted for the fruit, retrieving it just in time. We had too limited a supply to share with her. I'd have to find her a different snack. Chick-Chick, unaware of the alternate snack plan, decided her best option for retrieval was to start pecking at my ankles.

"Ouch!"

"Pass it back, Aunt Trixie!"

"Ouch!" I yelped, hopping from leg to leg, trying to avoid her pecks. "That feels like it would—ouch!—be highly irresponsible."

Bella frowned, sad not to be a part of the game, clearly not understanding the severity of the battle royale taking place between beak and ankle.

Beak: approximately 17; ankle: 0. I wasn't about to kick her.

"Okay, fine. I'll toss it to you, but stay on the move. You can outrun her. I'll use the distraction and free hands to catch her."

"What does distraction mean?" she asked.

"It means watching one thing so you don't notice something else."

Bella nodded and focused in on the lemon. I threw. The perfect pitch. Sign me up for Little League. Chick-Chick's head swiveled and her beady little eyes bulged as we all watched it soar. Bella stretched her hands out—it was headed right for them. It bounced off her fingers and rolled to the ground. Bella stared it down. Chick-Chick stared it down. She kicked her little legs back as though winding herself up. I crouched to grab her, and they were off. The three of us raced after the lemon, and as the scene played out, in my head I was like the Secret Service, diving to take a bullet, rather than a woman afflicting herself with rug burn and grass stains to stop a rogue chicken behind a lemonade stand in the burbs.

I managed to snag her, then bend and snap my way straight up to middle-school dance pose to keep her at arm's length so she wouldn't peck at my face in her frenzy to get to the yellow orb of deliciousness.

Across the street, a teen boy began to slow clap. I resisted the urge to stick my tongue out at him, impressionable minds nearby and all. He'd better come buy some lemonade once we got it made as a payoff for the show he'd just gotten.

"Do you guys still have a baby gate or anything?" I asked.

"Hmm, I think so," Bella said.

I temporarily placed Chick-Chick in the bathtub and went with Bella on a hunt for a gate. We found exactly what I was hoping for: some small gates that formed a little hexagonal pen. I penned Chick-Chick up in the yard with an apple as a treat, and we finally managed to get our lemonade made and open up shop.

"A dollar? Wasn't it seventy-five cents last time?" a gentleman who'd wandered over from across the street with his son asked, giving me a wink.

"Yes, Mr. Monroe, but that's inflation for you," Bella answered. "I also have a new business partner stealing my profits, so I had to increase my prices."

"How old are you again?" I asked her, shaking my head and already knowing the answer.

"Five and three-quarters."

"I can't believe you're throwing out words like *inflation* and *profit*."

"I watch *Shark Tank* with Daddy," she said. This kid. She was too much.

The rest of the lemonade stand was relatively uneventful, at least in comparison to the chaos of getting it started. The tiny entrepreneur even thought to charge people to pet and take photos with Chick-Chick, the new neighborhood celebrity.

By the time Fawn got home and we'd wrapped up our lemonade stand, we'd made sixty dollars. I was floored when I counted it out. Bella drove a hard bargain and insisted on a sixty/forty profit share in her favor. I hadn't actually planned on taking any, but she was insistent that as her business partner and "lemonade chef," I'd earned my keep, though Chick-Chick deserved a cut too, since a lot of the money was from people wanting to pet her. I promised Bella the money would go to Chick-Chick's care.

When it was time for me to go, Bella wrapped her arms around me in a tight squeeze.

"Will you come play with me again, Aunt Trixie?" she asked, hope in her eyes.

I started to say of course I would, but I didn't want to lie, and I worried I was intruding too much on Bear and his life. Fawn looked hopeful as well but didn't answer for me. The ball was in my court. I loved having this sweet girl as a part of my life, even if it was a small part for now, and Fawn was a great new friend. I was pushing the limits I was comfortable with in my relationship with Bear, but more than that, I was falling for his whole family. I was terrified, but I also wasn't sure there'd ever been anything I'd wanted as much as to keep feeling the way he and the rest of the Rosses made me feel. I swallowed the lump in my throat and pushed back my rising nerves and gave Bella my brightest smile.

"I'd love to."

CHAPTER TWENTY-TWO
BEAR

My phone buzzed with a notification. As I picked it up to check it, Trixie laughed from her spot next to me on the couch.

"This commercial always cracks me up," she said. In my peripheral, her hand moved to point, but my focus was stuck on my phone, where a picture of Trixie smiled back at me. Photo Trixie was seated at a folding table covered in a pitcher, cups, and a sparkly zip-up pouch, a poster board sign hanging in front of it. She grinned widely with an arm around my niece.

My roommate, who also happened to be the woman I found increasingly irresistible and was trying not to fall completely head over heels for, was posing for pictures and apparently hosting lemonade stands with my family, and I didn't even know about it.

"Why is there a picture of you and Bella having a lemonade stand on Fawn's Instagram?"

Trixie's eyes went wide. Her head tilted slightly as she watched me before she cautiously ventured, "You suggested I find other ways to make money, right? Fawn needed a sitter, and she suggested the lemonade stand too."

She had me on the suggestion, but I hadn't thought my niece would be the means she came up with. A sharp pang in my chest gave away my unease with the situation. I wasn't sure if that unease was because I was mad she'd crossed a line, felt excluded that I hadn't known, or was nervous about how close we were getting. Her spending time with my family, especially Bella, felt very personal. Maybe it was a combination of the three.

"So you're using my five-year-old niece to sell lemonade to raise money to pay your bills?"

Trixie's smile became so forced and cringey at her feared misstep, it looked like she was trying to show me her gums. "Well, when you put it like that . . ."

She waited for me to say more, but I needed more time to analyze the pangs in my chest. When it must have become clear I wasn't going to say anything further, she scooped up a cup of Play-Doh from the bowl on the coffee table and kneaded it with a nervous fervor while we watched TV.

I was angry, I thought. It seemed like I should be mad, but what I was experiencing didn't really feel like anger. Her lower lip was just the slightest bit swollen and red from her nervous nibbling at it. Fuck, she was beautiful. I was making zero progress in the emotional analytics. I needed a moment to myself to process.

I grabbed both of our glasses from the table and headed for the kitchen to refill our wine. The more I thought about it, the more certain I became that I wasn't upset about what she'd done. On the contrary, it felt good to see her in that context. She fit my family like a glove, but with her rules, she'd made it clear

I wasn't what she wanted. Seeing her get close with my family only made me wish we could be more, and that scared me.

"Thanks," Trixie said, when I set her wineglass back down on the table in front of her. She sipped her wine, then returned to the Doh, shredding it into little bits and pieces. Trixie always had a lot of energy, so playing with Play-Doh to keep her hands busy was nothing new to her. Normally, though, she absently pulled at it and rolled it.

As scared as my latest revelation made me, I couldn't leave her to stew in her anxiety. I sat down, edging closer to her so my leg pressed against hers. The small contact anchored my spiraling thoughts and quieted her fidgeting.

I'd worry about my growing feelings and what her friendship with my siblings meant another day. I wanted to enjoy being near her.

A thought occurred to me, and I barked a laugh.

"What?" Trixie asked.

If my mind was on how personal it felt to have her spending time with my family, my sisters were absolutely pondering the same, only multiply it by several.

"Good luck getting out of family meetings now," I said.

Then there was a pounding on the door.

CHAPTER TWENTY-THREE
TRIXIE

"Expecting company?" I asked.

"No. Are you?"

"Nope." I peered through the decorative glass alongside the door at the distorted image on the other side, as if that'd help. It at least told me it wasn't a family meeting. A lone man stood there.

I opened the door.

"Who the hell are you?" the man asked without preamble. He shook his head, his unkempt gray hair flicking out of his eyes. He towered over me, his skin sagging and leathery, like he'd been smoking for far too many years.

I glanced over at Bear, who looked pale, then back to the man.

"I'm Trixie. I live here. Who the heck are you?"

"Where's my son?" he asked, pushing past me into the house. His son?

"Excuse me—" I began, wondering if I should try to force him back out, but Bear spoke up, struggling to his feet with his crutches.

"What are you doing here?" Bear asked.

"I can't visit my son?"

It suddenly clicked. This must be Bear's biological father. I'd known his mom had remarried, but I'd had the impression his father wasn't around much, if ever. It was clear his stepfather, Russell, had acted as Bear's father figure for most of his life.

Bear's jaw worked. He looked like he wanted to say, *No, you cannot.* Instead, he went with, "A call ahead would have been nice."

That felt pretty generous a response. Even with my attempts at reconciliation with my parents, I wasn't sure how I would have reacted if they'd shown up without warning. Not well.

"Shit. Nice to see you too. What happened there?" He nodded at Bear's booted foot.

"Broken ankle," Bear answered. "Trixie, this is Lyle."

"Nice to meet you, Lyle," I said, unsure that it was.

"Be a darling and get me a drink," Lyle said.

The way he commanded rather than asked grated on me, but I went anyway, to give Bear a minute alone to talk with him.

"She's not your server," Bear said.

"Well, you aren't about to get me one, milking that ankle like you are."

Milking it? Bear's ankle was broken. I didn't like the direction this was heading. I tried to stymie the argument before it could devolve further and threw on my brightest smile. "It's no problem. I'll be right back."

"Nice catch," Lyle said to Bear as I exited the room. I froze on the other side to hear Bear's response.

"She's not a 'nice catch.' She's a person. One of the kindest I've ever met. She's beautiful and smart and fun. You don't know anything about her, so you can stop talking like you do right now."

My heart leapt to my throat. I had not been expecting him to defend me, especially with such vehemence. I hadn't enjoyed the way Lyle spoke to or about me, but it hadn't been terribly offensive. Did Bear really know me well enough to think I was beautiful, kind, smart, and fun?

I thought back over the last month and the time we'd spent together. Maybe he did. My attempts to keep my distance from him had failed miserably. He knew me at least as well as Lindsey did, given the time we spent together at work. My heart kick-started, and my cheeks flamed. I didn't think he'd talk about me that way if his feelings were casual. Worse, I didn't think I'd be reacting this way if mine were.

Those were emotions that would require further examination later. For now, I'd get Lyle's drink. I dug around the fridge and found a beer. Neither Bear nor I drank them unless we had company. Odds of us having it were a toss-up, but we kept them on hand for our visitors who preferred it, namely Ryan.

I handed the beer to Lyle, then turned my attention to Bear. We had a silent exchange, in which, through a series of eye widenings and nods, I asked if he wanted me to stay, and it was decided I'd make myself scarce in my room but pop out if voices rose. At least, that's what I took away from the wordless conversation. Hopefully I hadn't misinterpreted. He didn't react when I made for my room, so I took that as a good sign.

When had whatever this was between us progressed to reading each other so well?

I sat and snuggled with Chick-Chick, reading softly to her, trying to block out the muffled conversation outside my room.

"He'll be fine, right, girl?" I whispered to Chick-Chick.

I wanted so badly to be out there with him and protect him from his father any way I could, even if that just meant being a buffer in the conversation, or someone else for Lyle to direct his shitty attitude toward. Bear had stood up for me, though, something I got the impression he hadn't done before. So maybe in a small way, I had helped already. I'd just have to be ready to be there for whatever he needed when this was all over.

I let Chick-Chick wrap her foot around my fingers, like we were holding hands, and we waited.

CHAPTER TWENTY-FOUR
BEAR

"So how'd you meet her?" Lyle asked.

My hands clenched, and I wanted so badly to throw him out right this minute, but I knew if I did it would only set him off and make him more resistant to leaving. I'd indulge him with terse conversation a little longer and look for a better opening to kick him out.

"That's really none of your business."

"I didn't raise you to be so disrespectful, boy."

No, you didn't raise me at all. You treated me like garbage, then disappeared. Mom and Russell did the raising. There were limits to what I'd say to him, though. "She's in her room. I'm not going to talk about her like she isn't here."

"I can't believe you moved in with a woman and didn't tell dear old dad."

I ground my teeth. Dear nothing. I hadn't exactly broadcasted the news, but if I had, he would have been last on my list to tell. He'd be last on my list to share anything with. And Trixie wasn't some random bit of news. She was special, and I didn't want to share her with anyone who wasn't deserving of her light. Lyle did not qualify. All I wanted was for this encounter to be over so I could get back to spending time with Trixie.

"You haven't called or come by in a year and a half," I said. "And it's not like I could visit you when you're never in the same place." Not that I would want to.

"You kids are so unappreciative," he snarled.

"Was there something you wanted?" I was growing less and less patient.

"I was planning to stay the night on my way through, but I see the spare room is taken. Some information that would have been nice to know before I came all the way out here to see you."

"I'm sorry. Next time let me know you're coming, and I can try to work something out." I wasn't sorry. I hated myself for saying I was. He was the one who'd shown up without warning. Even if he hadn't, I didn't owe him a place in my house. I didn't owe him anything, and yet my first instinct was still to apologize.

Lyle shook his head at me, slammed the rest of his beer, and disappeared into the kitchen in search of another. I held my breath, waiting for a reaction.

He returned, carrying another beer. I waited for some praise, a comment, anything. My heart sank as I realized I'd been waiting forever.

"Why do you look like I pissed in your Cheerios?" he asked.

Don't say it. He didn't notice. It isn't going to make you feel better. It will only make you feel worse. Don't. Say. It. "Didn't notice the kitchen was remodeled?"

He turned, glancing in the doorway, not even bothering to look at the whole room again. "And?"

"I did it myself," I said. Home improvement was an item on the list of supposedly masculine activities he approved of. He ought to care. He ought to be impressed.

He ignored me. "Since your guest room is taken, where am I supposed to sleep?" he asked.

He didn't care. He wasn't impressed. He'd never been proud of a single thing I'd done and never would be, no matter what it was. I didn't know why I still cared or got my hopes up. It shouldn't hurt, but damn, it did.

"There's a hotel about a mile from here," I suggested, hoping he'd finish up the shitstorm of emotion he was throwing at me and be gone. As it was, it'd probably take me weeks to push this visit out of my memory.

"A fucking hotel? You want me to stay at a fucking hotel? How's that for goddamned hospitality?"

It had nothing to do with wanting to see or spend time with me. He just couldn't afford a hotel. He never came by unless it was not only convenient but also useful to him. Suddenly I was tired. So tired.

"I don't know what to tell you."

"You're still as useless as always. I'll try your sister," he said, downing the last of his second beer.

He shook his head and pulled on his shoes. Before he walked out the door, he nodded at my ankle. "Man up." Then he disappeared out the door without so much as good-bye. Good riddance. Hopefully I wouldn't have to see or hear from him for at least another year. My stomach was a giant knot I was ill prepared to untangle.

A door creaked, and I glanced up. Trixie tentatively poked her head out. "Did he leave?" she asked.

I fumbled to find words, caught up in my fury and disappointment. "I didn't know. I wouldn't have subjected you to that if I'd known. I—"

"Hey. No. Don't apologize. Never apologize for him. Are you okay?"

"I'm fine. He's still the same old asshole. Nothing's changed."

"He might still be out there. Want me to go chuck Gnomey at his head?"

Despite the heaviness I was feeling, I laughed. Trixie had brought the yard gnome home after spotting it for twenty-five cents at a yard sale, and he was her decorative pride and joy.

"It wouldn't be fair to Gnomey."

"You're right. He's far too valuable. I could probably find a big rock?"

"You don't need to throw anything at his head."

"I could kick him in the crotch," she suggested.

"I'd rather move on. But thank you. I'd better text Fawn a warning." She'd probably turn off the lights, lock the doors, and pretend she wasn't home. I wouldn't blame her.

"If you decide you want to talk, I'm here. I don't know exactly what it was like for you, but I'm familiar with shitty parents."

The sentence was a thread of insight into the enigma that was Trixie. I wanted to chase it, but I felt like I had nothing left in my tank. I'd have to ask her about it another time.

"Thanks, but I think I'm going to call it a night." I shifted my weight around and stumbled trying to get up.

"Here, let me help," she said, running to lend me her arm. *Still as useless as always.* I didn't need her help.

"No," I snapped, sure I'd regret it later, but right now I needed space and sleep. Trixie stepped back as if I slapped her. "I've got it. It's just an ankle. It's getting better anyway."

I turned my back on her.

CHAPTER TWENTY-FIVE
BEAR

The following weekend, I was settled on the couch, starting to feel like I'd merge with it if my ankle didn't heal soon. Chick-Chick was clumsily exploring the house, and Trixie was fixing drinks for us.

When she returned, she set the drinks on the table. My knee chose that moment to sting with the discomfort from constantly being locked in position, and I grimaced and shifted.

"What happened?" she asked. "Are you all right?"

Her eyes welled with concern as she leaned forward, wanting to help but unsure how to.

"It's nothing. My knee gets sore from being in the same position all day." I sat up and swung my lower leg a few times, flexing my knee.

"Here," she said, kneeling next to me. Her smooth, tiny hands found my knee and gently massaged. I bit the inside of my cheek, fighting the natural reaction to having her hands on me.

"Is this okay?" she asked.

I let out a grunted ascent. I didn't trust myself to form words while her hands did that. She pushed and pulled at the muscles for a couple minutes until they relaxed.

She looked up at me, those blue eyes as vibrant as her personality locked on mine.

My pulse quickened further at the intensity of her stare, and the way her eyes bore straight into my soul, as her skin grazed mine.

Trixie cleared her throat, breaking the moment. "Is that better?"

I nodded.

"You'll be up and running in no time." She smiled, pulling her hands free from my leg. I wasn't sure if I should be disappointed or relieved.

"Good. I don't know how much longer I can spend on this couch," I grumbled, knowing I was unfairly taking my frustration out on her.

"Eager to get back to work?" she asked.

"No," I said. Going back to work was the last thing I wanted. I'd never liked my construction job, but I hadn't realized just how much I disliked it. The time off from it while I healed had shown a spotlight on that, as had Mom's announcement and the opportunity it provided. All I longed to do was quit and take over Family Tree. If only things were that simple.

Trixie studied me as though searching for the deeper meaning behind my rejection but ultimately took it surface level and laughed. "A job's a job, right?"

I thought about my years spent at my mom's side, picking out flowers so we could arrange them together. I closed my eyes and could smell the sweet aromas, powerful enough to be dizzying. We'd have best-bouquet challenges, sketching out designs. The bright colors and smells always made me happy.

I didn't agree with the *A job is a job* sentiment. The way Trixie cared about the animals she worked with, I didn't believe she did either. Sure, everyone hated their job at one time or another, but in the right job, most days could be enjoyable. That didn't seem a likely possibility for me, at least not while keeping my life outside work intact.

Maybe I couldn't take over the shop, but at least I could be honest about my distaste for construction. I wasn't sure why I'd never enjoyed it. It was another form of creating, and I got to work with my hands. That was probably why I'd ended up doing it—that and the fact that I'd assumed it would be something Lyle approved of. Now I knew that wasn't the case. On paper, it had seemed like a suitable alternative to Mom's shop. In practice, it wasn't my bag.

"I hate my job," I admitted to Trixie.

She sat on the couch next to me, close enough to be in that magnetic field range that only made me want to draw her closer.

"The work you do or the company you're with?" she asked.

"The work. The only thing I have against the company is they don't have enough business to keep me working as often as I need to be."

"You don't like any of it?" She pulled her feet in all their cat-faced and rainbow mismatched sock glory up onto the couch, folding them under her purple dress to sit cross-legged.

I shook my head.

"Wow, I can't imagine that. I mean, I don't love cleaning out cat boxes and picking up the dog poop in the play areas. There are aspects of my job that suck, but I can't imagine hating all of it and still doing it every day."

I laid my head back on the couch and closed my eyes, letting my breath out in one large gust of air.

"Why do you keep doing it?" she asked.

"Lack of a better option, I guess."

"There must be something you're passionate about," she prodded.

Yes, there was, but the last time I'd admitted to being passionate about it had resulted in years of bullying and a black eye. Granted, I'd more than doubled in size and muscle since then. I wouldn't be such easy pickings now as I'd once been, but the pain of those experiences wasn't easily forgotten, especially when it had been all but encouraged by Lyle.

Trixie was studying me. I could sense her eyes on me. She seemed to hide her emotions from me, and maybe from herself, so I didn't owe her any explanation, but still. I wanted to tell her. There was no one else I'd consider admitting it to. I couldn't tell my family; it'd get their hopes up.

I opened my eyes and tugged at my beard, at war with myself. *Tell her.* She leaned a little closer. *No. Hell no. Not saying a word.*

Trixie's fingers tapped at the thin fabric of her dress like she was playing scales on a piano. I let my hand fall onto the couch next to her. She smiled to herself and danced her hand over to mine, continuing her drumming on my palm.

It relaxed me, and I was talking before I'd consciously decided to do so.

"I'm thinking about taking over my mom's store. Is that foolish?" I asked.

"I don't think it's foolish. I was wondering if you were thinking about it. You got so quiet at that family meeting, but that was weeks ago, and you haven't mentioned it since."

"It was a lot to think about. When I helped there as a kid or hung out while my mom worked, I always loved it." I glanced sideways at her, trying to get a read on her reaction. Was she judging me already, the sentimental boy that liked flowers?

Rather than judgment, I saw widened, hopeful eyes and a big grin. "It sounds perfect! If you used to help her, you already know the work, and she wants to retire anyway . . ." She trailed off, the light on her face dimming. "But your sisters were arguing, and you didn't speak up. How come?"

I craned my neck sideways. As bad an idea as being with my roommate was, I'd abandoned that concern. Trixie cared deeply for everyone and everything, even a stray chicken with a bad leg. Her quirky mannerisms muddled my insides. If I ever wanted to really be with her, which I did, I needed to open up to her. What if she had assumptions about who I was based on how I dressed and acted? What if Trixie learned it wasn't real and was no longer interested in me?

Trixie had seen behind the curtain. She knew the real Wizard of Oz wasn't so powerful, and she hadn't minded. In fact, she'd enjoyed watching soap operas with me, and had hugged me when I'd teared up watching Chick-Chick gain confidence and explore the house. A large part of the reason I was attracted to her in the first place was because of the way she accepted me.

I willed myself to stop overthinking. I focused on the sensation of those dancing fingers on my palm and let the words flow.

"So, as you've seen, I grew up in a house with mostly women," I began.

When I paused, she asked, "What about Russell?"

"Oh, he's great," I hurried on, not wanting her to get the impression he'd been an absent father once Mom had married him. "This was before him. Lyle wasn't very present, so between Mom and my sisters, my family was overwhelmingly female most of the time."

"Okay," she nodded, and closed her hands around mine, encouraging me to continue.

"You could tell that I lived with a bunch of women. I guess, from my mannerisms . . . and interests."

Her lips pressed together at this. Not quite a frown, but close. That was probably enough to tell her where this was going. I was tempted to leave it at that and let her fill in the rest.

"I used to make arrangements from the leftover flowers at the shop, the ones that were starting to die so we couldn't sell them but still nice enough to be beautiful for a time. I'd bring them to school and give them to my teachers, proudly announcing I'd arranged them."

Trixie smiled. "That's so cute."

"Yes, cute. Exactly what we men strive to be called by beautiful women."

Her smile widened, and a faint blush colored her cheeks. "Thank you for the compliment. And about calling you cute, we can come back to that. I'm not taking that bait right now. Finish your story." She gave my hand a small squeeze.

"It was fun until it wasn't. Other kids started taunting me and calling me things like flower boy. That would have sucked, but it wouldn't have been terrible. But then they started beating me up too. I told Lyle, and he took their side. Said I needed to 'grow a pair' and 'be the man of the house,' never mind that being his job, which he was failing miserably at."

Trixie's eyes widened, and she cursed under her breath. "I'm so sorry, Bear. That's horrible."

I waved off her concern. "It was a long time ago." She eyed me, that little brow crinkle making a return. "What?"

"Nothing," she said.

It clearly wasn't nothing. If she was going to judge me over this, I wanted to know now. She wasn't getting away with nothing. "Tell me," I insisted, my voice low.

"It's hard to picture someone beating you up. But I get that you were a kid then. You weren't always built like a mountain."

"Yeah, most of my height didn't come until high school. Until then, I was scrawny."

"And by then, you'd given up on the flowers," she added.

I nodded. "Among other things."

"And Lyle coming through town the other day, does he do that often?"

"Depends on your definition of often. Any visit feels like too much, but I won't hear from him again for months. I didn't even see him again while he was in town. He drifts and uses us as a free night's stay, getting in a few barbs to keep me from ever feeling good about myself."

As soon as the story was out, a weight lifted off my chest. It freed me to focus less on the words and more on the current situation. In Trixie's surprised lunge to seize my thigh in comfort or concern or whatever that was, she'd closed the remaining gap between us. Her thighs now pressed against the side of the leg she had grabbed, her feet tucked under her and to the side.

Though she was no longer squeezing my leg, her hand remained, and she leaned toward me, putting weight on my thigh. The light pressure made it impossible to ignore where—and how close to what—that hand was.

"Hey, Bear," she whispered. Her eyes were locked on my mouth.

"Mm-hmm?" I grunted, words suddenly difficult to form. If she didn't act on this soon, I'd have to make a run for the shower. I didn't dare move and scare her off.

"I don't think you're cute." She leaned in closer, so her breath kissed my neck as she spoke. "You're the sexiest damn man I've ever laid eyes on."

It was no longer a little blood rushing; it was all the blood, as heat spread everywhere.

"Trixie Ward, did you just swear?" I wasn't sure who this dirty-talking minx was, nor what she'd done with the sweet Trixie that used made-up curse words, but I liked it.

"Would you prefer I called you stud muffin?" There she was.

"I liked the first one better." I pulled her up onto my lap. "You like your men built like mountains, huh?"

"Man," she corrected. "And apparently I do."

She ground her hips over me, and I groaned.

She raised an eyebrow. "Speaking of mountains, seems like someone's reached peak elevation."

"No cheesy innuendos."

"*Butte* it's so fun." She tugged my beard up, forcing my eyes from her chest up to her face. "Quit staring down my crevasse."

"You're killing me, woman."

"I knoll." She smirked, and bent toward me. Then, as if neither of us could resist the pull of the last few minutes—or to be more honest, since the moment we'd met—our lips crashed together in a desperate kiss. Stars exploded behind my eyes. All my nerves were alert, firing and refiring the jolt of pleasure the swift kiss had brought and echoing their desperate pleas for me.

"I've wanted to do that for a very long time," I said.

"Me too," she agreed. Our breaths were ragged and charged with anticipation, exhilaration, and so many other emotions.

Our lips remained only a fraction of an inch apart, our faces close. She nuzzled my nose with hers.

I was dying to kiss her until my lips hurt, to bury myself in all that she was, but I forced myself to pull back.

"This is a bad idea," I breathed.

"Yep, but I don't care right now."

That was all the approval I needed.

Our lips met again, with all the urgency but less force, now carefully exploring. We sensed the right ways to move to match each other. She tasted exquisite. Flames of desire spread across my body. She ran her hands over my face, scraping her palms against my scruff. The friction paired with the desperation in her eyes had my own eyes rolling back in my head with pleasure.

We paused again, both gasping for air. "This is a terrible idea," I reminded her.

"Then we'll get it out of our system. One and done," she said, moving to kiss me again.

One and done? Was that truly what she wanted? What I did? The thoughts were mere wisps on the wind. A quiet alarm bell went off in my mind, but my brain was too fogged, or deprived of oxygen that was being spent elsewhere, to give the thought much attention.

"Does that ever actually wo—"

"Shut up, Bear," she said, and pushed her hips over me in a way that brooked no further argument. So I shut up, and we let our bodies do the talking.

CHAPTER TWENTY-SIX
TRIXIE

"Oh fish sticks," I cursed, pulling the blanket to my chest and blowing my hair out of my face after yet another round the next morning.

"Are your made-up swears only foods that you don't like? Or ones that you do like too?" he asked.

"Both," I muttered. "And other things."

I scanned his room, looking for an object that would make a good swear as an example, but came up empty. The walls were bare, and his dresser held only some loose change, receipts, a clock, and his phone charger. My heart stung to realize the extent to which his self-expression had been beaten out of him.

I let myself topple sideways, dropping my head onto his bare chest. He was warm and sturdy. Everything I wanted and was terrified of having.

He pushed his fingers through my hair and massaged my scalp, sending a fresh wave of pleasurable tingles coursing through my sated body.

"Was that an *Oh fish sticks, that was great* or an *Oh fish sticks, why did I do that?*" he asked.

"Why not both?" I asked, careful to keep my tone light. It *was* both. The sex had been amazing. The textbook definition of mind-blowing. Now that I'd floated down from my cloud and back to Earth, reality was setting in and quickly taking hold.

My pulse was racing fast enough to do an impressive rendition of "Flight of the Bumblebee" in a way that had nothing to do with arousal. What was happening with Bear was nothing like my platonic friendship with Julia, but my plan to not get attached was failing.

"So much for one and done," I said to the stucco ceiling. We'd had sex on the couch, then hydrated and powered up on granola bars before going for round two in his bedroom. After a quick anti-UTI bathroom run, I'd gone back to snuggle and fallen asleep there, only to wake up desperate to have him inside me again.

"Still within twenty-four hours." His deep voice rattled the caverns of his chest underneath me. "One day and done."

"Is that your way of tricking me into more?"

"I might use it as an excuse later. Right now, I've got nothing left," he admitted.

I didn't either. His fingers twisted in my hair. The soothing feeling melted my heart, a sensation that physically thrilled me but emotionally terrified me. I needed to put a wedge in this *now*, but in my puddle of bliss, devising a plan to keep from falling for Bear more than I already had was not something I could do.

All evening, he'd been sweet and vulnerable and perfect. I didn't understand how anyone could reject him, especially a family member. Yet this man, overflowing with a gentle but enthusiastic passion, had turned away from something he loved because of the ridicule of bullies and his condescending father.

Bear had said he'd turned away from the floral shop, among other things. In my preoccupation, I hadn't caught it before, but now those three words wouldn't leave my mind. *Among other things.*

I mulled over the last few weeks and everything I'd seen him say and do, and things clicked into place. Watching baseball until caving and switching to *Grey's Anatomy.* The way he drank beer in front of anyone else but drank wine when it was just us. The job he hated.

Had he changed his entire being to avoid the criticism of others? The idea that as an adult he was having to hide who he was made me want to vomit. My heart squeezed in complete agony for him at the revelation. He was the best man I'd ever known, and nothing from his father's warped conceptions about what that should be were worth anything.

A silent tear trickled down my face. I discreetly rubbed it away before he could notice.

"Bear?" I asked, my voice barely above a whisper. "If you want to take over your mom's shop, why don't you talk to her about it?"

The fingers weaving through my hair stopped moving. "I thought I explained that," came his terse response.

"I know," I said, backpedaling at his obvious annoyance with the question. "But . . ." I hesitated, struggling to find the right words. Things might still be uncomfortable with my parents, but they were far less explosive than before I'd confronted them. I still hoped I could someday be at ease in the same room as them. I was on a path to healing, albeit a long one. Even my eggshell conversations with them gave me a hope for the future and for myself that I'd desperately needed. Since his background was similar, I thought maybe he needed it too. "It's been a long time. A lot has changed. Would it be so terrible to be yourself?" I ventured.

He tensed up and wouldn't meet my eyes. Maybe I'd pushed him too far. We lay in a heavy silence that felt endless, until at last he rolled away from me and stood.

"I'm going to take a shower." He brushed past me and into the bathroom.

I once again retreated to my room while he showered. Last night had been emotionally and physically intense. I wasn't sure how I would separate those feelings and maintain a platonic relationship with Bear for the sake of our living arrangement and so I wouldn't lose him as friend. I needed the day to breathe and sort my thoughts. Bear probably did too, and not just his thoughts about me, but about his mom's store.

I spent the rest of the morning in my room, playing with Chick-Chick. I had plans this afternoon with Taya and Camila, some girls I'd met at a yoga class I'd taken a few months back whom I occasionally went out with. At least I wouldn't have to hide in my bedroom all day to get some space from Bear.

A knock sounded on my bedroom door. I wasn't ready to talk, but the image of his large frame outside the door, shoulder bent in, him scratching at his scruff, was too hard to deny. I pushed my confusion and overwhelming emotions away, made sure my smile was securely in place, then pulled open the door.

"Can we talk?" he asked. The hope and insecurity in his eyes tugged at my heart. I wanted to say yes, but if I agreed to talking before I processed my feelings, I was likely to agree to a new dynamic I wasn't ready for. I glanced at the clock on my nightstand. If I didn't leave soon, I was going to be late. I had a valid excuse.

"Sorry, I have lunch plans with my friends Taya and Camila," I said, feeling guilty at his sunken expression. "We can talk tonight, though, okay? We should."

"More friends?" he asked.

"Yeah, I don't think you've met them." The comment struck me as odd, but I brushed it off and grabbed my purse.

He nodded and stepped aside. I slid on my shoes and said good-bye. As soon as the door clicked shut behind me, I wanted to fall back against it. The mental wall I'd put up to shove the emotions back while facing him crumbled to dust, and I had to fight my body's inclination to double over. My heart clenched with guilt at leaving without talking to him. Images of our bodies entwined and words whispered in the dark made my head spin from an emotion I struggled to name.

Well, bubble and squeak. Now I wanted to go back in there and fold myself into his sturdy arms, but I couldn't. I didn't want to cancel on my friends at the last second, and I didn't want Bear to know how much of an effect he'd had on me. I wanted to be with him, but I had no other living options, so I couldn't leave. Eventually, I had to face my growing closeness with him and do something about it. What, I didn't know.

I trudged forward like I was wading through caramel, barely warm and melty enough to move through. Every fiber of my being wanted me to turn around, but I went.

At lunch, I sat and chatted pleasantly with the girls, catching up on what was new with them and bragging about my sweet new pet chicken. The whole time I had trouble focusing. My mind kept turning back to Bear. The feel of his hands on my waist, and how he'd scooped me onto his lap the night before. He'd studied me like I was some fascinating creature. I missed the sweet musky smell of him as I lay in the crook of his arms. And the sound of his reluctant laugh as I told him about my many failed attempts to sneak pets past my former landlord.

Taya and Camila kept talking, not seeming to notice I wasn't following the conversation. It was like they couldn't sense the monumental shift that had happened in my life in the last twenty-four hours. It must have been written all over my face. Then again, it wouldn't be so noticeable, would it? All they'd see would be my typical smile.

After lunch, we headed to the mall. The two of them wanted to go shopping. Given my financial situation, it was window shopping for me. I roamed through the racks while my friends picked out items. I ran my fingers over the soft cotton of a sweater I thought Bear would like.

In the next store, I tried my best to be attentive and give honest feedback on their clothes as they tried them on. Taya had to wave a hand in my face for my attention, though, when a song came on that I'd remembered Bear dancing to at the stove.

I wanted to go back in time and smack myself for agreeing to hang out with friends today. I wanted to be with Bear.

"That was so fun," Taya said as we stood to leave. Had it been? I'd been counting down the minutes until I could get back home to him.

"We have to do this more often," Camila agreed. Even though I felt guilty about it, I wasn't sure I felt the same. It wasn't fair to them. I'd always enjoyed their company before, and they were nice girls, but I'd been spending a lot of time with Bear lately. There was such a natural ease to time with him that felt missing when we weren't together. It had taken me far too long to notice.

I sped the whole way home.

CHAPTER TWENTY-SEVEN
BEAR

I hobble-paced around the house. I needed to get off my foot but had way too much nervous energy to sit. Chick-Chick hobbled and flapped about behind me. I cleaned and cooked, propping my leg up when I could. None of the things I normally did to calm myself down worked.

I'd thought about Trixie nonstop since I'd met her, and last night I'd finally gotten a chance with her. The air between us had been different when she'd left. Something was off. I worried I'd blown it in one day. Her nudges about the store made me uncomfortable. I knew what I wanted, but I wasn't sure I was willing to take it.

Her comment about being myself had rubbed me the wrong way too. It felt hypocritical. She was the one who hid in her room at the first sign of having an emotion. Then she'd gone out with more "friends." She had so many, I had a hard time believing any of them could be very close. It felt like an attack she didn't have any right to launch, even if that wasn't how she'd intended it. As a result, I'd snapped, and done my own running off. Could that have been enough to scare her?

I'd already been thinking about taking over the store. I'd thought about it on and off my entire life. Since Mom's announcement, I'd been thinking about it constantly. For the last week my mind had been an incessant loop of Trixie, florist, Trixie, florist, Trixie, florist. Both of which I'd been trying to keep myself from, because both were terrible ideas. No other thought I could call to mind was strong enough to nudge those out of the way, so I'd tried to think of nothing. Which was impossible.

I was beginning to think that Trixie was on the longest lunch date in the world. She'd been gone four hours. Did her friends live in Wisconsin or something? My hands were shaking, and if I didn't find some way to calm myself down quickly, I was going to crack.

It was time to break out the boxes. I'd kept them in Trixie's room before she moved in, but since then they'd been stored in the garage attic—an attic I couldn't get up to with a broken ankle.

I stood underneath the opening, staring at it and trying to decide what to do. Then Ryan strolled up next to me and mimicked my stance. We both stood together, silently staring at the attic.

"What are we looking at?" he asked.

"An attic," I said.

"No shit."

I waved at my leg. "Would you mind getting a couple boxes down?"

"Sure. How's that doing, by the way?" he asked, nodding toward my leg as he retrieved the ladder.

"Getting there," I said.

"And that?" he asked, this time nodding toward the house, and I knew he was referring to Trixie. Trixie, whom I'd finally had earth-shattering sex with last night and this morning. Trixie, whom I'd snapped at and who'd taken off.

I sighed.

"You've got it bad. I'll try not to take offense that you've been coming over less. Can't say I blame you if she's your alternative."

"I don't know what you're talking about," I grumbled.

"So she's fair game, then?"

My nostrils flared and my fists clenched.

"Whoa, struck a nerve." He smirked at me. Shit, he didn't even want to make a go for her. He was just gauging my reaction.

"You are such an asshole," I said.

"True, but I'm a lovable asshole. You know I was messing with you. I've got my eyes on someone else," he said. I'd heard him wax poetic about his girls of the week too many times before to take the bait on that one.

I pointed out where the boxes were and which ones I wanted. Ryan deftly climbed up and handed them down to me, then came down the ladder, and we carried them inside.

"What's in these, anyway?" Ryan asked.

"Some stuff for one of my projects," I answered, hoping he wouldn't push. Ryan knew I'd been getting fewer construction gigs lately and was picking up some side projects to compensate. Sometimes he'd sit and drink in the garage with me while I worked on a piece. As much of a dipshit as he could be about and around women, he was a good friend.

Ryan accepted this explanation and launched into a monologue about a trade the Cubs had made, then headed back home once all the boxes were in my room.

I opened them, looking for the materials I needed. The bins were overflowing with floral supplies. There was wire and wire cutters, vases and floral tape, foam and pliers. Setting out a few of the items, I grabbed some shears and headed to the backyard to gather some flowers for a bouquet.

Not only would making a bouquet ease my mind and expel the nervous energy in my hands, it would allow me an excuse to talk to Trixie, who, on her way out, had seemed keen on ignoring me.

There was so much more to floral arrangement than grouping flowers together in a way that appealed to the eye. The right grouping of flowers could talk. Mom had taught me how to tailor the arrangement to the recipient and about which colors drew out which emotions. I knew how to make arrangements that said *I love you*, *I miss you*, or *I'm sorry*. I could make them say any of those things, or simply evoke happiness. I'd been raised to believe that the perfect arrangement could sometimes express things better than words ever could.

Fortunately, I knew what the perfect flower for Trixie would be, and I had it on hand. Our backyard was full of the daylilies she'd admired the day we'd gotten treats from the ice cream truck, and which I'd caught her admiring a few times since. It was a bit of a gamble. Would she interpret it as invading on the tradition she had with her parents? Maybe, but I had a feeling she wouldn't mind a new memory to associate with the flowers and was confident enough this was the right move.

I trimmed a few of the flowers, leaving plenty to adorn our yard, and snagged some deep-blue speedwell to fill out the rest of the arrangement. Back inside, I dug through the binful of vases, studying my options. After narrowing down my selection to those about the right size, I was left with three. The simple cylindrical glass one was way too boring for Trixie. A unique woman needed a unique vase for her arrangement. The brown milk-jug-style one didn't feel right either. I went with the wavy turquoise vase with a bubbled surface.

I filled it with water and a packet of flower food. My fingers moved nimbly as I tucked each flower in, ensuring a balanced view from all sides. Then I sorted through spools of thick fabric ribbon and selected the yellow one. I measured out a length and cut it off, tying a small bow around the neck of the vase. I hobbled back a step to admire my handiwork.

Perfect.

I did the careful balancing act required to stand on my injured leg to go place the vase. The back door swung open, and Trixie walked into the kitchen, flinging her purse down on the counter. Concentrating on my work, I was caught off guard. I stumbled, and water sloshed over the side of the nearly upturned vase.

Trixie ran over to help. "Sorry, I didn't mean to scare you," she said, taking the vase and offering her arm.

I grabbed it, using her for balance, as I steadied myself on my good leg.

"I didn't hear you coming," I grunted. "You usually stand there for ten minutes digging through your bag for your keys."

"You were focused." She nodded at the flowers. "They're beautiful."

This wasn't what I'd intended. I wasn't supposed to have to fumble for words. She was supposed to find the flowers when she got home. The flowers were supposed to do the talking for me. I watched her for a reaction. She studied the flowers. Maybe they still would. Her chin tilted upward, and her eyes locked on mine. A lump formed in my throat. She was looking at me, at least. That was already an improvement over earlier.

I pointed out the table I'd intended to place them on. Trixie made sure I was stable before bringing them there. She set them down with a gentleness like reverence, then hurried to tuck herself under my arm and help me over to the couch.

Urgent need to get the vase and me settled aside, now we had nothing to do, and the awkwardness between us returned—and hung around. It was not only an elephant in the room, but a tap-dancing and trumpeting one. I didn't know what to say. Now that I'd been with Trixie, I knew what I'd be missing if we stuck to the one-and-done suggestion. That plan wasn't what I wanted. Keeping my hands off her was already torture. I had to tell her I wanted more, risks be damned, but first we had to clear up this awkwardness.

"You're good at that," she said, saving me from having to think of an opening line. Her face flushed. "I enjoyed watching you work. I might have stood there for a minute when I saw what you were doing."

"Thanks." How long had she been there? At least she'd enjoyed watching me. That sounded promising.

She turned back to the flowers again. From the other room, Chick-Chick warbled quietly, adding her own little flair to the silence.

"Are they for me?" She turned her face away, like she was worried the question would sound self-centered. Maybe it would have if she hadn't been right.

"Yes." I watched for her reaction, which was challenging to gauge when all she ever did was smile. What level smile was this? Small, but sweet. Genuine, but reserved.

"You remembered the lilies," she whispered, settling down next to me.

"Mm-hmm." I waited for her to say anything more, or for her smile to change and give me a stronger indication of whether my olive branch had worked. She traced the outline of a polka dot on her dress. She looked like she wanted to say more. Maybe she was ready to take this further. She felt so close, like it was on the tip of her tongue. The discomfort was eating away at my stomach. I couldn't take it anymore. Maybe this was finally our moment.

Her fists clenched and unclenched, and she shook her head. Her smile, as always, stayed in place, but it was different. Whatever she'd been about to say, she'd changed her mind, and I didn't think that boded well for me. For us.

"Anything good on tonight?" she asked brightly, launching herself off the couch and toward her room.

Even though I'd spotted the shift in her, the subject change baffled me. She was intending to watch TV with me, so I figured we were okay. The abrupt dismissal of the thick tension between us had the land-mine-type feeling of any conversation in which a woman utters the words *I'm fine*. Except instead of saying them, Trixie was retrieving a chicken.

She returned to the couch with her feathery armload, crossing her legs underneath her. "I won't pester you about it," she said, running her fingers over a contented Chick-Chick. "All I'll say is what I saw in there was a man with a passion for what he was creating. It would be a shame to see that passion go to waste, given such a perfect opportunity."

She still didn't meet my gaze, as though I couldn't argue if she didn't look at me. She stole the remote from my lap and started flipping through channels.

* * *

The next few days passed uneventfully. Chick-Chick and I kept each other company during the day. True to her word, Trixie didn't nag me about taking over the shop. She made it a point to stop and smile at or smell her flowers and slide comments about my mom, the shop, or flowers in general into our conversations, though. I was aware of what she was doing but didn't mind enough to challenge her on it.

She'd also unfortunately held true to the "one day and done" condition of our hookup. Every time I was near her, my skin prickled with longing. The desire had been difficult to fight back before we'd caved, but now that I knew what being with her could be like, it was even harder to ignore. That she might hold on to the rule forever terrified me, but I wasn't just lusting after her. She'd pulled me in with her charisma, and there was no turning back. We needed to talk, but the way she hid from her emotions, I knew that if I pushed, she'd run. I'd have to wait it out.

I went on, biding my time. I'd be her roommate and friend for now, if that was what she needed. I was relatively certain she'd come around eventually. At least I hoped she would.

In addition to all my pent-up and growing feelings for Trixie, who was set on preventing those from developing, my mind was stuck on what she'd said: "a man with a passion" and "it would be a shame to let that passion go to waste."

The day of Mom's retirement was still a way off, but it got closer every day. It didn't feel like I had much time to decide, and I had even less time than it felt like, because even if she wasn't retiring for another two months, the developers had made a decision. It might break her heart to see her little corner of the city knocked down and sold out to another cold business, but she couldn't work there forever. If another offer didn't come along, she'd take it. I knew she was hoping one of her children would step up before she finalized a deal.

Time was falling away like sand, only instead of slowly straining through an hourglass, a sinkhole had opened, and it was all dumping down in one fell swoop.

My family had barged in for one more meeting after the first. Trixie hid in her room, part of her *stay away from Bear* campaign, for reasons I did not understand. I hoped it was because she had as difficult a time fighting temptation as I did, but I worried it was something else.

"Uncle Bear, can I see Chick-Chick?" Bella asked.

"Sure, kiddo. Go ask Ms. Trixie." I knew Trixie wouldn't mind, nor would she turn Bella away or give up an opportunity to show Chick-Chick off and let someone else give her attention.

Bella knocked, and Trixie let her in. Once the door was open, my sisters sprang into action.

"Trixie! Come here. There's some pictures I wanted to show you." Fawn dragged her out, giving me a wink.

"Yeah, you can show her in a minute. I think Bear needed her help finding something in the kitchen first." Zoey shoved me toward Trixie in a way that was anything but subtle.

"Hi," she said.

"Hey." Our eyes locked, and my throat got tight. I held my breath, wanting to say everything and wanting to say nothing. I wanted her to take a step. Extend me something, even just a genuine smile.

She rubbed her lips together. "I'm just going to go . . . um . . ."

"Right." I stepped aside, and she took a few steps in one direction, then turned and took a few steps in another, then turned again. She had zero plan.

She quickly recovered and blended right in, laughing with Zoey and Fawn while keeping food constantly in front of my dad, elevating herself to goddess status in his estimation. She swapped stories with Mom, engaging everyone but me. She dodged me like a tornado that suddenly changed directions, hurling debris and windblown cows like little torpedoes at my heart. With me, she did an intricate dance, twirling away and making it look effortless as she wove from one conversation to the next, the amicable life of the party.

She'd said she'd been a dancer, but watching her and thinking back to how she'd moved at the club, I wanted to know more. She still had a dancer's grace, and it was probably why she walked on her toes all the time. The next time I pinned her down for a conversation, I was asking her about it.

Neither in that family meeting nor in our lively sibling group chats did anyone else volunteer to take over the store. It was either me, or the store was going to end up in a stranger's hands. Though that would crush my mother and me, I still wasn't sure I could do it.

Giving myself distance to decide wasn't helping. I couldn't base this on nostalgia. If I was going to do it, I had to be sure. Making one little arrangement with the flowers I had on hand for Trixie was not a good representation of what it would be like to run a florist's shop. I needed to remind myself of how it felt.

I was still on leave and Trixie was at work, so with the goal of deciding in mind, I headed out.

Family Tree was tucked between two taller buildings. Its faded brick was an anomaly among the gleaming surfaces of the surrounding newer developments. I knew Mom had received offers to purchase the property over the years, but she'd never caved until now. I didn't know how much the offers had been for, but I was fairly certain the land itself was worth a lot. Mom had said she'd be sad to see the store go, but if I couldn't come close to their offer, would she even let me keep the store? All this agonizing could be moot.

Over the years, I'd seen the neighboring buildings torn down and their cold replacements thrown up instead. Still, I couldn't imagine anything in place of the worn brick on the face of Family Tree. The store was ours. Anything else would seem wrong. I scratched at a stray line of window paint, where Mom's painted flowers and the advertisement of the current sale had wandered. Then I walked into the store, the small bell jingling on the door as I opened it.

It was a matter of instinct that once inside, I inhaled deeply. It was a habit ingrained in my soul after years of coming here, drinking in the sweet aromas, and letting the strong floral scent sting my senses and overwhelm my brain.

Mom popped out from behind the beaded yellow curtain that served as the door to her back room. She planted one hand on her hip and wiped aside a strand of her salt-and-pepper hair that had broken free from her loose ponytail with the other.

"Hi, Bear." She grinned at me. My nerves about the purpose of this trip were soothed by the honey in her voice. My mom could calm me with two words. "Nice to see you out of the house. What brings you here?"

"Just thought I'd check in on you," I said.

Mom raised an eyebrow at me, as if to say *You've never done that before* or *Uh-huh. Nice try, son, but I'm not buying it.* If the eyebrow hadn't done it, the quirk to her mouth as she riffled through papers on her register desk made it clear she knew I had ulterior motives. She didn't challenge me, though.

"As long as you're here, might as well make yourself useful," she said. She handed me a stack of orders. "Do you want to start on these?"

I gratefully accepted the order forms. The task was welcome, giving me something to focus on so I didn't keep staring around the shop, my mind running in an endless loop. In the brief time I'd been in the room, I'd already been analyzing every detail. There was a water stain on the ceiling tiles; would that be an expensive fix down the line? The sun shone through the storefront windows and hit the reflector ball wedged among the plants, sending brilliant beams of light dancing around the room. It felt like home.

The front window had tables with a variety of arrangements in vases of different sizes and shapes. She took special care with the window display. It was important for business, but she'd told me how making the windows look nice reminded her of taking us around to see the Macy's holiday window display. Viewing that and making a stop to walk around FAO Schwarz for Christmas wish list ideas had been a happy tradition for the family, before and after Lyle left.

"Do you remember where everything is, or do you need a quick tour?" Mom asked.

"I think I can find it," I said.

The bell tinkled over the door, and an older gentleman stepped inside. Mom glanced toward me to see if I wanted to take the customer. I gave my head a small shake. She nodded and waved me toward the back room, then smiled brightly to greet her customer.

The beaded curtain jangled behind me, muffling the sounds of their exchange. It was surreal to be at Family Tree again. I tried to remember how long it had been. Time went by so quickly. Guilt that I hadn't been in to help Mom or visit recently bubbled up in my stomach. I'd avoided the store since my days of being bullied, but I used to sneak in and help now and then. I hadn't consciously realized I'd stopped doing it.

Everything seemed at once new and the same. The back room was still plastered with wall-to-wall pictures of arrangement samples. Many of them I recognized, though their edges were more curled and frayed than I remembered. Some new ones had been added since I'd last seen them, following modern trends.

The shelves that held most of Mom's floral supplies were new since the last time I'd been in, but it looked like the organization system was the same.

I reviewed the orders, checked the wall for sample photos of what had been requested, and got to work. After grabbing some shears, I trimmed the bottoms of stems and used a thorn stripper to pull the thorns off the roses. I worked in a circle, starting in the middle and spiraling outward to ensure the bouquets were symmetrical. Once I got the flowers in place, I tucked in some greenery.

I tugged at a stem to raise up one of the flowers and display it more prominently, then stood back to admire my work on the third arrangement.

"Like riding a bike," my mother said.

"It's sloppy." The years of doing nothing but an occasional arrangement for my table using only the flowers from my garden had made me rusty.

Mom scoffed, then stood on her toes next to me. I bent my head down to let her kiss my cheek. "You're being too hard on yourself, pumpkin. They look great." She inspected them, making a minor adjustment to the first and nodding her approval at the other two. "A little slow, though," she added, side-eying me with a smirk.

I laughed. After carrying the arrangements I'd completed to the fridge, we returned to the table. She sat with her legs crossed, smoothing her apron over them. Then she patted the seat next to her.

I sat, and she gave me that knowing mom look.

"Are you ready to tell me what you're really doing here?"

"No," I said.

Mom laughed, a burst of *haha*s in staccato, the laugh lines on her face becoming more pronounced.

"That's my Bear. Both as blunt and as shuttered in as ever. Okay, we'll try a different tactic. How's Trixie?"

I scowled. I'd come about the store, not about Trixie. Then again, she had been on my mind. A lot.

"Aha, now we're getting somewhere." Part of me hoped there'd be a chime of the entry bell to rescue me from this question, but part wanted to answer and was working up the guts to. Mom seemed to understand the latter part and let the silence gather, until the weight of it crushed me and speaking became the easier choice.

"She's avoiding me," I finally admitted.

"I noticed that," she said.

I looked up at her, disbelieving. She nodded.

"Honey, she sure knows how to work a crowd and still avoid a person. I would have been impressed if it hadn't hurt my heart for you." Leave it to moms to always know what's going on. Mom Spidey senses. "What happened?"

I stared at a spot on the table, refusing to speak. I wiped stem clippings off the table, into my hand, and into the trash to fill the void.

"I'm not going anywhere," she said.

"Okay!" I threw my hands up. "I don't know what happened. Things were good—great, even. But she said something I wasn't ready to hear. I didn't have the best reaction, then a few hours later she came home and acted like everything was fine. Now she's avoiding me. I'd almost prefer she lash out. I'd know what to do with that. Then I'd know where I stood and could make a plan. Right now, I don't know what the hell is going on."

Mom watched and waited to be sure I was done with my rant before she spoke. She patted my arm. I expected her to ask what Trixie had pushed me on, but again, seeming to know exactly what I needed, she didn't. "Do you remember what Zoey was like growing up?"

I nodded.

"When she was younger, she was always so sweet. Rambunctious to be sure, but a heart of gold. Then she got to high school, and she . . . well, she—"

"Turned into kind of a jerk?"

Mom laughed. "I'd never use a word like that for my daughter, but yes. There were some challenging years in there. But in the middle of being defiant and doing everything she could to drive Russell and I up the wall, she'd be volunteering at the soup kitchen on the weekend."

I nodded. Zoey was always sneaking out. Once in a while she'd get into real trouble, but mostly when she sneaked out, she was off to do volunteer things, and she only sneaked to annoy our parents.

"Zoey acts out, and to this day can be a little over the top, but it's an act to hide her warm, gooey inside."

"I see what you're saying." I nodded. "Trixie's like that, but kind of the opposite. She's this . . . ray of sunshine around everyone, and I mean *everyone*. It's like she's friends with half the city. But I get the sense it's a bit of an act. I'm still not sure what she's burying with those smiles."

"Trixie, Zoey . . . lots of people use different personas to protect their real emotions." She tilted her head as if to say *look in the mirror*. I shifted uncomfortably.

"Son, you should see the look on your face when you talk about her."

My face heated, and I was glad to have my beard to partially hide it, not that it would get by Mom unnoticed. I scratched at my jawline.

"I . . . like her, but I'm not sure I know her." *Like* wasn't right. It wasn't strong enough. I knew the word I wanted to use, but how could I?

The bell chimed as another customer entered.

Mom patted my arm again as she stood. "You do. Give her time. Be her friend, if that's what she needs right now. She'll come around."

I stood too. I'd come here to decide about the store and wound up with my head swirling with Trixie. She always seemed to be in there nowadays. I was ready to go home. All this thought was a mental workout, and I was drained.

"And Bear?" Mom said, pausing at the curtain. "I'm holding off on selling the store for a few more weeks, but the developers are getting pushy. That's as much time as I've got."

With that, she slipped into the front room and focused on her customer. On the way out, I wove through the tables, which held an array of vases, sample books, arrangements, and a small collection of things for the garden, because Mom liked to appeal to all things floral, even if she wasn't a gardening store.

A few more weeks.

Nothing ever got past Mom.

CHAPTER TWENTY-EIGHT
TRIXIE

The shelter buzzed with the voices of the many visitors and the blend of the playful and anxious barks and meows of the animals who were excited or nervous about the influx of people for our adoption event.

Event days were always draining. I still had to complete the normal tasks in caring for the animals while also helping all the people who came in and processing adoption paperwork. I was exhausted but feeling good. I'd said good-bye to a lot of animals I loved, but I knew that finding them forever homes was the best thing for them. Placing the animals with good families who would love them like we did but be able to give them all the attention they deserved was always the end goal.

"Any luck with Felix?" Lindsey asked, returning from seeing a family out the door with one of our younger dogs. The puppies and kittens always went first. My heart broke for the older animals every time they got passed by. It was why I'd started making the "dating profile" posts for them on our social media. Being older and needing some extra care, Felix was a tougher sell to families, but he was so sweet, and I so badly wanted to find him the right match. I was a sucker for the animals who were a little rougher around the edges and needed some patience in getting to know them.

"Not yet. I've introduced him to a few people, but they've all gone another direction so far. There's a woman getting to know him now, though." I held up my crossed fingers, and Lindsey crossed hers in return.

A half hour later, my feet were aching and I couldn't help but watch the clock. It'd been a great day, but I was ready to go home and relax with Bear. With only a few minutes left in the event, I didn't think we were likely to have any more adoptions today.

"I'm sorry, buddy." I met Felix's amber eyes and scratched behind his ears. "Maybe at the next one. In the meantime, you've got me."

I was just about to close up when one of the couples who'd come in earlier in the day walked in the door.

"Sam and Georgie, right?" I asked.

"Yes, good memory!" Georgie said. "We got home and couldn't stop thinking about Felix. Is he still available?"

My heart dropped so low in my stomach I nearly retched. It was what I'd been hoping for all day, but I'd quickly adjusted to thinking I'd have another few weeks with him. *Pull yourself together, Trixie. This is for the best.*

"You're in luck. Our sweet little guy is right back here." I led them back to his cage, and he perked up in recognition, his tail thumping loudly against the side of his crate.

We sat down to go through the paperwork, a knife twisting in my heart the whole time. These busy days were so much more than physically draining. The emotional drain of saying good-bye over and over again through the day had me worn thin.

It was fortunate I had many years of practice at wearing a brave face and a smile. I fought hard to keep the tears at bay, giving Felix one last hug good-bye before watching him go out the door with his new family.

After helping Lindsey get the chaos of the shelter back under control and handing things over to the night crew, I drove home, eager for a Bear hug. The warmth and gentle strength of his arms around me would refill my emotional cup in an instant. Friends could do that for each other, though, right?

Bear stepped out the door to meet me on his new walking boot.

"Hey, Trixie," he said. My name on his lips was always a special kind of sweetness. It hurt to know there was probably a reason it sounded different coming from him than from anyone else; that it meant he was important.

My heart skipped a beat at the sight of him, something that happened all too often. He was exactly what I needed at the end of a long day. Even if I'd never admit that to him, I could admit it in my heart. My strength would come in not acting on those emotions. It'd have to do.

I ran over, crashing into him for the hug I'd been longing for. He stiffened in surprise, then relaxed, wrapping his arms around me. We sat close together on the couch on a regular basis, but I hadn't allowed myself to be in his arms since the one day we'd had sex. This wasn't me caving again, no matter how badly I'd wanted to.

Staying out of his arms these past few days had been one of the most difficult things I'd ever done. My body, my heart, my soul called to him on every level. I was still determined not to jeopardize my living situation by dating him, though. He'd become my closest friend, and I didn't want to risk losing that either, even if allowing him to get as close as he had was new and scary ground for me.

Succumbing to my desires here wasn't caving to lust. Simply a moment of self-care. I wasn't sure when Bear had become how I looked after myself. I was walking a fine and dangerous line. Too much was at stake. A friendship, a home, my emotional well-being. I never wanted to let Bear down, and that meant proceeding with caution.

"Hi," I breathed against his chest, inhaling the sweet floral scent of him. I hoped that meant he'd gone to talk with his mom. I squeezed him tight, luxuriating in the warmth and comfort of his embrace for one last moment before releasing him and stepping back.

He ran a gentle hand down my cheek, the contact exquisite and intimate. He tipped my chin up and searched my eyes.

"You okay?" His brow furrowed with worry.

"Just a long day." I smiled up at him and leaned into his touch the tiniest bit.

He nodded and withdrew his hand. "Ready to go?"

Did we have plans I'd somehow forgotten? Other than the occasional joint grocery run, we didn't make plans. Still, I was a go-with-the-flow kind of gal for outings. "I guess? Where are we going?"

He held up a *one minute* finger, then retreated into the house, leaving me alone standing awkwardly on the walkway to our front door.

"Hey, gorgeous, you lost?" Ryan shouted getting out of his car, having just gotten home from work as well. "I can point you in the right direction."

I rolled my eyes and shook my head with a chuckle. "I think I can manage."

"You're not still giving Bear a hard time, are you? The man's a fool for you."

I reeled at the comment, putting all my mental energy into keeping my smile in place. I'd been so caught up fighting my feelings for him, I selfishly hadn't put much thought into his feelings for me. Other than his family and me, Ryan was the only one Bear talked to. If Bear had feelings for me, Ryan would be the one to know. Then again, Ryan was such a casual flirt, I wasn't sure how much to read into it.

Behind me, the door opened. Bear stepped out with a picnic basket slung over the crook of his elbow, cradling Chick-Chick in his arms. Was there anything sexier than a tall, gorgeous man in jeans that fit him just right, with a button-down rolled up to expose muscled forearms, face spattered with the perfect amount of scruff, toting a chicken and a picnic basket?

"Speak of the devil," Ryan said.

Bear glanced at him. "I don't have to beat his ass, do I?"

"Nah," I said. "He's harmless."

"I don't know about that," Bear said.

"What are you lovebirds muttering about?" Ryan shouted.

Bear's face reddened, and he flipped Ryan off before returning his attention to me. "Ready?"

"Ready, Freddie," I said. Inside a tiny voice whispered that if I was going with Bear, I'd be ready for anything.

CHAPTER TWENTY-NINE
BEAR

"A picnic, huh?" Trixie asked as she drove.

"I thought it might be nice to get Chick-Chick some fresh air," I said.

Her face lit up with that real smile. She loved it when I included Chick-Chick. To think I'd considered throwing them both out when I'd found out about her.

After we parked, Trixie took Chick-Chick while I laid out the picnic on the grass. Once we were all settled, Trixie and I reclined on our elbows, watching Chick-Chick stumble around the park. Her little head was on a swivel, taking in her surroundings. She roamed back and forth, never straying far from our blanket, warbling happily.

We talked while we watched her, enjoying the end of summer weather, just cool enough to hint at fall. The city breeze cooled us, with Lake Michigan, the distant Navy Pier Ferris wheel, and the city skyline providing pleasant views for our picnic. As we ate the veggie sandwiches and sipped the wine I'd packed, I dug out a container full of chicken feed and sprinkled some in the small dish for Chick-Chick.

"You really thought of everything," she said. Arms tired of leaning, we sat back to back, using each other as backrests. I was probably reading more into it than I should, or than she likely was. One and done was all she wanted. I needed to remember our physical contact was strictly for practicality.

"I tried," I said.

"And succeeded." She held her glass to the side, and I raised mine to clink it. The three of us out for a picnic at the park felt like such a family thing to do. When we hung around the house, as much as we were spending time together, it was easier to brush it off as a roommate thing. Getting out in the world, us and her feather baby that felt as much mine now as hers, hadn't concerned me when I'd suggested it, but now I worried it was a mistake. I could feel the ridges of her back tensing against mine. I'd inadvertently pushed us into a gigantic leap forward I hadn't anticipated, and if I was reading her correctly, we were both beginning to freak out about it.

"Fawn stopped by when I stopped home on lunch," she mentioned.

I breathed easier. My family was a conversation topic I could usually handle. "That's nothing new. She stops by like twice a week."

"Yeah, but you won't like this one."

I frowned, already knowing my sisters had taken liberties with my generosity in letting them use my stuff all the time. "What'd she borrow?"

"You sure you want to know?" she asked. "May be better if you didn't know. And I should cook breakfast tomorrow."

Well, that was a statement it was going to be hard to respond generously too. She'd attempted to take over more of the weekend breakfast cooking while I was keeping off my ankle. Her gloopy pancake puddles had been less than impressive.

"What did she take, and what does it have to do with breakfast?" I asked.

A dog barked on the far end of the park, a distant siren blared, but no sound came from Trixie. Damn, it really must be bad.

"Trixie . . ." I scooted away to look at her, forgetting she was leaning against me. She toppled backward onto the blanket with a yelp.

I chuckled and leaned over her. Looking down at her sprawled under me like that brought back too many memories of our single night of ecstasy. The reminiscent position acted as a conduit for the ever-present chemistry between us.

Trixie's lips parted, and her pupils dilated. Her breath hitched, pressing her breasts against my chest.

I let out a rumbling growl. "I know that look."

A blush tinged her cheeks, and her shoulders lifted in a small acknowledging shrug.

I positioned myself over her, my knees on either side of her hips and my arms propped about her shoulders as if about to do a push-up.

My need for her was an ache that ran bone deep. I wanted her, I wanted her. But she didn't want me. She wanted to stay platonic roommates and friends. Mom was sure she would come around, but I didn't know how much of this I could take.

I bent lower. Her face was so close to mine that if she lifted her head the slightest bit, our lips would come together. Her hips rose to meet mine, brushing against me. She sucked in a sudden breath, and her hips pulled away from mine, back to the ground.

"What comes next?" I asked. "Ball is in your court."

"It's a public park," she whispered.

It was deserted, but that could change quickly, and neither of us could afford a ticket, but I wasn't worried about that.

"I could have you home and in either of our beds in a matter of minutes."

Her hips lifted again. She must be deliberately torturing me. Either that or she had no idea how she affected me. Hard to believe, since the evidence of it had just been pressed against her. I groaned and lay my head down on the blanket, my cheek resting against hers.

"Tell me what you want, Trixie."

"I . . . I don't know," she breathed. "And I'm not the only one here."

I laughed disbelievingly into the ground. "In case it wasn't clear, I want you."

My heart broke with each passing second she didn't reciprocate.

"Just sex?" she finally asked.

Disappointment. Incredulity. Frustration. Anger. The emotions whipped around me like balls in a bingo cage. I lifted my head up to look her in the eye. "No. I'm beyond that point with you. I want more. I want to call you my girlfriend, and I think you want that too, whether you're able to admit it to yourself or not."

Her lips moved as if trying to formulate a response and failing. She glanced away, and I knew I'd lost her, at least for the moment. Her eyes darted, wheels were turning, looking for a subject change. I lifted myself off her.

"She took your favorite spatula," she said.

Any last morsels of hope I'd had that she'd return my declarations of love fled. We'd have to talk about it eventually. It hurt that she didn't seem to feel the same, but she wasn't telling me no, so I wouldn't push it; I'd just bide my time and hope for the best. I resigned myself to following her subject change, then my eyes widened as I realized just what an effective one it was. I did not miss her quiet sigh when I sprang up.

"Fawn took my spatula?" Not much in the house was off-limits, but if one thing was, it was my lucky spatula, which I used solely for pancakes. It got a lot of use.

"I know. I told her not to, but she bolted before I could explain how critical an item it was. I'm sorry."

My annoyance that Fawn would take it fizzled as suspicion took its place. "She ran out the door? Doesn't she usually stay and talk with you?"

"Yeah, it was kind of weird. She didn't even seem like she needed anything, and she grabbed the first thing she saw."

Definitely concerning. Fawn might borrow things from me on a near daily basis, but she always had a purpose in mind. Grabbing an item at random was a red flag. "Oh no."

"What?"

"This has meddling written all over it. They're up to something. This is important. What did she say before she"—I hesitated, choking on the next words—"took my spatula?"

"She asked if we had any plans for the evening, but this was a surprise. I told her we didn't."

I pounded a fist into my palm. "Zoey texted me this afternoon asking the same. That's not a coincidence. They're in cahoots." I couldn't believe I had brushed off Zoey's text without a second thought.

"Bear Ross, did you just say 'cahoots'?" she teased.

She might think it was funny, but I was alarmed, and I didn't think my paranoia was unfounded. I scanned the park, squinting toward a small cluster of trees, where I thought I'd caught movement.

"I'm telling you the sisters are up to no good. Do you see someone with binoculars by that tree?"

"What?" She glanced around. "No, calm down. Hey, maybe we should pack up and go home? Chick-Chick seems tired anyway, and it'll be getting dark soon. The mosquitoes will come out."

There had been something by that tree. Definitely a figure there. "I swear I saw—"

That was when the nearby parking lot erupted with *sha-la-la-la*s and the unmistakable tune of "Kiss the Girl," as performed by Horatio Thelonious Ignacious Crustaceous Sebastian in *The Little Mermaid*.

"I am going to kill my sisters," I said through gritted teeth. "I'm so sorry, Trixie!"

Meanwhile, she was laughing hysterically. Glad one of us thought it was funny. We weren't about to kiss, and we were not going to end up in the relationship my sisters were hoping for, at least not anytime soon. Maybe in a few days I'd see the humor in the lengths they'd gone to in an attempt to be my wingwomen.

"Fawn! Zoey! Get out here!" I bellowed. A Fawn-shaped figure in black sprinted from the tree I had previously indicated and dove into what I now recognized as Zoey's car, which sped off. I knew it.

Trixie hiccupped another laugh.

"This is funny?" I asked.

"A bit."

I shook my head. "Come on. Let's go home."

If they only knew how close we'd come to the kiss the song suggested. And she'd shot me down—for the kiss, and the more I so desperately wanted.

CHAPTER THIRTY
TRIXIE

"I'm sorry about that," Bear said yet again, obviously mortified by his sisters' stunt. The ironic thing was, we'd almost kissed without their help. I wanted to, but it was too much of a risk. I didn't know if I'd ever feel safe enough to let Bear in, but I at least needed time. To his credit, he hadn't pushed. He was a patient man, but he didn't know what he was getting himself into.

Bear had only seen the senior superlative most friendly Trixie with the best smile. He'd never seen vulnerable Trixie who had feelings and cried sometimes. Whose parents had yelled about frowns and losses and ignored tears until she didn't remember how to show anything but a smile. The Trixie whose heart had been beaten to a pulp when her roommate broadcast her private feelings, stole her boyfriend, and left her feeling alone in this world. If the limited interactions hidden Trixie had engaged in were any evidence, he wouldn't like her.

"That's like the tenth time you've apologized." Despite all my fears, I wanted him. Of course I did. He was everything. He was gentle and strong. Kind and sexy. The man had become a poorly named superhero in an ill-fitting costume for me.

"Relax, it's okay," I said. "It was a great picnic, even with the surprise ending. I'm only sorry we didn't get to do any stargazing."

Bear went silent for a moment, processing this. I meant that we'd been lying on a blanket already and some stargazing would have been nice. I couldn't blame him if he was confused. I was confusing myself. I knew I was sending mixed signals but wasn't sure how to stop when my heart and my mind wanted two different things.

I imagined nestling up to him, my head resting on his shoulder, the sounds of crickets blending with those of the city, watching stars twinkle into existence in the sky. Granted, the light pollution would mean we wouldn't see many, but he was my star.

"I could set up the blanket in the backyard," he said. A tiny voice that stood guard at the wall around my heart told me to call it a night and go inside. I didn't listen.

I set Chick-Chick down in the yard, freeing up a hand to help Bear up to the deck in his walking boot. Once we were on even footing, I threaded my hand into his and leaned my head against his chest. We swayed slowly, the night sounds of the city our only accompaniment. He held me tight, and it felt like home. This was all I ever needed.

Then, as if the music of the night's soundtrack had ended, we both slowed to a stop. I lifted my gaze to him. His eyes reflected the moonlight back at me, and in them I could see how badly he wanted to lean down and kiss me. I could picture him doing it, and the temptation was intoxicating. I needed to sort out my feelings, and fast.

Bear swallowed, the edges of his mouth flickering down with disappointment, but he pulled me in close to hide it.

"How come you don't dance anymore?" he asked.

What I thought was, *Because it was so simultaneously wonderful and terrible that it became easier not to think about it.* But what I said was, "We're dancing now. I danced at the club. And I know you see me dance while I clean."

"You know what I mean," he said, not letting me off the hook as easily as I'd hoped. "You still love it. I can see that."

I leaned against him, hiding my face. I was about to attempt a subject change but remembered where we were, and how perfect an evening it had been, thanks to him. I owed him something. I sighed and glanced up to face him. "I do. I always loved the actual dancing. I didn't love the other stuff."

"Other stuff?"

Telling him was a risk. Letting him see the darker side could ruin everything, but years of it eating away at me, with no one to talk to about it with, was exhausting. The pressure was near bursting, and maybe he was my release valve.

"My parents were busy people, involved in their careers. They never paid attention to me, but I convinced them to sign me up for dance. I picked it up right away. I was a natural, but they had no idea because I carpooled with other families to practice. I earned solos, but they didn't have a clue. They didn't bother to ask. When they came to that first recital, they were shocked and so proud. Suddenly, I had their attention."

"That sounds like a good thing," he said.

I paused for a minute, gathering myself. I pressed into him, using him as an anchor to get through this story.

"You'd think, wouldn't you? So did I. And it was, briefly. But they did a total one-eighty. From distant and aloof to over-bearing, controlling, obsessive." My gut twisted at the memories, and at the difficulty in speaking about them, of exposing myself like this. Bear's hand moved in gentle circles on my back, encouraging me to continue. "Suddenly I was in double the classes and on a rigid practice schedule at home. My mom made me do smiling exercises in the mirror. I was put on crash diets. My feet were always bloody and blistered. They became extreme stage parents. I was popular at school but didn't have time to make good friends because everything was dance. If my parents ever caught me frowning, they'd freak out as if the judges were sitting in our house, waiting to mark down style points for expression."

It felt like a vise had been removed from around my heart, not carrying this pain by myself anymore. Sharing it with someone. I gasped in air that tasted clean and crisp.

My relief was short lived. My fears returned, and I hoped that unburdening this on him hadn't ruined the relationship I'd so carefully protected since moving in here.

"Trixie." His voice was so heavy, I could feel the weight of it. He knew my truths; was he judging me for it? His forehead was crinkled. Were those lines of worry or disgust? I couldn't take it if he rejected me. I had been wrong to share this. Appreciative of the evening or not, my throat was clenching with the anxiety of the potential outcomes. I had to distract him before he could draw the same conclusions the only other people I'd gotten close to had. My parents, Julia, and the ex she stole. My ups weren't worth my downs. If I couldn't keep that mask up at all times, I wasn't worth it.

I didn't want to find out. "Thank you for the dance. Good night, Bear." I stood on my toes. He bent within my reach, and I planted a soft kiss on his cheek. Before he had a chance to react, I turned and went inside. I glanced out the window as I shut the door and saw Bear's fingertips trace the spot I'd kissed reverently, as if he needed to make sure it was real.

CHAPTER THIRTY-ONE
BEAR

Everything was going wrong. The morning after our picnic, neither of us had said a word about the previous night, how real it had felt, how she'd opened up, how much we'd felt like an actual couple.

She'd hesitated like she might say something before she left for work. I'd wished I could kiss her good-bye. I wanted to tell her how much I'd miss her in the hours she was gone. And oh, how I missed her.

The third day after our picnic, I was anxiously awaiting her return from work when my phone buzzed with a text.

Trixie: I forgot to mention I'm helping a friend with deliveries for their restaurant tonight. Can you give Chick-Chick her meds?

Another odd job to help pay for rising vet bills. I walked into Trixie's room to retrieve Chick-Chick's medicine and noticed her food bowl was still full. That was unusual for her.

I gave her medicine to her and settled back down to watch TV.

As the night went on, I paid extra attention to Chick-Chick.

"Are you acting tired, or am I just paranoid because of the food?" I asked her, fully aware that I was absorbing Trixie's personality into mine more every day if I was talking to animals.

She only pecked at her feathers, but I could have sworn she seemed drained.

*　　*　　*

The next few days were much the same. I wasn't getting to see Trixie nearly as often as I'd hoped, and I had only just over a week left before my scheduled return to work.

"You look miserable," I said to Chick-Chick, and she squawked at me. I hadn't mentioned my concerns to Trixie the first night I'd noticed her struggling. I didn't want to alarm her over nothing. I knew how important Chick-Chick was and knew it would break Trixie if anything happened to her.

When she seemed worse the following day, Trixie's eyebrows had wrinkled with worry, before she'd brushed it off and said it was probably nothing. I'd asked if she wanted to stay out and watch TV with me. Or play Scrabble. If I could just spend time with her, I didn't think it'd be long before she was reminded of the picnic and drawn back to me.

Alas, she'd returned to her *push Bear away and pretend we aren't meant for each other* routine. It was exhausting, and I was frustrated. I could see the spark there. I was certain she felt it. I couldn't understand why she fought it.

She was worth it, so I'd wait it out. If she gave me any sign that she truly didn't want a relationship beyond friendship, I'd respect that, but she kept leading me on. We'd get close, and she'd draw away, but never completely shut me out. I could see the longing in her eyes. I saw it when she left for work each day.

Day five of Chick-Chick's lethargy, and I was really getting worried.

"Come on, girl, don't you want to walk around the house?" I sprinkled feed in a line leading out of the room in an attempt to bring some life out of her. Chick-Chick slumped to the ground and watched me, beady eyes full of sorrow.

"I don't think she's going for it. Sorry, man." Ryan stood up from the couch as Trixie's car rolled into the driveway. He'd gotten off work early and come over for a beer. "She needs a vet again. Which means you need to talk to Trixie." Ryan's eyes flicked to me. "And not just about the chicken."

I glared at him. It wasn't like I hadn't tried.

"Hey, don't take it out on me. You know you do." With that, he was out the door.

"Hey there, gorgeous," Ryan said as he passed Trixie on the way out.

"Hey yourself," she said. Trixie gave me the bashful smile that was her norm before disappearing to change out of her work clothes, giving me a minute to work up the nerve to talk.

She came out and picked up Chick-Chick, settling on the couch with her.

"Trixie?" I asked.

"Hmm?" She stroked at Chick-Chick's feathers, not looking up.

"Have you noticed she hasn't quite been herself lately?" I asked, nodding toward Chick-Chick. It wasn't the first time I'd mentioned it. I saw more of it than Trixie, since I was home all day in my final week before my return to work. That was making it easier for Trixie to ignore. Each time I'd brought it up, she'd changed the subject. Her refusal to meet my eye didn't have me hopeful that the night's attempt would get a better reception.

"I'll handle it. Anything good on?" she asked, nodding to the TV.

I sighed and turned on a game show.

She refused to talk about us. Conversations revolving around Chick-Chick had constituted almost all our exchanges this past week. If she took that away too, what more could we have?

I was absolutely worried about Chick-Chick. It had taken time, but I'd grown to love her, especially since I'd been injured. If we were to lose her, it would crush me. If she didn't improve, I hoped that Trixie's and my relationship with each other didn't hinge on our interactions with Chick-Chick. I knew there was more to us, but without any chance to communicate, there was no room for that to grow.

I watched Trixie, her eyes trained on the screen, the bluish glow from it splashing across her cheeks. Her uncharacteristic quiet gave me an ominous feeling.

CHAPTER THIRTY-TWO
TRIXIE

I stroked the feathers on Chick-Chick's head, holding her in my lap in defeat. It was the fourth day in a row that I hadn't been able to get her to walk around, and I knew Bear had been struggling as well. Chick-Chick still had the vibrant red coloring that had returned after her first course of medicine, but the other improvements she'd made were disappearing.

"What's going on with you, sweetheart?" I whispered.

Her beady little eyes were sorrowful, and the sounds she made in answer came out more like feeble squeaks than her usual clucks. She looked better, but her behavior was reminding me all too much of the day I'd found her.

I couldn't ignore the signs of a relapse in her condition any longer. Denial wouldn't help her. I'd scheduled an appointment with the vet for the next morning. I needed to be prepared to answer their questions. The problem was, I'd been so busy with odd jobs and my normal hours at work, I hadn't spent as much time with her as I'd have liked. I wasn't sure if she was always this lethargic or if it was only certain times of day.

I was going to have to ask Bear. He'd been keeping an eye on her and cleaning out her cage. He'd been so pissed she was here originally. In a short time, he'd come to the point where he was voluntarily caring for her when I was away, when I hadn't even asked him to. It made my heart all warm and gooey for him. That only made me panic and want to distance myself more.

I'd been avoiding him, spending less time watching TV with him and more in my room. Chick-Chick needed help, though. I walked into the living room. Bear was on the sofa, his leg propped up, an ice pack over his ankle. He didn't look up when I entered, but he startled when he realized I was standing there staring at him.

"Hi," I said. A safe opener.

"Hi." He dragged the word out with wariness.

"I'm taking Chick-Chick to the vet tomorrow." His face relaxed, and he sat up a little. Yes, this was something we could talk about. Something he'd wanted to talk about. These were safe grounds.

"I'm glad."

"I want to make sure I'm giving the vet the right information."

Bear scratched at his face. "Well, she's still getting her regular medication, and she's still eating, but not as much."

"Okay, and what else?" I didn't want him to think I was oblivious to the changes in her. I hadn't been around as much as I should have been, but I still took care of her, even if he helped. Okay, helped a lot. "I mean, I've noticed some things, I just want to make sure they're consistent with what you have."

He let out a low hum of agreement while he thought. "She won't walk around. She's lethargic, and she's making weird noises."

I blew out a sigh. It wasn't anything I didn't already know, but it still hurt to have it confirmed. I was worried. I was doing everything I could to keep her healthy and give her a good life. I'd spent far more money than I had to spare on this chicken I'd found on the street a few months ago, and I was terrified it wasn't going to be enough. If I lost her, it would tear me apart.

I forced an appreciative smile. "Okay. Thank you. Hopefully the vet will figure something out."

I spun on my heels to retreat to my room and cling to my ailing chicken.

"Trixie, wait—" There was a thump behind me that I assumed to be his ice pack hitting the floor. The idea of him hobbling after me, even if it was only a few feet, made me wince. He was essentially healed, but he was still supposed to be resting. If he was icing his ankle, I suspected he'd already overdone it today and it was hurting.

Averting my eyes from his face, I turned back to retrieve it for him. "Don't get up."

My voice shook. I was losing control faster than I was prepared for. My eyes itched with the threat of tears. Bear gently grabbed my wrist before I could run away.

His dark eyes looked up into mine, awash with concern. "Are you okay?"

"I'm okay," I said. Then, with a weak laugh, "She's the one that's sick."

"You're allowed to be sad," he said. "Talk to me."

"I'll let you know how the appointment goes."

I walked away.

CHAPTER THIRTY-THREE
BEAR

She turned and ran into her room, avoiding me again. Anyone who knew her even the slightest bit would know she was devastated, and I wasn't just anyone. As much as she tried to keep me from getting in, I knew her.

I knew the way she'd eat peanut butter sandwiches all day but detested jelly. I knew that if you got her started talking about the right books, she would go on forever and her face would light up with that special smile, the real one. I knew she had countless versions of the smiles she wielded like armor, and I'd come to understand what most of them meant. I knew she had dozens of friends, but none seemed to know her. I knew she loved daylilies and they reminded her of her parents, who were controlling, superficial jerks. I knew that her nose crinkled when she laughed, and that she always wore out the sides of her pant legs, dirtying them up the way she stood like a flamingo.

I knew she made the sexiest little moans when I kissed her in the right spot, even if I'd gotten that pleasure for only one special day. I knew she cared about that chicken with all that she was. If I knew anything, Chick-Chick's worsening condition was crushing Trixie. What I didn't know was what to do about it.

The rest of the night, the door stayed solidly closed. If she left the room, she managed to do it when I was up getting a drink, and I wound up going to bed early. Sometimes the best way to solve a problem is to sleep on it.

*   *   *

At some point in my restless sleep, I'd decided the best way to help Trixie was to take things step by step, and the first step was to feed her breakfast.

I figured she was going to wake up stressed. Waking up to breakfast might go a small way toward alleviating some of that. Pancakes were always a safe bet and kind of my specialty, so I went with those. Still, I wanted to make it clear to her that I was trying to help, so I needed to do something different too. More sugar seemed like the way to go, so I made a batch of cinnamon rolls too.

Trixie stumbled out of the bedroom in her skimpy pajamas, and I was proud I managed to avert my eyes quickly and focus on getting her plate ready, as well as a glass of orange juice. After a quick trip to the bathroom, she zombie-walked into the kitchen, rubbing at her eyes and yawning.

"It smells delicious," she said.

"Pancakes and cinnamon rolls. I've got a plate and drinks for you on the table there."

Trixie blinked, her brain still foggy with sleep, trying to process my words. In slow motion, she glanced down at the table, where her plate and drinks sat waiting for her.

"Wow . . . thanks, Bear."

"How is she?"

Trixie startled again, as if surprised that I would bother to ask. As much as I felt like I knew her, everything I did still seemed to catch her off guard.

"Still not great. She was quiet all night. Do you mind if I take this back to my room? I want to see if I can coax her into eating her own breakfast before I head to work. I'll be back to pick her up for the appointment later."

Step two: give her the space to do what she needs.

"I don't control what you do. Of course I don't mind."

She shrugged, that familiar blush dusting her cheeks. "I know, but I feel guilty cutting out on you when you went to all this trouble."

"Trixie, you're not cutting out on me. I did it so you could focus on Chick-Chick. We're good. Go ahead."

Her mouth parted, then spread wide. "Thank you. That's . . . very sweet of you."

I gave her a small nod as she whisked her plate and cup off to her room. As I sat at the table eating my own breakfast, I could hear gentle murmurs as Trixie tried to coax Chick-Chick to eat. I shoved a forkful of pancakes into my mouth and thought. Each chew was like turning the gears in my mind. Step three . . . I needed a step three.

I still wanted Trixie as more than a roommate, and more than a friend. Since the picnic, she hadn't even been giving me much of a friend zone to hang out in. My mom had said to be patient with her. That she'd come around. I knew Chick-Chick's health was the larger concern at the moment. So I needed to be there for her without being too in her face. I had only a few days left before returning to work. Be there for her, make sure she knew she didn't have to worry about Chick-Chick when she couldn't be there herself—that was it.

Minutes later, as I was rinsing off my plate, Trixie came in with hers. I held out a hand for it, and she smiled again, handing it over.

"Any luck?" I asked.

"No." Her face flattened, as close to sad as she ever let it come. "But I have to get to work."

"If you don't mind me going in there, I can keep trying while you're gone."

"Would you?" she asked, eyes full of hope and relief. "I felt guilty asking, but I'd worry so much less if I knew you were keeping an eye on her."

"Of course. I think she could use the company," I said. "Tell me what else I can do to help."

Trixie studied me, a tremble in her lip. As ever, she smiled, despite the tremble. The trick to deciphering the smiles, aside from their magnitude and tilt, was in studying her eyes. They were big and often gave away what she was thinking. Looking into her eyes in that moment was like falling into an ocean.

It was full of roiling, tumultuous seas, and then, like flipping a switch, there was a sudden calm. Trixie had reached a decision.

CHAPTER THIRTY-FOUR
TRIXIE

I stared back at Bear, my emotions on the verge of crumbling. I was operating on a lack of sleep and an abundance of stress. If Chick-Chick didn't snap out of this on her own, she wasn't going to. I couldn't handle it.

Then, as if making me breakfast hadn't been enough, he'd offered not only to feed her but said he knew she needed companionship. The offer and the sentiment had rocked me. Like I'd been lifted up and spun around in a tornado and spit out on the other side, everything different.

"Bear," I whispered.

He sucked in a breath and swallowed. Had he felt the shift too?

All my life, or at least about as long as I could remember, I've known one thing to be true. People valued other people who smiled and brought brightness to their life. Negative people were easily discarded, so I'd avoided becoming one. I'd hid my emotions from everyone until Julia.

Sharing a college dorm, there wasn't another room to retreat to, so I'd caved and let her in. She'd been the first person in years to see my real emotions, and we'd gotten so close. Apparently, all along, she'd thought my private breakdowns were ridiculous. They might have been a lot, but since it was the only place I ever let it out, when I finally did, it was like opening the floodgates. I'd thought she'd loved me as a friend despite that, but as it turned out, she hadn't. She'd used it to turn others away from me.

I was terrified to allow myself to get close to Bear. Letting people see my emotions had gotten me nowhere but miserable in the past. But Bear—sweet, wonderful Bear—he knew when I wasn't being real and supported me anyway. He was nonjudgmental and always there. He'd given me no reason to mistrust him, but I'd had such a hard time getting over my fears. I'd been so afraid to let him in, but in light of what was happening with Chick-Chick, it seemed like a waste to keep fighting it.

I was resisting something that, even if my brain was set on fighting it, my heart wasn't. Bear had been unfailingly kind to me, and I was pulled to him in ways I'd never been drawn to anyone before. I wanted him. I was tired. So tired. It was time to simplify things.

Tell me what else I can do to help. The ball was in my court. All I needed was for him to be him. Him by my side, that was all I wanted.

After far too long fighting it, allowing myself to feel for him was like blowing apart a dam. Emotion crashed through me, so hard it propelled me forward with the force of a riptide. I threw myself into Bear, and my lips crashed into his.

He tensed in surprise, but only for a moment. Then his lips were parting, moving with mine. He pulled me close with one arm. His other hand went around my neck, tilting my head back to deepen the kiss. My hands were in his hair as I tried to infuse all the joy and pain—the overwhelming sea of emotions I was experiencing—into the kiss.

We came apart gasping for air. My hands were on his chest, pressed over his beating heart, which thrummed wildly. He cupped my face in the warm embrace of his strong hands. His eyes searched mine for answers.

"What was that?" His voice was husky and low.

"I'm done fighting it, Bear. I want you." I leaned forward to kiss him again. I placed a soft kiss on his lips, which he returned before pulling back again.

"Want me . . . how?"

I laid my forehead against his chest. Could he not feel the monumental shift that had just taken place in my heart and mind? I thought for sure the tremors from this earthquake ought to have been felt for miles.

"I need you to tell me," he continued. "This isn't just physical for me. I'll take what you can give, but I care about you, Trixie. So if that's all it is to you, I need to brace myself for that." He cupped my chin and tilted my face up to his, his eyes scanning mine as if the answer would be written there, plain as day. "You want me *how*?"

Maybe it was clear in my eyes after all, because the worried furrow to his brow relaxed before I'd even spoken.

"In every way," I whispered. "Yes, I want your body, but I want the rest of you too. I have for a long time, and I don't want to fight it anymore. Will you be mine?"

"Hell yes," he grunted, then his lips were on mine again. Time is a void when you're kissing someone who makes your heart skip beats and your soul dance. We finally came up for air again, lips swollen but tipped into elated smiles. At least until I caught sight of the clock behind him.

"Almond butter!" I cursed. He glanced over my shoulder at it too and winced. "I have to go," I said. I tore off to my room to grab my purse, and he met me at the door with a thermos of coffee. The man thought of everything. "Thank you."

"Didn't you mention the vet is near your work? It's kind of out of your way to come home, isn't it?" he asked, leaning casually on the low banister that separated the small entryway from the living room.

He let the words hang in the air, not pressing me with an offer while subtly letting me know what he was open to. The ball was still in my court.

"Would you be willing to bring her and meet me there?" I asked tentatively. Even though I already knew the answer was yes, I still felt guilty asking it. He'd been catering to me all morning, and I didn't want to take advantage of him.

"You don't even have to ask. We'll be there. Text me the address."

I bent forward and gave him a final quick kiss, then ran out the door.

CHAPTER THIRTY-FIVE
BEAR

I watched her drive away, then fell back against the walls and pressed my hands to my eyes. If I hadn't known Ryan would already be at work, I'd have gone over there and made him punch me or something just to make sure I hadn't dreamt this morning.

Trixie wanted me. I thought she had all along, but there was still a part that hadn't been convinced, or that thought no matter how much she wanted me, she would fight against it forever. I ran one hand through my hair and laughed aloud in disbelief.

She'd kissed me and hadn't said it was a one-and-done scenario. *Will you be mine?* They were the best damn words I'd ever heard.

I turned around and looked at the room. My arms shook with the adrenaline rush from the kiss and her request. My heart thundered like a drum in my chest. My hand vibrated with energy, and I found myself staring at Trixie's name in my text messages.

She'd only been gone a few minutes. I was going to sound clingy as fuck, but I didn't care. Trixie wanted me, and I was so elated I wanted to shout it from the rooftops. If I couldn't do that, I at least wanted to shout it to her.

> *Bear: I miss you already. I'm allowed to say that now, right?*

A few minutes passed, and I managed to put a load of laundry in while I waited for her to finish her drive to work so she could respond.

> *Trixie: Definitely. I would not be opposed to hearing this every day.*
> *Trixie: And I miss you too. XOXO.*

I smiled so wide my cheeks hurt. Then I heard a squawk. Right, Chick-Chick. My joy over finally being in a relationship with Trixie beat steadily in my chest, even if it was dampened a bit by concern over Chick-Chick's state.

If Trixie hadn't been able to get her to eat, I wasn't likely to, but I'd at least promised to try. I spent the next hour doing everything I could think of to try to get our sweet pet to eat, without much success. She only nibbled a little when I'd finally given up. She was not looking good.

> *Bear: She ate a little more, but not much.*
> *Trixie: Okay, thanks for trying.*

*   *   *

An hour later I was watching a *Jeopardy* rerun and crushing it. Okay, not crushing it, but I was pretty sure I'd had at least a 5 percent improvement to the number of questions I could get correct with all the downtime I'd had at home thanks to my injury.

I wanted to take Trixie out. Showing her off wasn't quite my thing, but she deserved a date.

> Bear: We should go to trivia night at a bar. All this couch time, and I've watched enough game shows to be a trivia master.
>
> Trixie: You want to go to a bar? This is Bear, right?

I chuckled down at my phone. She had a point. I was really going to like the freedom to text her about everything and nothing throughout the day.

> Bear: I know. I blame you.
>
> Trixie: The club was Zoey's fault.
>
> Bear: I wouldn't have gone to the club if it weren't for you. And the baseball game was all you.
>
> Trixie: No, the baseball game was all Lindsey. The murderer screening, remember?
>
> Bear: Ah yes. Good thing you haven't discovered the organs in the freezer.
>
> Trixie: Gross. Is it too late to change my mind about the whole dating thing?
>
> Bear: YES. You're stuck with me.
>
> Trixie: Great. Remind me to clean out the freezer when I get home.

I stopped texting so she could get some work done and went back to my day of boredom and trying not to worry about Chick-Chick. I tried coaxing her into walking around. It didn't work. She looked too exhausted to even tolerate any further attempts to get her to do anything, so I settled for snuggling with her. If nothing else, I could at least make her feel more comfortable and loved while she wasn't feeling good. Chicken in lap, I sent Trixie an update.

> *Bear: She's still sleepy. No interest in the walking.*
> *Bear: But I'm keeping her company. [photo attachment]*

I petted her, and she relaxed on my lap.

"A couple more hours, then we get to see her again and hopefully figure out what's going on with you," I told Chick-Chick. She buried her head in her feathers and fell asleep.

CHAPTER THIRTY-SIX
TRIXIE

"Bye, Lindsey, I'm heading to the vet! I'll be back in maybe an hour and a half."

"Won't it take you longer than that?" she asked.

"I don't have to go home before and after. Bear is meeting me there with Chick-Chick."

"Oh really?" She raised an eyebrow. "I knew it'd been way too long since we'd caught up. How long has that been going on?"

"Mutual vet appointments?"

"Oh, come on."

I raised my hands defensively. "I knew what you meant. Actually, just since this morning."

"Seriously?" she asked. "I thought for sure you two would have gotten together a long time ago! You're so tight-lipped about everything, I didn't bother to keep asking."

I rolled my eyes. "Yes, seriously. I've got to go."

"I want more details when you get back!" she shouted after me as I walked through the lobby and out the door.

My phone chimed as I buckled my seat belt.

Bear: We're on our way.

Despite my worries, I grinned at the interaction with him and allowed myself an indulgent hug of my phone to my chest.

I'd made the photo he'd sent my screen saver. In retrospect, as much as I'd been on my phone, it was a wonder Lindsey hadn't asked me about Bear until I was leaving.

I pulled into the parking lot at the vet's office to find Bear's truck already in the lot. He exited when I did, cradling Chick-Chick's carrier in his arms.

"You ready?" he asked.

"No," I admitted.

Bear sat down in the waiting room while I signed us in with the receptionist. Then I took the seat next to him.

"Hey, girl," I cooed to Chick-Chick.

She warbled feebly in return. Bear reached out and squeezed my hand. I didn't let his go.

The tech called us back. Bear looked at me questioningly, unsure if he should come with, and I nodded.

As the tech recorded Chick-Chick's weight, I wobbled on my feet, trying to ignore the sensation that the walls were closing in on me. The rank smell in the air, so similar to the mix of cleaning products and animal scents that I was used to from work, suddenly had my nostrils flaring and my stomach queasy.

Bear noticed my stumble and guided me to a seat. I sat there, blinking, and tried to regain my composure as the tech finished up and exited the room.

Holding Chick-Chick, Bear sat beside me, placing a hand on my leg.

"Hey, you all right?"

"Yeah." I attempted a reassuring smile. "Worried about her."

I held out my hands for her, and he gently passed her off. Her weight in my arms and the sleekness of her feathers against my skin grounded me.

"I'm thinking pizza for dinner," he said.

I knew it was a distraction, but I ran with it. "Works for me, but don't even think about getting mushrooms."

"I won't get mushrooms if you won't get pineapple."

"Maybe I'll get sausage." I lowered my voice seductively. I didn't eat meat, so he took my meaning. The gutter was a lovely place for my mind to be. Anything to get it out of the exam room.

Bear leaned back and looked at me, wide-eyed. In his surprise, he choked on his words. "You're welcome to"—he coughed again—"some *sausage* anytime you want. That was naughty," he growled. He leaned in, hesitating. I leaned toward him, and he planted a soft kiss on my neck.

"Well, I'm a naughty girl," I whispered.

"Are you now?" He nipped at my ear.

The handle on the door jiggled, and we sprang apart. The gutter served as a nice escape, but the sight of Dr. McAlister stepping into the room, brows crinkled in worry and a clipboard tucked under one arm, snapped me back to earth with enough force to knock the wind out of me.

She took a pump of hand sanitizer from the bottle on the edge of the mustard-yellow counter and plopped herself onto her stool. The metal screeched against the ground as it slid an inch. She finished rubbing in the sanitizer and pushed her glasses back on her nose before looking up at me.

She gave me a small smile. I knew that smile. I'd worn it a thousand times. The edges of her eyes still tilted downward with sadness. It was well rehearsed and practiced. In her role, I imagined she had to give it a lot, to brace herself to be the bearer of bad news. It raised my hackles, and my chest heaved.

Bear must have sensed the change in me, because he straightened and reclaimed my hand, giving it a gentle squeeze.

"Hi, Trixie," she said. "And who is this?"

"This is my—" I hesitated. I'd never known what to call him. Roommate? Landlord? Friend? But now things had changed. I'd asked him to be mine. That made the label clearer. "This is my boyfriend, Bear."

I think I kept my voice from escalating in a question. Still, I glanced at Bear for confirmation, and behind his scruff he smiled, and his thumb danced calming circles in my palm.

"Nice to meet you, Bear. So, Chick-Chick has had some setbacks?"

I nodded. A lump formed in my throat. I wasn't going to help her if I didn't speak, though, so I focused on a heartworm poster over her left shoulder and tried my best to recall the things I'd wanted to mention: her general lethargy, her refusal to walk. I got a few things out, then froze. My tongue swelled, and try as I might, it was like my synapses were misfiring. A thought would be right on the tip of my uncooperative tongue and then would fly away as though caught by a sudden burst of wind. The poster was no longer doing its job. I searched around frantically—a jar of treats, a scale, the sink. I couldn't make myself focus on anything else, and if I tried to look at Dr. McAlister, my heart rate went skyward.

Finally, my eyes landed on Bear. I tightened my grip on his hands and fumbled for words. Bailing, I went silent and tried to implore him with my eyes.

He got the message and answered for me. "She's been eating very little. She isn't entirely starving herself, but her appetite has gone down."

Dr. McAlister frowned, checking her clipboard. "But she's still gained weight."

"And her . . . speech?" Bear paused, watching the vet.

She nodded at him to keep going.

"She's making different noises. It's more of a chirping than the *cluck, cluck* she had been doing." He was facing Dr. McAlister, but the skin on the back of his neck reddened. It tugged at my heartstrings, how he was constantly going out of his comfort zone for me.

"Like the sounds she made when I found her," I added, finally regaining my senses enough to contribute to the conversation.

I was stuck on thoughts of Bear's comfort zone, a welcome tangent during this appointment that I was struggling with. I absent-mindedly cooed soothing words to Chick-Chick as the doctor examined her in my lap.

Finally, Dr. McAlister returned to her stool. She faced us, no longer attempting the all-too-familiar smile. It was time for the bad news. I scooted myself a little closer to Bear, and he wrapped an arm around me.

My head spun, and the room went blurry. The words on the poster fell out of focus. I could sense the bad news coming, and I wasn't ready for it.

"Are you with us, Trixie?"

No.

"Mm-hmm," I acknowledged vaguely.

"I try to be very honest with the families of my patients. Sugarcoating doesn't help anything. Trixie, you and I have talked about her breed. She's a broiler chicken. It's a sad and harsh reality that her breed was developed with the sole purpose of becoming food, not to lead a long and healthy life. She's meant to gain weight and gain it fast. Some instinct must be telling her it's wrong, and that's why she's stopped eating, but she still keeps gaining."

This wasn't new information for me, but it was for Bear. His grip had tightened on my shoulder, and his voice was low and angry. "What about the lethargy?"

Dr. McAlister grimaced. Maybe not so practiced at concealing her emotions, then. She leaned in and examined Chick-Chick further, gently feeling along her wings. "Her wings have some damage that looks fresh—not from when you found her?"

Bear cleared his throat. "When she walks, she has a hard time balancing. She seems to use her wings for balance, but that means she smacks them into things a lot."

"Hmm. I'd like to take another set of X-rays to get a better look at her wings and her legs. Would you be all right with that?" she asked, turning to face me.

My heart sank. X-rays weren't cheap. So many extra hours at every odd job I could find, and it was only going to pile up on me again. I swallowed my dread and nodded.

*　*　*

Soon after, Dr. McAlister returned to the room with Chick-Chick, and a tech followed with a laptop, dark images on its screen.

"The good news is, the damage to the wings is external," she said.

I squeezed Bear's hand as tight as I could. "What's the bad news?"

"This is Chick-Chick's leg. This one over here is an image of another chicken's leg for comparison. You see the difference here? Her hip joint didn't fully develop. It's another common issue with her breed, possibly exacerbated by the injuries she sustained before you found her and the strain of all her excess weight on it."

"What does that mean? Is there anything we can do about it?"

Dr. McAlister hesitated. Whatever she had to say next, she didn't want to say it.

"She needs to stay off her leg. Especially at her current weight, but really anytime. Pain from trying to walk on the bad joint is likely why she's started to avoid walking. And trying to compensate for the limp with her wings and beating those up is causing her further issues. She shouldn't be walking around."

My hand went limp in Bear's, and the floor tilted underneath me. When she was confined to my room, that had actually been right? When Bear had said she could have free rein to explore the house and suggested it might be good for her, it had sounded like a miracle and exactly what she'd needed. All this time, I'd thought pushing her to exercise and stay mobile was the best thing for her, but I'd been putting her through pain and forcing her to further injure herself.

"Are you saying I've basically been torturing her?" I asked. My voice sounded cold, even to myself. This conversation hurt too much. I was having an out-of-body experience. If I didn't distance myself from the conversation, there was no way I was surviving it.

Dr. McAlister sighed and set her clipboard down on the counter behind us. She folded her hands together on her lap and leaned toward us. When she spoke again, her voice was softer.

"Of course not. You've tried so hard, harder than any pet parent I've ever seen, to give her a good life. You were doing what you thought was best with the information you had. Unfortunately, with her other injuries at the time, the deformed joint didn't present itself until now."

I'd hurt her. I was hurting her. He'd said she could walk around. I'd tried to help, but I only made it worse. My consciousness floated above the room, nodding at her words, knowing them to be true. Somewhere down below, my body closed its eyes and took slow, even breaths. If I stayed detached, I'd get through this appointment. If I kept the knowledge apart from the emotion, I could keep from crying.

Bear turned toward me, scanning my face and waiting for me to react. When I didn't, he turned back to Dr. McAlister. "What do we do? How do you keep a chicken from using her legs? And what about stopping her weight gain? Where do we go from here?"

I pressed my leg against his, needing the touch to stabilize me. I was so grateful for him, that he was asking the necessary questions when I was too shaken to process everything.

"For the weight gain, I'd like to put her on a special diet that I can give you an info sheet on, and I have a medication we can try. I can't make any promises that it will work, but we can try."

"And what if it doesn't work?" I asked. "What if she just keeps gaining?"

Dr. McAlister swallowed. "Then we'll have another conversation, but we're not there yet."

Another conversation. I knew what that meant, and I wished I didn't. I couldn't—I . . . I was going to be sick. I bent forward and put my head between my knees, breathing in deep through my nose, out through my mouth, to tamp down the nausea. Bear's hand quickly moved to my back, gently rubbing in soothing circles.

"Trixie?" His voice strained with concern.

"I'm okay," I whispered, and sat back up. After searching my face, presumably to make sure I wasn't about to keel over, Bear nodded to Dr. McAlister to continue.

"As far as keeping her off her legs goes, there are wheelchairs for chickens. You could look into getting her one. We don't have any here, but you can order them online. In the meantime, I can give you some painkillers for her to make her more comfortable."

Dollar signs. So many dollar signs. All these medications and special foods would cost me a fortune. Today's visit and the X-rays would cost me probably three odd jobs to pay for. I didn't even want to think about how much a custom wheelchair would run me. My heart thumped faster with stress, but I'd do anything for Chick-Chick, even if it meant subjecting myself to enough debt I'd have to do a thousand birthday parties to dig myself out of it.

At the back of my mind was a deeper worry that hurt too much to think about. I could do all of this, and it might not matter. I could still lose her.

They both watched me, waiting for acknowledgment. On an intellectual level, I knew Bear was here to support me, but at a whopping few hours old, our relationship was too new for him to make these decisions for me.

Words wouldn't come, so I nodded. Dr. McAlister tilted her head sympathetically, then wrote out the prescriptions.

Bear accepted the slip for me, and I went through the mechanics of checking out. He tried to pay, I suspect because he knew I was foggy and it was likely the only time he might get away with helping me financially, but I came to life enough to swat him away.

"Nice try." I shot him a smirk I didn't feel and handed over my card, then went back to zoning out. *I hurt her. I could lose her.* The thoughts swirled through my head in a never-ending cyclone.

We swung by the grocery store so we could get Chick-Chick's medication from the pharmacy. He suggested I wait in the car, and I went along with it. Trudging around a grocery store sounded like a lot of effort, and I didn't want to leave Chick-Chick alone. I never wanted to leave her alone again, but the mountain of bills I'd have to pay made that impossible.

I turned on the radio, and a voice crooned. The beat thrummed through me. Crushed as I was, the music still brought life to me, and my dancer's feet wanted to move. I sucked in a breath, and even the lemony air freshener that usually made me gag smelled sweet and wonderful. For a moment, I'd allow myself to forget. For a moment, I'd let the beat of the music shape the beat of my heart, my own personal life support.

The air freshener also made me aware that I'd wound up in Bear's truck, even though we'd driven separately to the vet. I didn't remember having that discussion.

Bear slid into the car with a bottle of wine, a small, stapled paper pharmacy bag, and a Twix bar in tow. He handed me the Twix bar. "Eat."

I accepted the candy, tearing into the wrapper. "I'm supposed to go back to work."

"I already talked to Lindsey. She said you can be done for the day."

I narrowed my eyes at him and snapped off a bite of the Twix. He watched me, his hands tight on the steering wheel.

"What?" I asked.

"Nothing." He pulled out of the lot and drove us home.

As the radio, now several songs past mine, faded into a commercial, I pretended for a minute longer that everything was all right.

CHAPTER THIRTY-SEVEN
BEAR

Trixie was freaking me out.

She'd been near comatose on the ride home from the vet. I'd walked her to her car, and she'd stood there looking at the door. It was like she'd forgotten where she was, what she was doing, or maybe even what a car was. Just stood there staring. I asked her if she was okay. I waved a hand in front of her face. She didn't seem to notice, only muttered, "My fault."

I ended up guiding her to my truck by her shoulders, then Googling the shelter she worked at to call Lindsey and explain what was happening.

When we got home, I'd guided her inside. I went into the kitchen to grab her something to drink, and when I came back, she was washing her face. She patted it dry, and when the towel came away, she looked normal. It was eerie.

But the tiny quiver of her lip did not escape my notice. She was a live human land mine, and I wasn't sure if it would be better to set her off or walk on eggshells around her and hope not to trip the wire.

She loved Chick-Chick more than life itself. The vet's outlook hadn't been optimistic, yet she hadn't shed a single tear at the vet. Months living with Trixie, and she acted like I didn't know her. Like I didn't know her fear for Chick-Chick was eating her up inside.

"You okay?" I asked unnecessarily.

"Yup." She didn't meet my eyes. If I hadn't been able to read her already, the fact that Trixie, who could ramble cheerfully for minutes at a time before catching herself, was monosyllabic would have been evidence that she wasn't anything like okay.

"Come here," I said, wanting to fold her in my arms. She might have been keeping it together on the outside, but inside I knew she was crumbling to pieces. I wanted to hold those pieces together with every ounce of strength I possessed.

"Do you want some tea?" she asked, her voice jumping up an octave. No, I didn't want some fucking tea. I wanted to sit her down and let her pour her emotions out to me. If she wouldn't let me hold her together, I wanted to pick up all the tiny pieces. I wanted to listen to her talk about Chick-Chick for hours so I could glue those little pieces back together again and make her whole.

"Trixie, I can get the tea. You've had a rough day."

"It happens," she snapped. "I'll be all right. We'll do what we can for her and hope for the best. What will happen, will happen." The smile she gave me was the least sincere thing I've ever seen.

Her hand trembled as she walked the full kettle toward the stove. It slipped from her grasp and crashed to the ground, water spraying everywhere.

"Shit!" she yelled, grabbing the hand towel off the counter and bending to mop it up.

"See? Right there. We've lived together for months, and I've never once seen you swear outside the bedroom. Let me do this. You sit down and we'll talk."

"I don't want to talk, Bear. I'm fine. It's just a little spill."

"I'm not worried about the spill," I said, gently taking the towel from her hand. "I'm worried about you. I need you to talk to me."

"I've got this!" She was still smiling, and it was so forced as to be frightening. Her eyes were bloodshot and wide with a wildness that I'd never seen before, in her or anyone else. She was cracking, and I was losing her.

My muscles strained without purpose. I was itching to act. To do something. The woman I loved was in front of me, sinking into an abyss of depression. I needed to save her, but I didn't know how. Doing nothing but watch her fall apart was going to put me over the edge right alongside her.

"Trixie—"

"I said I've got it," she hissed through gritted teeth. She looked at me then, really looked at me, and hiccuped.

She thrust the towel into my hand and took off at a run, rounding the corner toward her bedroom. I tossed the towel onto the counter and chased after her. The door slammed behind her before I got there. I stood there staring at the grainy wood of the door.

Stubborn woman couldn't just let me love her. If I wasn't allowed to be there for her when she was having the shittiest day ever, what was the point of being with her at all? I clenched and unclenched my fists to tamp down my frustration before giving the door three solid and distinct knocks.

"Trixie . . ." In my head, there was more. A whole speech. Something along the lines of *I love you. I want to help you. Please talk to me.* But I was so worn out. I'd been trying to work emotion out of her for weeks, and it was taking its toll on me. At some point, if she didn't open up, I would have to admit defeat and realize she didn't want me to be a part of her life.

What other explanation could there be? If she couldn't let herself be vulnerable with me now, then when? If not with me, with whom could she? Not the parade of acquaintances she was constantly going out with. They didn't know the real her. I bared my soul to her on the regular, and the only time I'd seen a sliver of something real was when she'd told me about her parents.

I thought I loved her, but how could I say that when I couldn't be sure if the person I loved was real? I'd only seen the mask.

I was so mad that my mind was screaming at me to give up. If she wanted to be alone, let her. But my heart was screaming too. I'd never felt about anyone the way I did about Trixie. I wanted her to let me in. I wanted to be her person because she was mine. One last try. I'd allow myself one last-ditch effort to draw her out from behind that plastic smile she was so keen on holding on to. I knocked on the door.

"Go away, Bear."

"I live here," I reminded her.

"You know what I mean."

I pressed my thumb to my temple in frustration. "Trixie, I'm not trying to be the bad guy here. I want to help. You asked me to be yours. Isn't that what I'm here for? You're going through difficult shit right now. I want to be there for you. Please, tell me what you need."

I didn't know what she needed, but I knew staying alone in her room wasn't it. She'd been coping like that with little things since moving in here. This wasn't a little thing. My plea was met with silence. It dragged on. It radiated in pulsing, mocking waves from the door.

Finally, I heard a sniffle that split me in two. For God's sake, she was crying in there and wouldn't let me help. I was going to explode. I thrust open the unlocked door to see her crumpled on her bed, tears streaming down her face. A handful of tissues were balled in each hand.

I dashed to the bed, prepared to hold her close and let her cry into me until her eyes burned with the exhaustion of it and no more tears came. As I drew near, though, she bolted upright in alarm.

"I didn't tell you to come in!" she shrieked.

"You don't have to face this alone. I'm here for you. We'll take care of her together," I said calmly.

"You said she should walk around. You said." Thick wet tears streamed down her face now, uninhibited. The dam had burst.

I stepped back as though shoved. All I wanted was to help, and she was blaming me for Chick-Chick's health, all because I'd felt bad the chicken was stuck in a small room and said she could roam the house? No, Trixie couldn't mean that.

Even if all I wanted was to provide her comfort while she was crying, she clearly didn't want me here. No was no. My whole body tensed up, every inch of me fighting to stay with her. Fighting not to abandon the love of my life when she was clearly in crisis. I tilted my head to the side to stretch the taut muscles in my neck and ease the strain, turning to leave.

"Go!" she yelled. She snatched one of the little sculptures she kept on her nightstand and hurled it at me. I ducked, narrowly escaping. It crashed against the wall, shattered, and sprayed tiny shards of clay in every direction.

Not wanting to wind up in the hospital from another projectile, I closed the door behind me.

I knew she was having a hard time, but how could I ever help her if she wouldn't let me in? How was I ever supposed to know if she didn't let me see the real her? How could we ever truly be together if she never let me see beyond her carefully curated surface?

Even though it was what she'd asked for, abandoning her made me feel like a bad boyfriend. I was trying to be a good one, but maybe that wasn't what she really wanted after all.

I paced across the room, still awkward on my injured ankle. My footfalls landed with a heaviness that caused small earthquakes to rumble through the house.

I was helpless, growing ever surer that I was not, nor would I ever be, enough for her. My hands shook nearly as much as hers, with nowhere else for the nervous energy to go.

As she shifted between silence and sobs, I continued my fidgeting. Back and forth I went, my heart rate ratcheting higher with each lap. I shared her pain. Knowing how badly she hurt was agony for me. I was going to wear holes in the carpet if she didn't cave soon.

A muffled wail was audible through the wall. The sound of it ripped me to shreds. I couldn't sit here while she was suffering. I had to either get in that room and help her or get out of here. Idly listening while she experienced that kind of pain was the kind of torture I couldn't withstand. I lifted my hand to knock once again but dropped it back down. She'd set a boundary. It killed me not to help, but I wanted to respect it. I shouted through the door so she'd know I was leaving.

"Trixie, you asked for space, so I'm giving it. I'm going to leave for a while so you can cool off. If you want to suffer in there all alone, that's fine. But you don't have to be alone. Everyone has problems. I don't know what you're so afraid of showing me, that you can't let me take care of you. But—"

I rubbed at my beard in frustration, unable to find the words I needed. My throat felt tight, and emotion welled up in a way it hadn't in forever. Before I'd met her, I couldn't remember the last time I'd cried. This damn woman had me tearing up left and right and was going to have me sobbing any minute.

"I'm not enough. I don't know why. I tried to be. I thought . . . Call me if you need me." I turned, grabbed my keys, and ran out the door.

CHAPTER THIRTY-EIGHT
TRIXIE

Outside my room a door slammed, and sobs racked my body. He thought I didn't want him. That was the exact opposite of how I felt. I needed him, desperately. I needed him more than I'd needed anything in my life. Somehow, in trying to hide my emotion so he'd only see the happy, likable me, I'd convinced him there was some problem with him.

Maybe I wasn't ready to let him see this side of me, but I couldn't let him keep believing he wasn't good enough.

His truck rumbled to life in the driveway. Crumpled tissues still in hand, I ran over to my window, not sure what my intent was. I watched, tears streaming down my face as his headlights bounced off the driveway and then onto the street as he pulled away.

He'd left. He'd walked in on me crying, and he'd left. He was just like everyone else.

My stomach twisted into a knot as I scooped Chick-Chick up and snuggled with her on the bed.

"Please be okay," I whispered to her. "I need you to be okay."

Through bleary eyes, I followed the bright wavy orange lines of my comforter dancing across the white background. The pattern, which I normally found fun, dizzied me. I closed my eyes and let violent sobs tear through my chest.

It was all closing in on me. An ill and injured Chick-Chick we might not be able to help, who needed a wheelchair I had no hope of affording, and no Bear. It was his house, he couldn't stay away forever, but when he came back, I wasn't sure I'd be allowed to stay.

I was terrified of losing them both. I'd felt so sure around him. The way he'd shown me the things he normally hid from others, I thought maybe I'd been good for him too.

And then I'd blamed him. The guilt over Chick-Chick's injury ate away at me, and I was scared, so scared, and I'd made it worse by blaming him.

Numb, feeling like all the tears and all the emotion had been wrung out of me until there was nothing left, I drifted off to sleep.

*   *   *

Air hissed out of my mouth. My heart beat loud in my chest. The mattress groaned as I shifted, rolling away from my snoozed alarm. Every movement was harsh and loud in my ears, calling attention to how quiet the rest of the house was. There was no floor creaking, no dishes clanging, no shower running outside my room.

I gently moved Chick-Chick to her bed on the floor and set out some of the special new pellets we'd gotten her.

I crept out of my room, hoping Bear had come back last night but doubting that was the case.

"Bear?" I called, wandering from room to room. The smell of coffee was noticeably absent. His bedroom door was ajar. I knocked, then peered around it. No Bear. To be sure, I walked out the back door and checked the driveway. No truck.

I trudged back into the kitchen. Tears pricked at my eyes and I doubled over, clutching at my stomach as if I could fill the hollowness there. From my bedroom, my phone dinged. Bear? I ran back to my room and scooped it up. Lindsey's name glowed on the screen.

Lindsey: How are you holding up?

My brows furrowed. *How are you holding up* wasn't the kind of question you asked someone if you didn't already know they were struggling with something. I was debating my response when the phone chimed again.

Lindsey: You don't have to come in today if you need time. I can take care of things on my own.

While considering this, I forced my sluggish body, still in yesterday's clothes, back to the kitchen to start coffee. I felt like crawling back into bed and never leaving the house, never leaving Chick-Chick's side.

Coffee brewing, I jumped in the shower. I scrubbed hard at my face, rinsing away the crustiness around my eyes from a night of hard crying. As the warm water pelted my back, my mind swam with Chick-Chick and Bear, and soon my own tears were blending with the water from the shower. With effort, I toweled off. Hoping that bright clothing would cheer me up, I dressed in my hot-pink pants and a bright-yellow top.

Coffee finally in hand, I glanced at Lindsey's unanswered text. The coffee wasn't helping. I still wanted to hide under my covers and not face any people today. Smiling and putting on a brave face sounded exhausting. Still, every minute my mind wasn't busy, it drifted right back to thinking about all my fears and guilt, making fresh pain stab my gut. As difficult as pretending everything was all right would be, at least I'd have work to distract me. Without it, I wasn't sure I could take the pain of my emotions pinning me down.

Finally, I responded.

Trixie: I'm good. I might be a few minutes late, but I'll be there.

It was hard to see through my puffy eyes. A little extra time to clean myself up wouldn't hurt, but then work and Lindsey would be the perfect distraction.

* * *

I made it through the workday in a fog, throwing myself into my tasks to keep my mind occupied. I smiled at Lindsey, and she watched me, a worried crinkle to her forehead. When I returned home, I wasn't sure what I wanted. I was drained from having to keep my emotions bottled up all day, and I knew that as soon as the door shut behind me, they were going to leak all over the place. I didn't have it in me to hide them, especially not from Bear.

I missed him. I missed him so much, and it had only been a day. I hated that we'd fought. I hated that I'd told him to go away and that he'd listened. I'd hated that he'd somehow felt like me not wanting his comfort was a fault with him. On some level, I knew he was right. He was my boyfriend, or at least, he had been. I wasn't so sure now, after I'd blamed him for Chick-Chick's injury. As he'd said, comforting me was kind of what he was supposed to do, and it wasn't his fault that it wasn't something I could accept.

I wanted him to be home so I could apologize. Somehow I wanted to make him understand, and do it quickly so I could go back to falling apart. I wanted to feel his arms around me. I wanted to know we'd be okay.

The driveway was empty when I pulled in. The house was dark. After making sure Chick-Chick was all right, I did a quick scan of the rooms in case he'd had to take a cab here or something, not that I knew why he would have. That made it nearly twenty-four hours he'd been gone. I kept wondering if he was okay. Bear wasn't a heavy drinker, but I still couldn't help imagining the worst. Him indulging in too many drinks after our fight and getting behind the wheel. Suddenly I was less worried about *us* and more worried about *him*.

I pulled out my phone. The urgency of my worry almost made me call, but the idea of hearing his voice and having to put together words without falling apart was too much, so I started with a text. I'd call if he didn't respond.

Trixie: Are you okay?

While I gave him a few minutes to respond, I set myself to work. I pulled up a browser and began a Google search for wheelchairs for chickens. After going through page after page of unhelpful information, I finally located one on a website in Australia. Even after the price of the chair, the international shipping was going to crush me. I'd need to look for a local alternative, and I was going to need a lot more odd jobs. My phone buzzed on the nightstand.

Bear: I'm fine.

My feelings were a jumble. I was relieved that the worst-case scenarios I'd envisioned were untrue, but I was disappointed he hadn't said more.

Ever since I'd beamed through my first-ever dance recital and won my parents' approval and attention, I'd known that happiness, whether feigned or real, was how to earn love. It was how I'd become the most popular girl in school. The one time I'd let my facade drop in an audition, when I'd been sick with a cold and miserable, I'd wound up losing the dance solo. Being happy was what I'd done to keep my parents' attention, no matter how hard on me they'd been, because I'd decided that being their perfect puppet had been preferable to being invisible to them.

Smiling was everything. Nobody wanted to be around unhappy people. I'd thought that I'd found my person, but then he'd burst into my room and seen me miserable for one minute, and it had been enough for me to lose him.

I tried to search for some more things I could do to make some extra money. I felt so sluggish, I wasn't making any progress. I could continue tomorrow, but for now I needed rest.

CHAPTER THIRTY-NINE
BEAR

"Uncle Bear!" Bella ran down the stairs and dive-tackled me on the pullout sofa.

I groaned under her sudden weight and sat up. "Hey, kiddo."

"Mama says you need to shower, because you're getting stinky, and you'll never get Aunt Trixie back like that."

"Did she now?" *Gee, thanks for that, sis.* You skip a shower for one bad day and everyone's a critic. Then again, looking down at myself, I realized perhaps she was right. A shower sounded like so much effort when I was devoid of energy. Trixie had rejected me. She wouldn't let me help. She was incredible and capable, and there were many things she could do without help. Shouldering the emotional burden of possibly losing Chick-Chick was not one of them.

I couldn't be with someone who didn't trust me enough to be the slightest bit vulnerable with me. What was a relationship without trust? But I still couldn't imagine a life without her.

"Yeah, but she said not to tell you that, and to tell you breakfast is ready."

"Remind me not to tell you any secrets," I laughed. My heart felt like it had been torn out and stomped on. I was miserable, but leave it to Bella to put a smile on my face anyway.

She pouted. "But I'm good at keeping secrets."

"Oh?" I asked, and she nodded eagerly. "In that case, come here."

I pulled her into a hug, then whispered in her ear. "Your mama had an imaginary friend until she was fifteen."

My sweet niece's eyes bugged out.

"Really?"

I nodded. "Tell your mama I'll be up in a few minutes."

Bella skittered back up the stairs, and I flopped back on the bed. Maybe I should shower, but I didn't care enough to do it. Depression hung over me like a cloud, and everything felt like it would take too much energy. I was worried about Chick-Chick, and it'd only been a day, but I missed Trixie. It felt like it had been weeks.

I didn't know if I should even try to get her back or not, but if I should, I thought a heavy dose of space would be necessary first.

I finally dragged myself to the shower before heading upstairs.

"Good morning." Fawn handed me a plate when I walked into the room. "Showered and dressed, I see. We're peopling today?"

"That might be a stretch," I said.

"Any plans to see Trixie?" Fawn cleared Bella's plate and rinsed it with her back turned to me, feigning indifference. She was dying to outright ask what *exactly* had happened and try to smooth things over.

I'd told my family that we'd had a fight, but I hadn't been more specific than that. I hadn't shared that I'd tried to be there for Trixie and she'd rejected me.

"No," I said. "But I could use a favor."

Fawn stopped washing and shut the water off. "You mean besides staying here?"

I grimaced. "Yeah."

"I'm messing with you. You're welcome here anytime. How can I help?"

"Can you please stop by my place and get some clothes for me? She needs space, so I don't want to run into her, but I didn't think to pack for more than a night."

"Owen could lend you some clothes," she said.

I glanced over at Owen, who was several sizes smaller than me.

"You realize men's clothes aren't one-size-fits-all, right?" he asked her.

She glanced between us and frowned, apparently just now realizing we weren't even remotely close in size.

"Well, all right. Bella's going to a friend's tonight. I'll go after I drop her off there," she said.

"Thanks."

"Did you talk to Mom?" she asked.

The last thing I needed was a family meeting regarding my love life. I was at risk of that as it was, coming here. I definitely hadn't talked to Mom.

"No, she doesn't need to know. She'll find out eventually." I hoped Fawn would take my meaning and not tell her, if she hadn't already.

"Not about you and Trixie. About the shop. The developers called. They gave her one more week to sign the paperwork or they're pulling their offer. Looks like it's really happening."

My stomach lurched, and I set down my fork. I hadn't had much of an appetite, but Fawn's news had just killed it. She couldn't have known how much it would sting me, or she wouldn't have kicked me when I was down like that. At least, I didn't think she would have.

I was losing everything. Trixie, and Chick-Chick, and now my hope at taking over the store, a dream I'd never been brave enough to act on. It was more than I could handle.

"I'm not hungry." I shoved my chair back and cleaned off my plate.

Intent on her hurry to get out the door and the resulting argument with Bella, who was insistent on tying her own shoes, an impressively slow process, Fawn didn't seem to notice my reaction. I was ready to retreat to the basement.

The store. Chick-Chick. Trixie. *Trixie.*

Fawn grabbed her keys and ushered Bella out the door.

"Fawn?" I asked.

She hesitated in the doorway and turned to face me.

"Can you just . . . make sure she's okay?"

She tilted her head to the side with a compassionate smile. "Of course."

CHAPTER FORTY
TRIXIE

After work, I checked on Chick-Chick, then took a neighborhood dog for a walk for a little extra cash. I hadn't walked for the same family as when Bear had been injured out of fear of another incident, but dog walking reminded me of him and only made it harder to keep my mind elsewhere.

I missed him, but he'd left after seeing me crying. I still didn't know how to be in a relationship and keep my true self buried. Nothing had changed, so I hadn't reached out to him, as badly as I wanted to.

When I got home, I tossed my purse to the side, heated up some pasta, and brought Chick-Chick to the couch to snuggle. I was just settling in to watch TV when headlights flashed through the edges of the curtains. Bear!

Despite my concerns, my heart leapt, and I raced to the door, Chick-Chick cradled in one arm. I flung the door open, and my grin fell. Fawn and Zoey stood on the other side of the screen door.

"Oh, hi." I tried to muster up the requisite enthusiasm for receiving guests and forced a smile into place, albeit a less enthusiastic one than I should have mustered.

"Sorry to intrude," Fawn said. "Needed to pick up a few things for Bear."

"And he didn't want to get them himself?" I asked. I didn't want to admit it, but that hurt. It felt like he'd sent his sisters to do his dirty work. He couldn't face me on his own? Then again, I'd sent him away; I clearly couldn't face him either. Was he afraid to talk to me? Respecting my wishes? I didn't know whether to be mad, or disappointed, or glad. I needed a guide to tell me how to navigate my emotions in this situation.

"May we come in?" Fawn asked, avoiding my question.

I stepped out of the way to let them past. Zoey nodded to Fawn and headed off to Bear's bedroom, his duffel bag in tow.

"He wanted to come, but he said you'd asked for space. He's . . . well, I've never seen him like this. But I think he's trying to give you some time. He seems to think that's what you want."

Fawn let the statement hang like a question, watching my face for confirmation. Only I wasn't entirely sure what I wanted. When I didn't answer for an uncomfortably long time, she changed tactics.

"How's she doing?" she asked, petting Chick-Chick.

I resisted the urge to fold in on myself. "Time will tell. The painkillers have her seeming less miserable, and she's been eating her new food."

"That's good."

"Do you want something to drink or anything?" I asked, politeness winning out. I liked both the sisters, but after a full day of trying to hold myself together at work, I desperately needed the evening to decompress, and I couldn't do that with them here.

"I'm okay, thanks. Do you . . . want to talk about it?" Fawn asked.

About what? Bear? Chick-Chick? The fact that I was failing in every relationship in my life and was losing hope that I'd ever be able to have a healthy relationship?

"How is he?" I asked.

Fawn smiled. "How do you think?"

I didn't have the energy for guessing games. Fortunately, she seemed to sense that and carried on. "Look, I don't know what happened between you two, but that man is smitten. He is head over heels."

Zoey stepped back into the living room, duffel bag packed. "What did he do? Do we need to smack some sense into him?"

I shook my head, a lump forming in my throat.

"Look, you asked, so I'm going to tell you the truth. It's not to make you feel bad, I'm just trying to be honest. He's a mess. Is there anything we can do to help?" Fawn asked.

They couldn't help. There was nothing they could do that could fix things. I was about to break. Tears began to well at the edges of my eyes, fighting to the surface.

"I'm pretty tired," I said in a hurry.

They both frowned but seemed to take the hint.

"We're around if you change your mind," Fawn said. "Whatever happens, we're still your friends."

I nodded, struggling to hold back the flood.

"We're here. Anytime," Zoey agreed.

I nodded again, fearing my voice would waver if I spoke. They left, and I just caught Ryan's "Hey, ladies," as they walked to their car before I closed the door behind them.

CHAPTER FORTY-ONE
BEAR

"You know you were asking for trouble telling her to check on Trixie, right?" Owen asked, passing me the bag of chips.

I sighed. I had to know she was okay. The ends justified the means.

"I know."

The door burst open, and sure enough, Fawn and Zoey both tromped in. They pulled kitchen chairs over and sat in front of me and wasted no time getting to business.

"It isn't over," Fawn said.

"You don't know that," I said.

"Yeah, actually, we do." Zoey stuck a finger at my chest. "So you just sit your butt down and listen."

"She's miserable," said Fawn. "She was doing her smiling thing, but she looks like she's done nothing but cry."

This news stabbed at my gut. I had the feeling they'd thought this was going to make me feel better. While it would have sucked to hear she was happy and thriving without me,

I wanted her to be happy. The last thing I wanted was for her to be miserable and crying.

"That might be because she's worried about Chick-Chick, though." I hoped it didn't mean anything had gotten worse with our pet, and I wished I could be there to help.

"She asked about you," Zoey said, her eyes wide, as if this should be all the evidence I needed.

"So what? I asked about her too."

"Exactly." Zoey looked like she was ready to smack me for being dense. "And do *you* want to move on from her?"

"No," I admitted. At the very least, I would need time to let it sink in that she was never going to trust me before I could convince myself to move on. Even with time, I didn't think I'd ever be able to forget Trixie.

"I rest my case," she said.

"How does that help him?" Owen asked. "So she still likes him, what does he do about it?"

I nodded at him appreciatively. It had felt a bit like the women were steamrolling me. It was nice to have another guy on my side.

"We were getting to that." Fawn subtly scooted her chair, uninviting Owen from contributing further to the conversation. So much for that.

"On the way out, we ran into Ryan," Zoey said.

"Oh, here we go." I threw my hands up.

"He said he heard her arguing with someone," Fawn said.

"Yeah, me." I shook my head. Thank you, Captain Obvious. How was this helpful?

"No, this morning." Zoey leaned forward and met my eyes. "She was on the phone, arguing about her credit. Something about needing to get a wheelchair. He said she was still upset at the end of the call. If she was trying to get help paying for a wheelchair, she didn't get it."

"This feels intrusive," I said. "Her finances aren't any of your business."

"I'll wipe it from my memory as soon as I'm done telling you," Fawn said.

"Same here," Zoey nodded.

Owen crunched away at a potato chip, his feigned ignorance acting as his own agreement.

"I still don't see how this helps. She won't let me give her money or buy her anything. I've tried."

"Think outside the box," Zoey said.

"You've got some builder skills that could put the Pinterest moms to shame." Fawn raised an eyebrow at me, waiting for me to catch on.

Finally, the lightbulb clicked.

"I need to make a store run for some supplies."

"Yeah you do!" Fawn shouted, and gave Zoey a high five. Sometimes their meddling was all right.

* * *

I had cut the PVC pipe down to the sizes I needed and sanded down the edges. I hadn't worked with fabrics much before, but Fawn always made Bella's Halloween costumes from scratch, and she helped me with the hammock. All that was left was to put them together.

I jumped when the door from the kitchen into the garage opened.

"Did you pull an all-nighter?" Fawn asked, ushering Bella past her and into their car. I checked the time on my phone. Seven in the morning already. The time had flown. The stress of the fight with Trixie and of Mom selling the shop had been snowballing inside me. Having this as a creative outlet and a way to do something about one of those problems had burst the snowball apart.

"I slept some." For a couple hours. I'd woken up in the middle of the night and been unable to fall back asleep with the wheelchair build calling to me. Making a project I actually cared about had me energized. I still couldn't say I fully understood why Trixie had asked me to leave, but I hoped the wheelchair would be the olive branch I needed to open up that conversation.

Fawn and Bella left, and I put the finishing touches on the chair, then stood to admire my work. I gave it a nudge with my foot, and it glided smoothly over the floor. My heart swelled. I'd created something I was proud of and that I hoped would bring joy to the person I loved. And help the chicken I loved too.

Barging in on Trixie didn't feel like the right move. The way she hid from serious conversations with me, I was fairly sure she would need to gear up for that, so I decided to leave the wheelchair as a gift, with a note.

I stopped home and gave Chick-Chick some snuggles, then left the wheelchair in plain view so Trixie would see it as soon as she got home. I couldn't wait, though. Building this gift had reminded me how important it was to be doing and creating something I loved.

It meant facing a fear I'd had almost my entire life, but I knew what questions I needed to ask next.

Maybe there was still time.

CHAPTER FORTY-TWO
BEAR

"There you are," Mom said as I walked in. "How are you, sweetheart?"

"I'm good." I kissed her cheek.

"Oh no, not girl trouble again?" she asked. Mom with the sixth sense again. I'd talked to her on the phone and over text since Trixie and I had gotten together days before. She'd even resisted saying *I told you so* about Trixie coming around.

"I'll figure it out." I waved her off. I was still stressed about Trixie but trying to retain optimism that my gift would help. As much as her motherly wisdom was welcome, between my own worries for Chick-Chick, Trixie's and my relationship, and the looming deadlines of my intended return to work and my mother's plan to proceed with selling to the developers, I was overwhelmed. I needed to focus on one thing at a time.

She nodded, taking the hint. "You said you wanted to talk?"

"Yes. Fawn told me the developers upped their deadline. Did you already sell?"

"Not yet," she said slowly. I felt like I'd been holding my breath since deciding to come here and had only just been granted permission to breathe. There was still time. I hadn't completely blown it.

"If it isn't too late, I'm thinking about taking over the store. I wanted to talk logistics."

Mom smiled and turned toward the back room. "Come, let's go sit. We'll hear the bell if anyone comes in."

We stared each other down in silence, each of us waiting for the other to start. I scratched at my face.

"I wonder what you did before you had facial hair," she said. "Sometimes it feels like I remember every little piece of yours and your sisters' childhoods. Other times . . . I've gotten so used to that little tic of yours, I can't remember what you did before you had the beard to scratch at."

Self-consciously, I pulled my hand away from my face, laying it in my lap instead. I had to resist the urge to look like a child and sit on my hand to avoid doing it again. "I don't realize I'm doing it."

"I know," she said. "It's endearing. But you don't have to be nervous. Ask what you want to ask."

"I'm not nervous about talking to you, I'm nervous about letting you down," I said. I thought I knew what I wanted, but I'd been fighting it for so long, and taking over the shop was a big deal. If I was going to do it, I needed to make sure it would work logistically. Now that I finally felt ready, I had to make sure I didn't commit to something on an emotional whim. "I don't know if after this conversation I'll want to go through with it. I need to know more, but I didn't want to get your hopes up."

"What's holding you back? Aside from the details."

I stared at her. Her mom sense was not a newly acquired skill. My mother was a smart woman. I'd never discussed the reason I'd been bullied at school, but she'd heard Lyle's admonishments and seen how I'd distanced myself from the store. I was confident she'd put two and two together.

She sighed. "It's been a long time, sweetie. The world isn't perfect and still has some skewed gender stereotypes, but it's getting better. And you're not a child anymore. Look at you! I know when you were younger, your life was made miserable by all this, but you can't let the past keep you from enjoying your future. You need to do what will make you happy."

I swallowed, glancing away from Mom and around the room, studying the place that could be mine. Was it what I wanted?

Mom cleared her throat. "I need you to know that I want you to do what will make you happy. If that means taking over the store, I'd be thrilled. But if it doesn't, that's okay too. I love you, and your happiness will always be more important to me. The store is just . . . a store."

Mom's tone was sincere, and even though I did want the store, her giving me permission not to take it was freeing. She hadn't sold it yet, but she still could. Knowing she would be okay if I chose not to proceed allowed me to think about what I wanted. It helped me get a clearer picture.

What I saw in that picture was that, to me, the store wasn't just—as she'd said—"a store." It was so much more. It was a place where I felt at home. The work was something I could get lost in and enjoyed doing.

My gut was telling me what I wanted to do, but I couldn't make this decision based solely on my gut. If I was going to do this, I wanted to make sure I was doing it for the right reasons.

What would kill me and my mom even more than her selling the business was if I took it over and failed.

"Thanks," I said. A thank-you that meant *I appreciate that you're selfless enough to give me freedom and that you're trusting me with this.* There was so much more that I didn't have the right words to say, but because she was Mom, I was confident she knew anyway.

"Do you still want to talk?" she asked, a little hesitantly, but her face was full of encouraging warmth.

"Yes." My voice got caught on the word, and it came out garbled. I cleared my throat and tried again. "Yes I do."

So we talked. We talked about how much I would pay to buy the business from her, and how we could space out those payments so I could afford it, given my lack of savings. We talked about how long she'd stay on to help make sure I was comfortable running all aspects before taking off on her whirlwind adventures with Dad. I asked her to walk me through the financials, and she smiled proudly before leading me over to the computer. She sat in the small computer chair that would crack in half if I tried to sit on it and pulled up her profit-and-loss statements. I stood behind her shoulder, watching as she called out key figures and explained them.

I breathed a relieved sigh when she closed the document, and it struck me that I'd understood it all. Not only that, but I'd asked questions that I thought were the right ones to ask and hadn't embarrassed myself in front of my mother.

"Son, my ability to read you has its limits. What are you thinking?" she asked.

I slowly ran my hand back along my jawline and tilted my head to stretch my neck. I wanted to answer her, but my mind was still a swirling mess. Hurricane-force lines of thought whipped around my brain, flinging stray messages. I tried to grasp at them, but they all flew past my fingertips and got away. I didn't know what I was thinking because I couldn't hold on to a single solid thought.

This was a lot to take in, and while I was doing my best to stay focused on it, because this was what was in my control, Trixie and Chick-Chick kept fighting for stage time.

Apparently her mind-reading capabilities were still working to some extent, because she nodded. "Need to let it ruminate. Let's make some arrangements. It'll help you think, and I can give you some pointers to help get you back into the swing of it."

"Sounds good," I said.

We worked together, side by side, churning out order after order. Mom stepped back and let me try the ones with less direction and more room for creativity. As my hands moved, trimming stems, banding flowers together, and placing them into vases, each movement was like catching one of those stray thoughts. I forced them to stay still and banded them together with the other thoughts I'd caught, just like I was banding together the flowers. With each new arrangement, my decision became clearer. When we finished up the last of her orders, I had a crystalline picture in my mind. I knew what I needed to do.

"You look like you feel better."

I stood and stretched. "I do."

"And do you know what you want to do?" she asked.

"I know we're out of time, but there's one more thing I need to do. Can I come by the house with my decision tonight? I'll bring dinner."

Mom patted my hand. "We'd love that."

CHAPTER FORTY-THREE
TRIXIE

My rounds of cleaning up cages and filling food and water complete, I wandered into the play area with all the dogs and puppies running around and sat on the floor. Immediately, I was ambushed by a horde tackling me and slobbering on my face. I fell to the ground, laughing. This was the kind of therapy I needed. This should be a service you can purchase. Puppy kiss therapy.

Lindsey heard my laughing and came to stand by the gate to the play area, smiling.

"Having fun?" she asked.

"Yes," I admitted. A huge weight had been removed from my chest. Bear and Chick-Chick were still at the back of my mind, but the puppy kisses had pushed them far enough back that I could breathe.

"Good to hear you laugh," she said. I could have sworn I'd maintained my smile at work. Apparently my struggles were still seeping through. Of course, she'd known I'd had a hard day after finding out Chick-Chick didn't have the best prognosis, but it felt like she knew something was wrong beyond that.

I got myself up and ineffectually brushed off my clothes.

We went back to our desks, her processing paperwork, me putting together info packets for the families that would eventually adopt animals from us. For a while, we stuffed in silence. I still felt a little lighter than before, but some of the effect of the puppy love had faded, and the heartache was returning.

"How did you know?" I asked.

"Bear was worried about you. He texted to give me a heads-up."

The papers I'd been about to stuff slid from my grip as I froze. This was the only logical explanation, so I wasn't surprised that was how she'd heard. Still, after I'd pushed away Bear's attempts to comfort me and he'd stormed out and spent the night elsewhere rather than returning to his own home and risk facing me, I was surprised that he cared enough to watch out for me via Lindsey.

Maybe all hope wasn't lost.

"Penny for your thoughts?" she asked.

I startled and resumed my packet stuffing. "Oh, thinking about Chick-Chick."

She clicked save on the document she was working on and spun to face me.

"I'm sorry about her, sweetie," she said. "You're doing your best. That's all you can do."

I nodded. I knew that. It didn't stop me from feeling guilty, but I did know I'd done my best by her. I turned my face away to continue my stuffing.

"Ah," she said. "Don't want to talk about her?"

I shook my head and worked my little assembly line. Paper, paper, paper, stuff. Paper, paper, paper, stuff.

"What about him? I know she isn't the only thing on your mind."

My shoulders tensed, shifting my hands enough for me to give myself a paper cut while sliding them into the folder.

"Horseradish!" I cursed, squeezing the finger.

Lindsey grabbed a box of Band-Aids from under the desk. I got a lot of paper cuts on envelope-stuffing days, so we kept them handy. She handed me one and waited patiently for me to handle my mini crisis.

"Thanks." I wrapped the finger, then returned to my project, now considerably harder to accomplish with a Band-Aid on my finger.

The little cut was such a common occurrence, it shouldn't have even phased me, but with all that was going on in my life, the minor inconvenience and short-lived pain felt like more than I could handle. I was shaken and struggling to regain control of my emotions. My heart rate was rising, and my breathing had picked up as well.

I wrestled with the Band-Aid, grabbing several pieces of paper from a stack rather than one. My already disproportionate frustration grew exponentially with each failed attempt to isolate a single sheet. By the seventh attempt, I was gasping for air, and I couldn't take it anymore. I threw the papers down and shoved my chair back. I wanted to make it to another room to cry. Lindsey had never seen me as anything other than cheerful, and I didn't want that to end today, but I couldn't make it.

Stress shook my legs, and I couldn't stand. I fell back into my chair, and the waterworks started.

For someone who'd never seen me emotional before, she didn't seem surprised. She calmly rolled back and opened the drawer of her filing cabinet. She pulled out a bag of Hershey's kisses and spilled them out onto the desk in front of us. Then she handed me the box of tissues.

I accepted the box, wiping away my tears. Lindsey peeled open one of the chocolates. "I've been waiting for this day for a long time. I was beginning to think it would never come." She popped it into her mouth and let out a quiet "Mmm."

I stared at her blankly, tears streaming down my face. "W-what do you mean?"

"You are a human being, not a machine. Nobody can be happy one hundred percent of the time. It isn't realistic. It's not what we're made for."

"Sure we can. I'm always happy," I said through my tears.

"Uh-huh." Lindsey popped another chocolate, then gestured at me as if to say, *Exhibit A.*

"Okay, I'm happy most of the time," I said.

"Are you?" she asked. "I can never tell. But it seemed more real when Bear was around."

I buried my face in my arms on top of the desk and sobbed. I hated that she was right. I had been happier when he was around than at any other time I could remember. The way he looked at me had made my whole body go warm in anticipation long before we'd started dating. I had fun around him. I could tell I was pulling him into things he'd never do otherwise, and he seemed okay with it. It was exhilarating and made me feel special.

Now all that was gone, because I couldn't let him see me cry. Yet here I was, crying my eyes out to Lindsey.

"Have some chocolate. It helps." She shoved the pile closer to me, and I unwrapped several and stuffed them into my mouth at once.

"Maybe one at a time would be good. I'm a little rusty on the Heimlich."

I glared at her, and she laughed.

"Okay, sorry. Are you going to tell me what happened?"

I sucked on the chocolate, debating my answer. Lindsey walked out of the room and returned with Snowflake, a tiny white kitten who had been dropped off a few days earlier.

"It doesn't look like chocolate is going to cut it. This calls for kitten snuggles."

I accepted Snowflake, who immediately curled up on my lap and started purring. I smiled down at her and ran my fingers through her soft fur. Lindsey was right. It calmed me immediately. With my free hand, I cleaned the tears off my face and pulled myself together.

"And she's back," Lindsey said. "Well?"

"I was upset about Chick-Chick. Bear tried to help, and I wouldn't let him near me, so he said something about not being enough and took off."

Her jaw tensed. "He left you after the vet?"

I shook my head. "No. He tried over and over again to comfort me, and I kept turning him away. He left me alone for a bit and gave it one last try, and he stormed off after I turned him down again."

Her jaw relaxed, but her frown remained.

"How come?"

"Because I knew as soon as he saw me unhappy, he wouldn't want to be with me anymore," I said.

The door to the shelter swung open, and Ali, one of our regular volunteers, came in. Our conversation was put on hold while Lindsey got her checked in. I hid my tearstained face, and Ali went back to take a couple of the dogs for a walk. The door shut behind her, and Lindsey turned back to me.

"Did he say he loves you?" she asked.

I shook my head. "But I think he does. I could feel it, you know?"

She smiled and patted Snowflake, who had settled back down to sleep after our brief interruption. "I do. But you honestly think he'd stop because he saw you unhappy once?"

I popped another Hershey's to give myself time to consider. "Yes. Maybe. No?"

"That's a crock of shit, Trixie. I don't know who hurt you, but nobody stops loving people just because they see them unhappy."

"Yes they do!" I protested. It had been proven countless times in my life. Smiles brought me friendship wherever I went, and my parents' attention. Frowns led to failure.

"No they don't." She was emphatic. "I'll agree with you that people tend to be drawn to friendlier, generally happy people. They are more approachable. But everyone has down moments. No one is happy all the time. And of course he thought you were keeping him at arm's length if you couldn't let him see that. You've done the same to me."

She was right. I'd known her for years and spent forty hours a week in an office with her, but I'd refused to let her get close.

"Do you want to be with him?" she asked.

I nodded.

"Darling, opening up to people isn't easy. I'm not saying it won't be hard. But if you want him back, you have to think about if you're willing to let him in. Because, if he isn't seeing the real you, then what's the point?"

The door opened again, and a family came in. We had a few families scheduled to come look at animals for adoption today, so this was the end of our discussion, but she'd given me a lot to think about.

CHAPTER FORTY-FOUR
BEAR

It was as if the universe had conspired against me. All of the important things in my life were boiling down to these few days. One of those was Mom's deadline with the developers. I had my answer, but If I was going to do things right, there were two things that needed resolving first.

One of those was my miserable construction job. Following my injury, I was supposed to be returning to it tomorrow. I wasn't going to be staying with it for long, but after leaving them short-staffed while I was injured, I owed them some notice.

I pulled up a number in my contact list and hit call.

"Bear, I'd been about to call you," my boss, Carlton, answered.

The repetition of my rehearsed quitting speech in my mind came to a screeching halt.

"I know you're supposed to be back tomorrow, but a job got canceled, and I don't have a spot for you until next week."

I froze. This news had zero effect on me, since I'd been about to quit anyway, and yet it still irritated me that I was just coming back from leave, and rather than asking how I was or letting me get in some hours to make up for the time I'd missed, the first thing he was doing was taking away a job and a week's worth of work.

"I knew you'd understand," he said.

Anger grew at the assumption. "In that case, go ahead and find someone else for the next job too. I'm done."

I hung up, tossed the phone down on the table in front of me, and scrubbed at the sides of my face. That had been simultaneously exhilarating and terrible. I hadn't meant to actually burn the bridge, just walk across it. It was flaming now, though.

At least one of my two tasks was done, even if the execution had gone off the rails. I was leaving the job I hated to pursue my passion. Trixie would be proud.

You drink a lot of beer for someone who isn't much of a fan of it, the Trixie in my mind said. Trixie felt I wasn't true to myself. Well, maybe I could fix that too.

Next on the list was Lyle. I might have stood up to him for Trixie, but rarely had I stood up to him for myself. If I was going to make some changes in my life, I needed to do it free from his voice, and that meant confronting him. Face-to-face wasn't an option, since I had no idea where he was, but it was likely far from Chicago. I found him in my address book and called, hoping his number hadn't changed.

"Hello?" he answered.

My jaw clenched at the sound of his voice. I wanted to punch the end-call button, but it was time to face him. I needed to say it. Get it out in a rush.

"Lyle, it's Bear."

"Oh, it's you." Classic Lyle, ever enthusiastic to speak to one of his children.

"I thought I'd let you know I'm taking over Family Tree. Mom's retiring."

The silence dragged on so long, my ear itched from straining to hear his response. If I hadn't known better, I'd have wondered if he'd heard me.

"Pathetic," he finally said, and hung up with a click. I stared at the phone screen in my hand and shook my head. The response should have hurt. At so many points in my life, it would have. As I looked down at my phone, though, I searched for the pain inside myself and couldn't find it. Instead, I felt free.

For years I'd let his judgments weigh down on me. I'd based decisions about my own life on the approval of the person least deserving of that kind of ownership over me. His approval didn't matter because his priorities and biases were all wrong. If he wanted nothing more to do with me, I'd be okay. In fact, I'd be better off than I'd been always waiting for the next insult. Finally, I felt like myself.

I was ready.

CHAPTER FORTY-FIVE
TRIXIE

My mind continued to whirl as I drove home from work, mulling over my conversation with Lindsey. The closer I got to home, the more I hoped Bear would be there, so I could talk to him and try to figure out if I'd been lying to myself this whole time.

I held my breath as I turned down our street and then up to our driveway. Empty. My heart sank, and it was no one's fault but mine. I'd told him to go. I couldn't be surprised that he'd listened. Still, I'd hoped.

I went in through the front door and tossed my bag aside as usual, then froze.

No. It couldn't be.

On the floor, in the middle of the living room, was a small contraption that weeks ago I'd have been unable to identify. But after countless hours of research in the past few days and arguing with pet care credit providers, I knew exactly what it was.

A chicken wheelchair.

I ran to it and knelt down. I recognized the fabric on the hammock from Fawn's craft supplies. I'd seen it when I was babysitting Bella. There was a tiny plastic vase mounted on the chassis with a tiny marigold in it, the perfect treat for Chick-Chick. Teeny, tiny floral snacks in an itty-bitty vase. Not only had Bear taken the time and effort to make her a wheelchair, he'd thought of everything. There was a note tucked into the hammock. I picked up the piece of paper and unfolded it.

Whatever you need, whenever you need it, I'm here.

Love,

Bear

Instant monsoon. Tears poured out of my eyes the second I finished reading the note. He hadn't left because he'd seen me sad after all. It really was just because I'd pushed him away. He still wanted to help. He still wanted to be there for me.

Love, Bear.

LOVE.

He'd signed the note *Love*! All hope wasn't lost. I pressed the note to my chest, ran to the bedroom, and carried Chick-Chick over to the wheelchair, gently settling her in. She stood there, pecking at it, twisting around confused, exploring it. She tried to flap her way out of it, and the wheelchair moved.

Her neck extended, and she looked at me like, *What the heck was that?*

I laughed through my tears and moved across the room, where I sat down and called her.

She glanced down at the chair again, untrusting, and took a tentative step.

"Yes! Good job, baby! You can do it!"

She let out a stream of clucks and tapped at the small metal food bowl affixed to the front of the chair, then took another small step.

"You've got it! That's it! Come here, girl!"

She took four hurried steps toward me, and more laughter bubbled out of me. My shoulders relaxed, an enormous weight off of them.

I spent a few minutes soaking in the joy of watching Chick-Chick test out her new chair, rolling around the room, clucking up a happy little storm. It was the most energetic I'd seen her in a while. She still had a long road ahead, but this would go a long way toward helping her maintain a good quality of life.

My bills were still overwhelming, but the cost of a wheelchair was one less thing I'd have to worry about.

And Bear had signed his note with *Love*. It wasn't quite the same as saying *I love you*, but it felt like it. Our relationship wasn't irreparable. There was still a chance to fix things. Knowing he wasn't scared off or judging me for my meltdowns and knowing he still cared made everything suddenly crystal clear.

I had to fix things. I dug out my phone and texted Zoey.

Me: I want him back Zoey. What do I do?

The phone rang almost immediately.

"Hello?" I said.

"A family meeting isn't a family meeting if the whole family isn't there," she said.

CHAPTER FORTY-SIX
BEAR

"Bear! Hi, sweetheart." Mom kissed my cheek when I arrived at their house and took the bag I was holding, freeing up one of my hands to shuffle the pizza box around. Deep-dish Chicago pizza was the answer for any occasion, especially for big, life-changing talks. Lou Malnati's was my family's favorite, and we were prepared to throw down with anyone who disagreed.

"Your father is watching TV in the other room," she said. "I'll go get him."

I nodded but set the box down and followed Mom halfway down the hall, pausing so I could see the two of them in the living room.

"Russ—"

Before she could get the rest of the sentence out, Dad's arm shot out, snaked around her, and pulled her down into his lap.

"Oh!" she gasped, letting out a laugh as she fell into his arms.

"You look beautiful tonight." He pulled her lips down to his for a quick kiss. "I saw a commercial for a resort in Jamaica. Want to go there first?"

"Anywhere, so long as it's with you," Mom said.

Dad liked his TV, but he was a completely different person when Mom was around. His light shone entirely on her. He couldn't help but have his normal, grumpy self cheered by her. I couldn't help but be reminded of the way Trixie made me feel. She was my sun. I wanted what my parents had. Grunts, giggles, and all.

"Bear is here," she said. "No more TV."

"Yes, ma'am." He swatted playfully at her backside when she stood. Twenty years of marriage and they were as into each other as newlyweds. Again, Trixie's face appeared in my mind. I had to focus. If nothing else, I could live with knowing this decision would have made her proud.

I crept back to the kitchen, hoping my parents hadn't caught me spying on them. I started unpacking the food I'd brought over as they walked in.

We kept the conversation casual while we ate, not getting into the real reason I was there. We talked about our days, and I asked them about their plans for retirement, and feigned surprise at Dad's suggestion that they might take a trip to Jamaica.

Forks scraped against bare plates as we polished off our slices, and I could stall no longer. Time to talk about what I'd come here for. I set my fork down and took a deep breath. Mom caught my shift and dabbed at her mouth with a napkin. She tapped Dad's arm to get his attention and sat up straight, her hands folded in her lap. They both waited patiently for me to begin.

"I've decided I'd like to take over the business," I said. "If you haven't changed your minds about that being an option, that is."

Dad sat back in his chair, his arms crossed. His grin was proud. Of course I wanted to make Dad proud too, but this was Mom's shop. She was the one whose reaction I wanted to see. She shot out of her chair, dashed around the table, and threw her arms around me. Tears sprung to her eyes as she held me close. My shirt was damp with her tears, and I hugged her back.

"These are happy tears, right?" I asked, knowing they were, but not sure what else to say in the moment.

A muffled laugh vibrated against my shoulder. "Mmmf oofed oo ooofed afed ift."

"Words, Mom."

She stepped away and smiled up at me. "I'd hoped you would take it. You've always belonged there. I knew you had reservations, and I didn't want to push you. I'm so glad."

"Me too. I'm excited about it. And there's no going back. I quit my job today."

That got an eyebrow raise from them both.

Mom shook herself back into the moment. "Well then, we'll start training you tomorrow."

"Thanks, Mom," I said.

Mom's sob fest over, Dad stood and gave me one of those handshakes that pulls into a hug.

They both stood back, smiling at me, and I suddenly felt like I was back at high school graduation, standing in a crowded parking lot in my cap and gown, my parents standing and watching as friends came by with their shared congratulations and wishes for a good summer and good luck at college.

"I would have been okay if you'd decided not to take it. You do know that, right? You're doing this for your own reasons?" Mom asked.

"Yes, Mom. I know. I'm doing this for me, but I'm glad it makes you happy too."

"It does. It really does," she squealed, tears welling up in her eyes again. "But you're positive? Because I want you to be ha—"

"Carrie," Dad barked. "The boy said he was doing it for himself. Relax."

"What he said," I agreed.

Mom pressed her lips together, quirking them upward at the ends, and nodded.

"Can we come in yet?" Zoey shouted from outside the side door that led into the kitchen. "We've been out here for like ten minutes!"

I looked at my parents questioningly.

Dad shrugged helplessly and pointed at Mom. Mom hunched sheepishly. "I got a little excited after we talked earlier and may have told them to come for a family meeting to celebrate."

"Come on in," I yelled.

The door flew open, and Zoey, Fawn, Owen, Bella, and even Lexie all poured in, everyone talking at once.

Bella shouted, "Grandma!" and ran into Mom's arms. Owen went to the fridge and got out a beer for him and my dad. "One for you?" he asked me.

"Actually, I think I'll have a glass of wine," I said.

"I'll do you one better." Zoey winked and pulled a bottle of champagne out of her enormous purse, followed by a bottle of sparkling grape juice. "I've even got one for the kiddo."

"Thanks, Zoey," I said.

"Proud of you, baby brother." Fawn patted me on the back and went to help Zoey get the glasses down.

"Hey, Lex," I said. "I didn't know you were in town."

"I'm on my way back on a work trip. I was going to have a layover either way, so I changed my flight to make my layover here so I could visit tonight. It was a happy coincidence this happened too. Congrats!" She hugged me. "I'll get Rose on a video chat for the toast."

I accepted a glass from Fawn and waited for her and Zoey to finish handing out the rest. Then the doorbell rang.

I glanced up. Dad shrugged. The only one missing was Rose, but I could see her already on the screen with Lexie. Everyone else seemed distracted, so I walked to the front door to answer it, passing the ever-present arrangement of fresh flowers on the small table in the entryway. It was a hallmark of my family, and now that I'd be at the shop every day, it could become a tradition in my own home.

I pulled open the door and watched as a shadowy figure emerged under the archway over the front stoop. Turquoise sneakers hit the welcome mat that said *Family*. Sprouting from them were smooth legs that led to a purple dress, and a yellow belt cinched the waist over hips that I knew well and could still feel in my mind, bare in my hands, the skin giving way to my gentle squeezes in bed.

Her hair was tied to one side, trailing over her shoulder. Her smile was tentative and nervous, her eyes wide with hope.

I realized I was staring and leaving her to stand there awkwardly, unsure of my reaction. She shifted, and I finally noticed her hands were full, weighed down with grocery bags.

"Trixie?" I asked. Brilliant first line.

"Um, hi," she said. Her foot slid up her calf into her flamingo stance as she continued to balance the bags in both arms. I leapt forward to take them for her, wishing I was jumping forward to kiss her instead. She hadn't called or texted with a reaction to my gift. I didn't know where her mind was at. As much as I was dying to taste her lips right now, the timing wasn't right.

"What are you doing here?" I asked. Inwardly, I grimaced. Hopefully that hadn't come out accusatory, or like I didn't want her here. I very much wanted her here. I'd missed her so much, she could have been here to throw tomatoes at my head and I'd still have been happy to see her.

Her eyes settled behind me, where all seven members of my family who were present were crowded around the edge of the kitchen, watching us through the living room. I took the rest of her bags and set them on the table.

"Owen, can you grab these?" I called over my shoulder, then turned back to Trixie. "Do you want to take a walk?"

Trixie relaxed. For someone who had a tendency to be in the spotlight, she seemed relieved she wasn't going to have my whole family as witnesses to our conversation.

I grabbed my jacket off the coatrack near the door and stepped out into the cool evening air, shutting the door behind me. Trixie hugged herself against the cold, and I draped the jacket over her shoulders.

"Thanks," she said.

"Sure."

"I hear congratulations are in order?" We shuffled along the sidewalk, the occasional dry leaf crunching under our feet.

I laughed. "Who told you?"

"Zoey," she said.

I grinned. Zoey could be a pain in the ass sometimes, but she had her moments.

"What was in the bag?" I asked.

"Ice cream," she said. "Zoey suggested I bring some brownie batter. I'm guessing that's her favorite. I got you vanilla with salted caramel."

"Yum." We walked on for a while in silence, letting the barks of neighborhood dogs do the talking for us.

"Thank you for the wheelchair. It's perfect. I can't believe you made it."

Trixie's hand fell to her side and grazed mine as we walked. She didn't jump away. She continued walking just as close, allowing it to happen a second time, so I took a risk and ran my hand along hers. She slid it into mine, intertwining our fingers.

"I wanted to help. It was something I could do. Did she try it?"

"She did! She was rolling all over. She loves it."

"I'm glad. I miss her," I said.

She nodded her agreement.

Zoey had given me this opening. I needed to take advantage of it. If I was going to put myself out there, there wouldn't be a better time. "I miss *you* too."

Trixie sniffled and glanced away. Still not opening up to me, then. That wasn't a good sign. My stomach dropped.

"Could we sit down somewhere?" she asked.

We'd rounded the block and were nearing my parents' house again. The old swing set from our childhood still stood in the back. I led her around the side of the house to the backyard, and we each took a swing, reluctantly letting go of each other's hands to do so. The rusty chains squeaked as she kicked backward, sending herself into a gentle sway forward and back.

"It was nice of you to come, even if things haven't been great between us," I said.

317

Trixie planted her feet to still herself and looked at me. I stared back. Her eyes were set with determination but wide with the depth of emotion. I sucked in a breath, feeling like we were on the edge of a crater and about to fall in.

"When Zoey told me that you were going to take over the shop . . ." Trixie hesitated. Crickets hummed, and I waited for her to gather her thoughts.

She looked down at the ground and kicked at the dirt, which had never managed to recover and yield to grass after years of abuse from our use of the swing set. Maybe it was Bella's more recent use that had worn it down again. The toes of Trixie's sneakers traced lines in the dust.

She took a deep breath. "You'd been afraid to take it over. It had a lot of bad memories for you. I'd accused you of not being yourself, and well, the way you reacted the other day, I guess you probably thought I was a hypocrite."

"Sorry—" I began.

"No, don't," she said. "You were right."

I scratched at my face. I wasn't sure how to respond to that. Fortunately, she wasn't done, so I had a minute to compose my own thoughts.

"Over the past few days, I've realized I don't have any friends who know me like you do. You've known me for only a few months, but some of them I've known for years. I don't let anyone see me or know how I'm feeling. You were able to see through that."

I nodded. I still had no idea what she was thinking half the time, but I could tell when what she was showing me wasn't real. Now was probably the realest she'd ever been, other than when she'd been out on a dance floor, lost in the music, having completely forgotten about everything around her.

"I care about you, Trixie. I wanted . . . I *want* to see the real thing. You don't have to hide from me," I said.

"I know. And knowing that you were facing your own fear and deciding to do what you were passionate about in taking over the shop, it helped me realize that. Then, when I got your note, I knew you didn't like me any less after seeing me crying. I finally got that I'd just made that assumption—thank you, trauma."

"What are you saying?" I asked.

Trixie bit her lip, a rare glimpse at the vulnerability she worked so hard to hide with her constant smiles. "I'm saying that if you'll have me, I want to be with you. That if you'll let me, I want to try and be more honest with you. Be real and give us a chance."

My heart was racing. A part of me had kept wishing for something like this to happen, but I hadn't dared to hope, hadn't thought it was possible.

"I'd like that," I said, tripping on my words.

"Then the honesty starts now." She glanced up at me through her long lashes, and my heart was pounding so loud in my chest, there was a real concern I might not hear what she said. "Bear, I think I'm in love with you."

All the walls in me came crashing down. My heart liquified and her words sang in my mind, again and again, pounding their beautiful melody in my ears. Trixie loved me.

I lifted out of my swing and fell to my knees in front of her. "I love you too," I breathed, and pulled her to me. I engulfed her in my arms, and our lips met with all the urgency of two people who had denied ourselves this emotion for too long and had missed each other too much.

She pressed her lower lip between mine, and I bit softly down. She moaned my name. I fell back, off my knees, and into a seated position, and she fell with me, straddling me. I pulled her in close, running a hand up through her hair.

She froze.

"What's wrong?" I asked, both of us panting. "Did I—"

"No, it's not that. We're good, but your entire family is crowded around the window, watching us make out. Including Bella."

"Shit," I groaned.

"Yup." She leaned her forehead against mine and laughed.

"We should probably go in there," I said.

"The ice cream is probably melting." She sighed.

"And they all had champagne glasses ready for a toast."

"Those bubbles are history," she said.

I grinned and kissed her again, deep and slow, exploring her mouth with my tongue. Let them watch. Fawn would have to cover Bella's eyes if she didn't want her to see it. "We could disappear into the night. I could whisk you away back home."

Her smile spread wide and true at the mention of home, our home.

"We shouldn't leave them hanging like that." She sighed again. "But I wouldn't be opposed to an excuse to leave soon."

"I've got you covered. Tomorrow's a big day. My first day of training at Family Tree."

"Uh-oh, does that mean you need to go to bed early?"

"To bed? Oh yes. To sleep? Hell no. If you send me to sleep early, I will be very disappointed."

"Is that so?" She stood and brushed herself off. It was a lost cause. In the moonlight, I could see the faint patches of dirt on her knees, and her hair was pulled free from its ponytail in patches where I'd run my hand through it.

"I want all of you, Trixie," I said, taking her hand as we walked to the house. "The good and the bad. I want you at your happiest, and though I share your hurts and hope that our life is filled with happiness and little pain, I want you at your saddest too. I want you."

She glanced over at me, pausing and taking my hand to make sure I saw her and felt the weight of her words before we went inside. Her eyes were watery, and as I watched, a single tear slid down her cheek. She held my gaze and let it fall, her lips curved in a warm smile. "I want you too. All of you."

EPILOGUE
TRIXIE

One year later

I gave Captain Blackbeard a hug. "Don't worry. Mommy and Daddy will be home in a couple hours," I said. The cute Lab mix wagged his tail enthusiastically, glancing at the door, hoping for another walk and not yet grasping that I was leaving.

"You make sure he stays out of trouble." I ruffled Chick-Chick's feathers and set her in her pen.

Our pup had come to us at the shelter a couple months ago. Given that he had one eye, a pirate name had been the obvious choice. Bear didn't even try to object when I brought him home.

Chick-Chick had taken to him immediately. The two would chase each other around the living room, her gliding along in her chair, him pouncing around her. When they were all played out, they'd curl up together on the couch next to us.

Chick-Chick's weight was down. Her special diet had helped, and the mobility the wheelchair allowed for had been a game changer. She was our little fighter, and she was thriving.

Captain Blackbeard was full of spunk, and Bear was a total sucker for his sad little pleas for treats and attention. Little did Bear know that I was buttering him up for more fur children, but I didn't want to push my luck quite yet.

I swung by our favorite Mexican joint to pick up dinner on the way to Family Tree. It was wedding season, and Bear was busy. He had a couple of high school kids working part-time through the summer to help him get through the spike in orders and to run some deliveries for him. Tonight was going to be a late night. I was bringing him food and planning to keep him company and try to help him without butchering any of the arrangements. He was teaching me, but I wasn't exactly a prodigy.

"Someone order an absurd amount of burritos for two people?" I asked, gliding into the back room.

"Hey, beautiful." He stood and pulled me to him for a kiss. His body pressed against mine, and I could feel his enthusiasm as the kiss drew out.

"I hope this isn't how you treat all your delivery drivers."

"Gotta tip 'em somehow," he teased.

We ate our food and talked about our day. "Hey, Fawn was wondering if we could babysit Bella again on Sunday so they can have another date night."

I smiled. We'd been spending a lot of time with Bear's family. I always felt so swept up and embraced by the chaos of them. Things with Owen's job had been stressful lately, and it had been rough on him and Fawn. Bear and I had been doing a little babysitting to get them some time together. I loved being a part of his family.

"Sounds good. I'll pick her up after class." A teaching job had opened up at the community center. I'd picked up a few dance classes on Sundays and had almost paid off all Chick-Chick's bills. It felt amazing to be back on the dance floor again. I'd tied my feelings about my parents to dancing so wholly, I hadn't realized how much I'd missed it. I wouldn't be leaving my job at the shelter, though; I loved it there.

A slow song came on the little radio that Bear kept in the back room, and he pulled me up to dance. We danced for three songs in a row before I reluctantly whispered, "Don't you have to get to work?"

He grinned, pressing a kiss to my lips. "I finished them all up earlier."

"What?" I pulled back to frown at him in confusion. "Then why are we here?"

At that moment, the bell on the front door jingled, and with it came raucous voices.

I laughed. "Family meeting?"

"Family meeting," he confirmed.

Carrie ran over and pulled me into one of her amazing mom hugs.

"How was the trip?" I asked.

"It was amazing!" she said. "It was so beautiful. The mountains are breathtaking, and we did so much hiking!"

They'd just gotten back from their second trip since she'd officially handed the business over to Bear. They'd gone to Jamaica one week after she officially retired. This more recent trip had been to Colorado for some fun in the Rocky Mountains.

"I've got Lexie and Rose," Zoey said, wielding a tablet. Lexie and Rose waved from the screen. I'd met each of them only once—Lexie the night Bear and I had gotten back together, and Rose when Bear and I had taken a weekend trip to go visit her, our first getaway together. It felt like I knew them both, having been at so many family meetings with them now. Everyone called out greetings and waved at the screen.

"All right everyone, settle down," Carrie said, gaining control of the wild crowd as always. "Your meeting, Bear. You've got the floor."

I looked to him in surprise. He'd called the meeting? I'd been to so many meetings, but I didn't think he'd called any of them.

He turned to me, scratching at his face, his telltale nervous signal. I braced myself.

"Trixie," he said, taking in a deep breath. "From the day I first met you, you felt like one of the family. Since I'm a man whose family comes as a package deal, it only felt right they be here for this, so you'd know what you're getting into."

"Eee, it's happening!" Lexie squealed.

"Shh!" Zoey hissed.

"Sorry!" Lexie yelped.

"Let the man talk," Russell grumbled.

I laughed, my eyes already watering. My heart was skipping beats in anticipation of what I suspected was coming next.

"You make me feel like the best version of myself. You push me to do new things, and I'm never happier than when I'm around you. I used to hide in my house and avoid people in general. Since you've been in my life, everything has changed for the better." He sank down to one knee, pulling a ring box out of his pocket. "I love you, and I want to spend the rest of my life with you and experience all the madness that comes with it."

Happy tears were pouring out of my eyes now, and I laughed through them. Madness indeed. He'd put up with a chicken, a costumed birthday party, a broken ankle, and so much more.

"Trixie Ward, will you marry me?"

"Yes!" I shouted, wiping away the mess of tears on my face. "Yes, yes, yes!"

He stood and slid the ring onto my finger, then lifted me off the ground for a kiss that blew my mind.

Around us the family cheered, but my whole focus was on Bear, the taste of him, the feel of him, and the idea that he was mine forever.

I couldn't wait.

ACKNOWLEDGMENTS

One day I called a friend to see how she was doing, and when I asked her what was new, she said, "Well, I've got a pet chicken now." Growing up in the Chicago suburbs, chickens were not a typical pet, so that would have been shocking enough if I hadn't also known she lived in a flat downtown. She told me the story of how she'd adopted a chicken she'd literally found crossing the road and nursed her injuries, even getting her a wheelchair. I immediately knew this belonged in a book, and my friend Gretchen Buhrke gave me her blessing to write about it. While Trixie, Bear, and the whole Ross family are entirely fictional, the story's opening was inspired by Gretchen and her chicken, so she is absolutely owed the first thanks. Thank you, Gretchen, for inspiring this story, letting me run with it, and taking the time to tell me about Chick-Chick's journey and what it was like living with a chicken.

The real-life Chick-Chick's story sadly did not have a happy ending. Even though she had the world's best chicken-mama, the nature of her breed meant she was not intended for a long life. This is a harsh reality that many animals face, but you can help remedy it by exploring a vegan or vegetarian lifestyle, or even starting with scaling back on the amount of meat you consume.

I dedicated this book to my mom, because she has been so incredibly supportive of me on this journey. I am not a patient person, and anyone in publishing knows that so much of the process requires patience. She has listened to my endless anxiety and been my first reader and cheerleader. I need to thank both of my parents for my lifelong love of books. My parents are both avid readers. Set foot in their house, and the stacks of books in every corner make that evident. Thank you, Mom and Dad, for introducing me to this passion, and for the family read-alouds that were so precious to me. I wouldn't be doing this if it weren't for both of you. To my brothers: Jake, thanks for always supplying excellent book recs and sharing your enthusiasm, and Alex, thank you for being an early reader to help me iron things out. And I'm sorry about that—haha.

Thank you to my husband, Jeff Ohlert, and to my daughters, Alice and Lillian, for giving me the space and time for this endeavor. I love you all so much. Thank you to all my extended family—my own and my in-laws—for your constant support and excitement, and to Taylor Kelly for answering my floral questions.

Thank you to my amazing agent, Emmy Nordstrom Higdon. You've talked me down from my panics so many times and been so patient and encouraging. Thank you for dreaming big with me. Much thanks to the rest of the team at Westwood Creative Artists as well for everything they do behind the scenes to support my writing.

Acknowledgments

Thank you to my editor, Melissa Rechter, for taking a chance on my little chicken book, and for your absolutely brilliant guidance that made it so much stronger. Thank you to Carolina Melis for the completely adorable cover that is everything I'd hoped for and more, and to Jeff DeBlasio for the gorgeous jacket design.

Thank you also to Rebecca Nelson, Madeline Rathle, Dulce Botello, Matt Martz, Rachel Keith, and Westchester Publishing Services for all your hard work to make this book a reality and help me share it with the world.

Thank you to Meika Usher for being my first IRL writing buddy, answering my questions, commiserating, and writing with me. Thank you to Lyssa Kay Adams for your little free writing workshops, for answering my questions when I was struggling with what to do with early feedback, and for all the writing sprints. Much appreciation to Kelly Siskind and Denise Williams for their support as well.

I would still be querying agents with some absolutely terrible books if it weren't for the endless support and wisdom of the members of the writesquad and the forge. Thank you all for sharing this writing journey with me. I really don't know what I would have done without the general support, writing sprints, critiques, cheerleading, and commiseration from you all. Thank you to all of you, including but not limited to Falon Ballard, Shannon Balloon, Joel Brigham, Audrey Burges, Jen Ciesla, Amber Clement, Laura Chilibeck, Kelly Kates, Keira Niels, L. Nygren, Michael Nelmark, Rachael Peery, Christy Swift, Ruth Singer, Esme Symes-Smith, Megan Verhalen, and Kyra Whitton.

To the booktokkers, bookstagrammers, bloggers, and reviewers, you do so much for the bookish community, and it is often thankless work. Thank you for your enthusiasm and for doing so much hard work to share the word about all the incredible books out there. I hope you enjoyed and will continue to enjoy mine. Regardless, I thank you for reading and sharing.

Thank you, dear readers, for taking a chance on my debut book. I appreciate it more than you can possibly know. I hope this book put a smile on your face. If it did, I'd love to hear from you, so please come say hi on any of my socials or join my reader group (links in all my bios).

To anyone I may have forgotten or who helps with the book after I've written this, thank you. From the bottom of my heart, thank you. I hope to have many more books to acknowledge you with in the future.